Herman Newton's passion ~~wicker laundry basket in h~~ sadly hampered when his fa~~ heard from again. Herman~~ been brilliant at mathematics, if a bit oafish in other respects. By the time he was hired by Major Shark to work in a British Intelligence Service laboratory, he had developed a sophisticated 'bug' that would have put Intelligence forward absolute eons. Only Herman decided not to mention it.

His other obsession was the development of a drug that would make people truly fall in love with each other: not an aphrodisiac, but the real thing – like Titania and Bottom. This was of particular interest as the failure of his first marriage had left him impotent.

So when Major Shark sent Herman to 'bug' a Barcelona sex clinic, it was as if two of our hero's dreams had merged into one. He had always seen himself as a spy in the classic mould – the exploits of Sir Richard Burton and Mata Hari springing to mind – though Inspector Clouseau might have been nearer. Still, in bungled attempts to lay hold of 'Aphrodite's Girdle' (the aphrodisiac), Herman drifted into contact with a suspect Russian called Kolowski and obtained evidence of a drugs-for-arms deal. With firm grasp of the wrong end of the stick, he spied on, bolstered by a sudden love for the Major's unremarkable daughter, Doris.

Ah, Doris. Was it the vapour inhaled from a phial at the sex clinic which impelled him to embrace mediocrity? How could he love a girl whose interests were fashion and Space Invaders – who didn't like opera 'because of the voices'? The answer came back with conviction: Doris was an angel. And so Herman follows her into the world of punks and street-fashion, where he tangles with her milieu – and her boyfriend . . .

BY THE SAME AUTHOR

AMONG THE THIN GHOSTS

CAREFUL WITH THE SHARKS

Constantine Phipps

Happy Birthday

from

Adam

to

Katie!

33   1992

BLOOMSBURY

First published in Great Britain 1985

Copyright © 1985 by Constantine Phipps

This paperback edition published 1992

The moral right of the author has been asserted
Bloomsbury Publishing Ltd, 2 Soho Square, London W1V 5DE

A CIP catalogue record for this book
is available from the British Library

ISBN 0 7475 0850 X

10 9 8 7 6 5 4 3 2 1

All rights reserved: no part of this publication may be reproduced, stored
in a retrieval system, or transmitted in any form or by any means,
electronic, mechanical, photocopying or otherwise, without the prior
written permission of the publisher.

Printed in England by Cox & Wyman Ltd, Reading, Berks

To My Mother and Father

Itaque tunc primum Dorida vetus amator contempsi . . .
Then for the first time I despised my old passion for Doris . . .
Petronius, *Satyricon*

Chapter 1

The first time I met Doris Shark, I didn't think she was the most beautiful woman I'd ever seen; I'm not even sure if she struck me as particularly pretty. Still, I have a very clear picture of her in my mind as she appeared on that occasion, as though my memory had picked her out prophetically and stored her away for future use: a large girl, almost ungainly, with a mass of reddish-yellow hair and hazel eyes, sitting at the foot of her father's armchair.

I can visualise her position exactly. Arms by her sides, her legs are thrust out, and the sitting position is achieved by the curve of her back rather than her bottom, like a rag doll bent in the wrong place. There is something of the rag doll, too, in the way her hands lie with the palms turned upwards and in the big brown eyes which remind me of two shiny buttons sewn on. When I speak she turns them on me, though it is not clear whether I have really caught her attention (she seems to look just short of me in a peculiar, unfocused way); but when her father speaks and she lifts her head in that languid manner there is no mistaking the fixed adoration in her look then.

Yet the odd thing about this is that although the picture is exact, I somehow managed to see it all wrong at the time. From the tapered bottoms of her trousers I see protruding her solid lower calves, rather thickset ankles, and big plimsolled feet splayed on either side. Probably it is the tapered trousers which are making me see her as fat-bottomed. Then there is that pink nylon polo-neck sweater, so bright, and clashing so remarkably with the reddy-gold of her hair that I have no recollection whatever of the beautiful little breasts, or of that small white waist. Or perhaps rather than the colours it is something in the rag doll posture which makes me remember her on that first occasion as being shapeless. I was Sir Isaac Newton watching the apple fall and thinking, 'Damnit. I forgot to fix the loose

7

tile on the roof'; like a fool I looked at Doris Shark and failed to see her for what she was. But I did notice her complexion. Yes, even in the smoky gloom of the Major's study I couldn't help noticing the pallor, and the wonderful freshness of her complexion.

As a conversationalist, the Major was stern stuff; he liked arguing, and even more than that, he liked to lecture. Above all he liked telling stories about himself. He wasn't very adept at the sort of conversation we were having now – the sort of talk it is polite to make with someone whose relatives you know, however vaguely, as a prelude to getting down to business – and he betrayed his impatience with repeated flicks of his cigar. He remembered my father, now dead, and asked after my mother, still living in the dark, vast flat behind the Parc Monceau with her widowed and aged elder sister. He told me a story about my father which I hadn't heard, an episode in the war-torn capital of an Asian country I had never visited and which he called rather quaintly by its old colonial name. When he spoke of my mother, it was with frank admiration for her beauty; the beauty I remembered in my childhood when she came into my bedroom at night to kiss me, silk dress rustling, diamonds black and prickly in the dark. I wondered if the Major had loved a great many women and recalled that his wife was dead.

'I haven't seen your uncle for years,' he was saying, 'not more than a couple of times since the war, I shouldn't think. Do you go to Hawtree much?'

I have to explain here that the man whom the Major referred to as my uncle was really my third cousin twice removed. I didn't as yet understand why the Major wanted to relate us more closely.

'Hawtree,' I said. 'That's his house in the country, isn't it? No, hardly ever. I don't think I've been since I was a boy.' I had no recollection of the visit at all beyond a distinct vision of being sick in a lavatory at the age of five or six, after eating too many sausages at tea – I have always detested them since.

'I visited it once in 1956,' the Major was saying. 'I remember the date exactly because it was the time of the Suez Crisis. I was Chief of General Staff to General de Witt in those days and we were called back to the War Office in the middle of dinner. But

I've never been back since. Your uncle hardly comes to London at all any more. In the old days I used to see him quite often at the club. We're both Knights of St Expeth, you know.'

There was something in his voice as he said this which suggested he would like to be asked back to Hawtree; and that when he did bump into my distant relative at the club he was more pleased than the distant relative – but these were only guesses on my part, since I knew the Major little, and my 'uncle' if anything less. As for the Knights of St Expeth, I knew nothing at all about them; nor was I much enlightened by the Major's explanation. As far as I could make out they were some sort of fraternity which admired right-wing governments and professed a devotion to chastity. The Major didn't ask me much about my own life, though he alluded to my marriage and made a remark about my period at the University of Paris. It surprised me that he knew even these facts about me, seeing we'd never met before.

When we finished our tea he patted Doris on the shoulder and said, 'Run along now, my dear. Mr Newton and I have business to discuss.'

'Yes, Daddy. Shall I take the tea away?'

Apart from an initial 'hello,' the first sentence I ever heard spoken by Doris Shark. The voice was deadpan, and strangely babyish. I thought, is she quite a lot younger than I imagined? Doris set the cups back carefully on the tea-tray while the Major and I observed a silence. Her hands were the same sort of white china as the cups, and I noticed her fingers were a strange shape: short and tapering down to little square ends. When she had gathered all the paraphernalia of teatime – plates with cake-crumbs and wobbling knives, and crumpled-up paper napkins on which the Major had wiped his lips as one might scrub a shoe, and a special silver contrivance the tea-strainer reposed on – Doris picked up the tray and began to leave. I remember very clearly noticing as she walks away from us towards the door how her red-gold hair hangs down her flaming pink back and how, as she passes the side-table, she perilously shifts the entire weight of the tray on to her right hand and with her left picks out a chocolate from a box that is lying there, pops it into her mouth, readjusts the tray and disappears behind the curtained door of the Major's study.

Perhaps these little details stick in the memory because they are so typical; or perhaps because they are so typical our imagination supplies them, rather as the early photographers would touch up their black and white postcards with certain colour highlights.

When she was gone the Major stood up and walked over to the window, where the deathly cold light of a London winter's day arrived down a sort of pit to the level of the basement study. In the rest of the room electric lamps gave out a dim yellow illumination, but here the smoke from the Major's cigar took on a blueish tinge as he moved into the daylight. He was of medium height and good figure, with dark receding hair combed back, and big perfect teeth and bloodless lips set in a grey complexion. The eyes were dark and hard, the irises surrounded by a faint fatty ring; his hands were short and rather pudgy, covered in very black hairs, and with perfectly manicured nails. He wore a gold signet ring on his little finger.

The Major was by no means a dandy, though it was clear that he took care over his appearance: he was clean-shaven and wore fresh linen and highly polished shoes. Today he had on a pair of dark grey trousers immaculately pressed, and a navy-blue blazer with gold buttons. When he walked it was with a slight limp on the right side, the vestige of a wound which had won him the medal now displayed in a case on the mantelpiece.

He didn't strike one as having a particularly military bearing, yet in his speech, as in his gestures, there was a certain clipped decisiveness which marked him as a man of action.

'As I mentioned to you in my letter,' he said, 'I have a proposition to make.' He paused, and regarded me keenly for a few seconds, before continuing, 'But before I can tell you anything about it, I must ask you to sign this. It will of course bind you to nothing beyond secrecy.'

He lifted the flaps of the blotter beside him and let them fall open on the desk. I walked over and saw a document which was headed 'Official Secrets Act' and marked in the top right-hand corner with a computer code reference. I sat down and began to glance through it.

The Major hovered beside me flicking and tapping his cigar over the ashtray, then he said, 'Look here, just sign on this line, you can read the rest later on,' and as soon as I had affixed my signature to the three copies, 'Good,' he said, 'let's get going immediately. We can talk in the car.'

In the hall he put on a navy-blue city coat and took an umbrella from the rack. Outside the sky was thick and grey and low, and though the streets were wet it couldn't have been more than a degree or two off freezing. We both thrust our hands into our pockets and walked round the square garden to where the Major had parked his car. I noticed that he could walk briskly enough despite his limp: for a man of sixty-odd he was surprisingly agile.

We got in, and set off westwards away from central London. The Major began to explain that he was offering me a job, and that though my role would be purely one of research, it would be under the auspices of the Intelligence Service.

'I understand,' he said, 'that there was some question of your being interested in Intelligence work a few years ago in Paris.'

'They were very rude to me. To be quite frank I think I was dealing with bureaucratic fools.'

As soon as I had spoken I regretted it. It seemed unlikely that the Major, who was clearly a member of the Intelligence Service himself, would take kindly to my remark. But in fact he didn't appear to be the least disturbed.

He gave me a wry sort of smile and said, 'Yes, bureaucrats are always slow-moving. But in the end we must have come to the right conclusion, or you wouldn't be here now. As a matter of fact, we've been aware of your work for some time. Personally I'm not an expert in the field though I did have some experience of it during the war. I was in North Africa at the time. We did a good deal of wire-tapping in the ports where most of their spies were, but mainly we relied on intercepting radio messages and decoding. All very primitive by your standards, I know, but it makes me appreciate the sophistication of what you're doing. That listening device which FBQ developed for you ... '

'Which they stole from me,' I interjected.

'Well, yes, quite so. All the same, our experts were very impressed by it. Very impressed indeed.'

We had left the city centre and were moving west along a

piece of raised freeway across the suburbs. I looked out of the window at the clapboard and plate-glass façades of the industrial estates and the residential districts with their depressing rows of boxlike houses. Alongside the road itself stood blocks of offices bearing their company's name on big neon signs, old, down at heel buildings for the most part, and somehow symbolic of an economy in decline. We swung off the motorway and found ourselves by an odd quirk in a village high street, a purlieu of the eighteenth century washed over by the outer London sprawl.

'What I'm offering you,' the Major was saying, 'is probably the most advanced and sophisticated laboratory of its kind in Europe. You'll be nominally responsible to Codrington, but as far as your work's concerned, you'll be your own master. We want you to work for us, and we're prepared to put everything at your disposal. I think you'll find the salary attractive.'

He named a figure that compared surprisingly well with what I would have got in the private sector.

We stopped outside a walled enclosure marked 'Ministry of Defence'. The Major showed a pass at the gate and we drove into a large compound dominated by two big factory buildings. Scattered around the edge of the precinct stood a number of prefab offices.

'Ostensibly, the place is for storing army equipment,' he explained. 'Our operation takes place underneath.'

We left the car in a covered park, took a lift down, were screened at the bottom by a security officer, and finally emerged into the argon-lit, ultra-modern, subterranean world that was to be mine.

It was clever of the Major to bring me in person to see the laboratories. He probably guessed that I was short of money and that the salary was a big incentive for me; but the thing that really decided me was the sight of this sophisticated equipment. People often think that an inventor needs nothing but his ideas, and in some senses this is true, but there are a hundred things which must be tested and tried out before a listening device is perfected, and I saw in front of me everything I needed for this, and more. I felt like a child in a toy shop. No, I could no sooner have refused a job in a laboratory like this one than I would have refused my first pair of long trousers. (I remember I wore them for a lesson with Dr Fitzer; a pair of bottle-green corduroys, uncomfortably stiff and hot, with huge turn-ups.) How I loved at first sight the daylight-free environment, and the mute swish of its air-conditioning. The walls with their green waterproof paint! The linoleum floors!

The only sour note in all this is Codrington. Ambitious, bureaucratic, free of any hint of originality, he spends his day wandering in the maze of departmental regulations. At just thirty he is already the executive head of the research department. Always, just when you're most absorbed in some piece of work, he appears as if from nowhere, rosy-cheeked, with back-slapping *bonhomie* and a footling memorandum which he presses into your hand. He is almost touching in his enthusiasm for his own self-aggrandizement.

'Success is a virtue,' he explains. 'Everyone should try to be top in their field.'

And just exactly what is his field, one would like to ask? He has never invented anything of consequence, but climbs in the department by appropriating other people's research. Is plagiarism the field he dominates so triumphantly? But one checks oneself in mid-sentence for fear of being constrained to listen to any more of this rubbish; instead, one inquires after his love life, which is his other great talking point and every bit as trivial. And already he's away, like a racehorse from its stall, recounting some triumph or soul-splitting difficulty. Naturally Codrington has never loved a woman. No, no inklings of infinity will ever trouble that chubby brow. He comes round like a nanny, ostensibly to supervise, in fact, so as to be able later on to claim credit for everybody else's research. I'm sure that a good deal of my subsequent secretiveness can be explained largely in terms of my aversion to him.

13

Chapter 2

I've been an inventor for as long as I can remember. I was one of those prodigiously advanced children of whom everyone says, 'How brilliant,' and then talks about Mozart. My earliest distinct memory is mathematical: that of realising that the rudimentary abacus on my playpen was wrongly designed and didn't allow one to resolve satisfactorily questions of fraction and proportion. Before the age of eight, I had a hundred mathematical ideas which I later learnt were renowned laws discovered by other men, centuries, even millennia previously; I remember thinking it surprising that my parents and their friends found this unusual or clever: if only they could have seen how obvious it was! As to Mozart, I couldn't help being envious. Sitting on the floor in front of our big wooden-boxed gramophone listening to his requiem mass, I knew he had done something beautiful beside which my simple tricks with numbers were clever and even elegant, but not more than that.

I never took to schools. When I started at the *lycée* I used to be sick every morning on the way there. How I dreaded that gaping *porte-cochère* which signalled one's passage from civilian life to prison! The minute you went through it a whole different order obtained: suddenly some obscene bully whom I would have run away from in the Jardin du Luxembourg was a janitor with prison authority; the desks reminded me of prison walls, where the previous generations of internees had scratched their names; the playground was nothing but an exercise yard. The maths lessons were farcical. I was put in the top class straight away where I astonished the geometry teacher by pointing out that Euclid's ideas on parallelism might be problematic as a picture of the real world.

One day he said to me, 'Herman, I'm not going to teach you from now on. Instead you'll be going to see somebody who'll give you a private lesson. You'll be able to learn at your own speed.'

I can see him now, sandy-haired, red-faced with wire-rimmed glasses and dressed in a voluminous pepper-and-salt suit. The poor fellow couldn't bring himself to admit that he knew less than I did. What an odd notion it is that children are somehow inferior, lesser beings than grown-ups. But I didn't particularly blame the teacher because I had learnt already that he wasn't the only grown-up to suffer from this idea. Even my beloved mama would say of love, 'but that's something only grown-ups can understand,' and her beautiful grey eyes under their dark brows would assume a distant, hazy look which always made me think that perhaps she didn't understand either. And when I pointed out that I was in love with little Louise Lambert, my mother just pinched my cheek and laughed and said that grown-up love was different.

To me Louise Lambert practically was grown-up. Six years old with a snood and white socks, she wore pretty cotton dresses and little gold studs in her ears. With her chocolate eyes and her strawberry mouth all the boys thought her marvellously beautiful, even those in the class above us. As for me, when I was alone in the locker room, I couldn't resist touching her satchel and loden where they hung on their peg beneath her school number, 92. Round her neck she wore a silver heart-shaped locket with a picture of an older boy in it who she said was her boyfriend: later we discovered it had been cut out of a magazine. Louise was a terrible *allumeuse*: there was nothing to compare with the joy of her suddenly, without any reason, coming up and asking you to play with her. But if in the next break you dared to approach her she would toss her head like a horse and unleash some terrible put-down and a whole circle of onlookers would whinny with laughter and gallop away. When I wrote to her she brought my letter to class and read it out to everyone. She called me stupid and said I had special tuition because I was so behind in maths, which was the opposite of true but which everyone believed. The trouble was that I wasn't quick and witty in the way Louise was and because I now took mathematics privately I had no opportunity to shine in class either. In fact Louise took to calling me 'the dunce' and somehow, with the devilish ingenuity she had, she managed to make it my school nickname.

The new maths tutor lived in a series of dark, sprawling rooms in the rue du Mont Thabor. With its black-leather-covered Empire furniture and nineteenth-century oil paintings (dubious artistic merits, dubious gender of subjects portrayed), it was a very different sort of place from my parents' apartment. And how delightful to discover here not only mathematics, but harpsichord, piano, two spinettes and a harmonium, not to mention a plethora of chessboards between which Dr Fitzer flitted, pitting himself against the various machines he had invented. (These were the early days of computer chess, and Dr Fitzer was one of its pioneers. One of these machines, a regular clodhopper as a matter of fact, later made him a great deal of money.)

My mother brought me to my first lesson. Dr Fitzer's maid served tea, and my mother sat uncomfortably in her chair, making conversation with Dr Fitzer. I sat next to her with my legs straight out in front of me. I remember the soft, slightly clammy leather of the chair seat under my knees, the eagle-headed lectern by the fireplace, a very glorious painting on the wall of a blue man with a single woman's breast sitting under a cobra's head (in reality a poster of Shiva pinned to a shelf of the bookcase). Everything here was a sort of centaur turning into something else: the sofa with leopard's skin, the lamps with yellow-petalled shades and long glass leaves, the chest of drawers on its four ball-clasping lion's legs. I could tell in the way children always can that there was something my mother didn't like about the place, or was it the Doctor himself? Nevertheless, of all the mathematicians in Paris, Dr Fitzer was the one reputed to be capable of training my sort of mind to become something useful. So dutifully, saying goodbye with the very effusive and totally false voice she uses on such occasions, my mother left me on Mont Thabor in the hope that I would undergo a suitable transformation.

One thing about Dr Fitzer pleased me beyond measure: unlike my dear mama and the sandy-haired dunderhead, he treated me absolutely as an equal despite the thirty years' difference in our ages.

He had a dark complexion with crinkly dark hair combed

back, a long straight nose and olive green eyes that seized on one with eager, almost promiscuous attention. I can see him now, sunk in an armchair, his long legs wrapped around each other, the thin ankles lost in the folds of his trouser turn-ups. I am sitting at his feet on the floor sucking my thumb. (He doesn't think this babyish.) Then I make a suggestion which pleases him. Suddenly the legs unwind themselves, his long frame unbends, and he lurches to his feet saying, 'Ya, ya,' and pacing the room with stooping, gangling steps. 'My tear boy! Quite lovely!' He pronounces English and French with a trace of something else. German, is it? I could never tell: people said that even in his mother tongue he spoke with a foreign accent. He belonged to all Europe but to no country in particular.

Or else I am sitting at his big leather-topped desk with its gold and red chessboard squares and Dr Fitzer is towering behind me like the cobra in the poster arched over Shiva's head. He has the thin snake-hipped figure, the venom-sharp mind, the wisdom (snakes were always wise in myth). And from time to time his hand slides down the inside of my airtex shirt like a snake's tongue or up the leg of my short school trousers.

It was he who introduced me to Bach, sitting at the harpsichord in his sleek, black leather coat, his long fingers running over the keys like mice. When he had finished we went over the score together and he taught me to read the curious notation of music, with its black-tailed dots lined up like starlings on the wires. It seemed an awkward, yet oddly poetic way to put the clear mathematical relations of Bach on to the page. Dr Fitzer told me how Mozart had been ignored, and said I was to remember it if people in my life set themselves against me. For, as he always insisted, 'My tear, it were the world that were small, not Mozart.' When he said 'small' in this way it was his greatest pejorative.

When I was eight my parents were posted to Mexico; I was entrusted to English boarding schools and other special tutors, none of whom I liked as much as Dr Fitzer. For the next years I yo-yoed between cacti and cricket fields, between bougainvillaea on the veranda and straw boaters over pink faces at aquatic events. Then my parents went to Guyana (my father an ambassador now) followed by Honduras, his final posting, where he was kidnapped and never heard of again. My schools also changed regularly but like the embassies they had a curious way of resembling each other. In most of them I was in trouble for insufficient dedication to outdoor games, and for spying.

My passion for spying began years before I invented my first listening device. I started by spying on my father as he returned from his nights with Madame du Barrier, but before long I was peeping at everything in the Embassy. I used to lie under the table in my father's study, and listen to him dictating letters; I was hauled out of the kitchen cupboard by the chef, chased from the boiler-room by the butler, and caught by the secretary in the stationery cupboard of her office. Often what I overheard on those occasions was nothing I couldn't have listened to normally, but at that age the very fact of overhearing made it thrilling. Even more interesting were the insights into sexuality and grown-up love. In my parents' bathroom there was a wicker laundry basket, cylindrical in form, into which I could creep and peep out through a slit where the wickerwork was torn. Squatting in here on some dirty towels and shirts, a stiff collar digging into me uncomfortably, I saw first my father, then my mother having their baths. I remember being astonished by the ridiculously huge size of my father's sexual organs, and, on my silken-skinned mother, by the extra-ordinary coarseness of her genital hair. My parents slept in different rooms so I never saw them make love. I did see one of the maids do it in the pantry though, hiding behind a crate of sweet-smelling apples. She pulled up her skirts and leant across a wooden table, and to my absolute amazement the bodyguard took out his cock and put it inside her. This was easily the most eccentric piece of behaviour I'd ever seen. I suppose I must have sensed its importance though because I tried it myself with one of the girls at school and this got me into trouble when she told her parents.

But spying appealed to me quite apart from the discoveries it brought. From a very early age it seemed to me that this was a vocation worthy to be pursued since it pitted the single man against the whole world, and because simply by knowing more he might change the course of a war more than a whole army. 'Kim' was the greatest hero of my early days, with his brave independence and his chameleon-like ability to put on *alterae personae*. And I naively supposed that if my father had been a spy Madame du Barrier wouldn't have left him. At that time I had no idea how intimate the connections were between espionage and ordinary diplomatic institutions.

I was about sixteen when the tiny spark of originality I had shown in pure mathematics began to fade. People often say they feel sorry for the child prodigy whose talent fades in adolescence. Actually youth is accustomed to change and so it hardly matters; I began instead to invent all sorts of listening devices which were if anything even more exciting than pure maths on account of the forbidden insights they gave me. Often I had the school so wound up with bugs I could have had the masters expelled, let alone the boys; and once or twice I overheard exam papers being set, and won prizes for subjects like history and Greek at which I was known to be no good. I was expelled from two of my schools for this snooping.

My first real love affair was with a girl called Matilda. It was really on her account that I went to University in Paris, and it was through her, too, that I met my Venezuelan first wife, Pilar.

I met Matilda in my last term at school. It was a dismal establishment and more than any other I went to, beset with that particular brand of obscurant philistinism which seems to be *de rigueur* in English public schools. Matilda was the daughter of my music teacher. When her parents went up to London for concerts I used to climb out of a ground floor window and meet her at her house. She had a mischievous smile and a hairy belly and she loved danger. Sometimes she concealed me under her bed when her mother and father came back and I listened to them come in and say goodnight to her.

Somehow Matilda got the wrong idea about me in a way that reminded me almost of my old love, Louise Lambert. I don't quite know how this happened; possibly it was to do with something that occurred the first time we made love. I suppose at first I was a little slow because when we'd been sitting on the bed chatting for a while, she said, 'Please stop talking and take off my clothes now,' and then I was a little too fast in trying to get off her jeans and they somehow got twisted round her ankles and so I pulled, and suddenly they came off and I fell backwards off the bed giving my head a nasty crack. Matilda was kinder than Louise Lambert. She said, 'Hopeless men are so sweet,' and kissed me on the floor.

Another time, soon before she went away to France, she said, 'My father says you got a scholarship to your school. Is it really true?'

When I told her it was, she let out a peal of laughter. 'Good heavens!' she said, 'I'd never have dreamt you had a brain in your head!'

When she got her own scholarship to study music in Paris I followed her there and enrolled at the University. But as luck would have it, Matilda took up with her teacher, a filthy old queen with an ambiguous reputation for his fingering. I must say I took it badly: for weeks I pestered her to come back to me, I was haunted by dreams of his horrible hands on her back and her belly, clamping her like a waffle iron. She told me to get lost; we agreed, on the Pont Neuf, not to meet again. I was as good as my word, or almost: the only time I bumped into them during the next years was soon after that when, quite fortuitously, I almost ran them down in the street one day. The old man, graceless to the end, hurled abusive nonsense at me through the car window; I drove on without a word.

Chapter 3

I was very lonely when Matilda left me. I didn't live with my mother at the Parc Monceau flat, but in a little room on the rue Pascal where the rue de Valence joins it. The building was at the apex of this confluence, so that the traffic divided to each side of me, like water to each side of an island, and the cars parked down below looked like driftwood that had caught there. From my sooted window above I could see the women go by; but even the pretty ones hadn't Matilda's smile, that lovely slow broadening of the mouth which seemed to say as we used to say at the lycée, '*Chiche!* I dare you!' Where would I find another girlfriend half so daring? Come to that, where would I find another girl with so many hairs on her navel? It came down the inside of her thighs too, where I persuaded her not to shave.

This particular morning at the rue Pascal must have been May, though it is certainly cold enough to be March. Outside in the street it is drizzling and a gusty wind every now and then throws a handful of raindrops against my window. Across the street a shutter bangs irritably. Pulling the eiderdown around me like a cloak I get out of bed and go through into the tiny kitchen. Smell of coffee, clatter of saucer to stop the milk boiling over, stale baguette, apricot jam. Then a shave and wash under a dribbling shower. It's important to look correct today: inconspicuous yet correct. With loving attention I remove the photo of Matilda from the mirror where she sits with her knees drawn up and her arms around them, propped in the angle of the frame. Then, relinquishing the eiderdown I survey the basic material. The hair is not too bad. Thick and unruly, it has a good blackish colour and mercifully no grey. But the rest is definitely less impressive. White immature legs with goose flesh; sex shrivelled up by the cold and looking like a frightened mouse; stomach rather distended already, a chest

21

which in contrast to the stomach remains boyishly diminutive, the neck with a cluster of hairs by the Adam's apple which the razor has missed. The worst bit, one has to recognise, is the face. There's something about my skin which refuses to settle down and be either oily or dry. Then there are the buck teeth which my mother never bothered to have fixed; and finally the beetling brows over thick black spectacles with chunky lenses which make my eyes (otherwise my best feature) look goggling and somehow distant.

Displeased with this unprepossessing reflection, I am none the less uncowed; unlike the ugly man of glossy magazines and cheap station novels, I do realise that women are not solely attracted by suntanned brutes and lissom dunces. With this in mind I pull on my warm winter underwear and then a clean shirt which I ironed myself the night before on the kitchen table. With my longjohns and big shirt tails I look like some awakened Victorian ghost ... but wait! Now comes the suit made specially to measure by a tailor in Scotland. If the cut is a little rustic for Paris, no matter: the sober grey cloth transforms me immediately into the inconspicuous, correct, serious being that I need to be. Also the colour goes well with my spectacles. Next come woollen socks, unfortunately with both big toes emerging, but this won't matter in a minute because here come the shoes, a pair of thick brogues equally at home in the *maquis* and the drawing-room. Taking my umbrella from its place on the radiator, I let myself out of the flat and descend the old staircase with its stairs splayed like the shelves of my mother's *coiffeuse* and its sink on every landing, and then out into the street.

In the cold, wet rue St Honoré there are few pedestrians. Of course I have looked carefully behind me all the way from the Métro to make sure no one is following me, but nevertheless I stop on the opposite side of the street from the British Embassy for a minute and observe. Nobody. Only a solitary policeman huddles in a glass sentry box, smoking a cigarette behind the palm of his hand. Above him the Union Jack flaps about on its pole like a wet dishcloth.

Fifteen years before this my mother and I used to stop just up the road opposite the American Embassy to buy soap at Roger & Gallet; then, as a special treat for me, we would visit my father at his office in the Chancery. As I stand here now I recognise the sculpted lion's face over the door and the alternating men's and women's heads over the first-floor windows, the men with their flowing stone moustaches and the archaic-looking woman on the right whom we used to call Geneviève after my aunt. My biggest excitement as a child was when the gate of the embassy opened and a shiny black limousine slid out bearing the ambassador himself or some foreign dignitary.

It felt very grand to imagine my father might one day be an ambassador himself; somehow it wasn't quite so impressive when I was older and he really was an ambassador, though the embassies in Latin America were also very splendid. When we had seen the limousine disappear, mama would take my hand and we would laboriously climb the stairs (they were so high I could only manage one step at a time) to my father's office. This was always rather a disappointment when we got there, though I would never have admitted it. The fact was that my father's office was a tame affair: there were no maps of the world or big game trophies (both of these would have impressed me enormously: my idea of international affairs was not on a par with my grasp of higher mathematics). Instead, there was a blue-haired secretary and a bearded man called Colonel Wrench who were both easily impressed by a few simple tricks with numbers. At school I said my father was a spy and had a gun.

Which was ironic, now that I came to be standing outside the Embassy fifteen years later, about to propose myself in exactly this capacity. As a precaution, to make quite sure no one is watching, I walk on up the street in the direction of the Elysée for a hundred yards. I cross the street to the embassy side and turn back, walking at a steady pace right up to the gates, and then unhurriedly, with a minimum of ostentation, turn into the Chancery as if nothing in the world has happened.

It seems smaller than it was in my childhood, and rather more mundane. I ignore the officious porter and make straight for the stairway which leads to my father's old office. At least there I'll be sure of finding somebody competent to deal with my rather special proposal. But infuriatingly the porter starts yelling at me to stop, thereby drawing attention to something which ought to take place inconspicuously and with a minimum of fuss. I wait for him to catch up with me:

'*Monsieur, où allez-vous?*'

His French accent is as filthy as his breath. I reply in English, 'I am here on important business. Please do not create a scene or it will reflect very badly on you later.'

'The public isn't allowed in this building. Apply up the road at the Consular and Visa section.'

'I'm not looking for a visa. I'm looking for the Chief Intelligence Officer!'

I had hoped the words 'Intelligence Officer' would inspire in this moron some semblance of respect, not to say urgency. Instead, he merely thrust his hands into his pockets and gestured with his head, 'Well, he's not on this staircase. You'll have to apply up the road.'

This was rather a setback. I didn't know the name of the Chief Intelligence Officer so I said, 'Listen here, I don't want to make a scene. In fact it's vital that I should remain inconspicuous, so I'll wait wherever you tell me to wait and you go and tell the Chief Intelligence Officer that I'm here.'

'Sorry, sir, I can't do anything for you. You'll just have to apply up the road. Number 109, fourth floor.'

I had no alternative but to do as he said. The consulate was in a concrete building with green-tinted glass windows, just before St Philippe du Roule. I took the steel lift to the fourth floor and went into the room where visas were issued. There were already a lot of people waiting their turn on the plastic-upholstered seats, their raincoats and umbrellas still wet beside them. For half an hour I waited opposite the notice-board with its sign about rabies and its table of consular fees and a warning that 'In France the penalty for drug offences can be eight years in gaol.' Then, over the loudspeaker my number sounded: '*Soixante-seize.* Seventy-six. *Soixante-seize.*'

I went up to the counter and wrote on a piece of paper 'Must see Chief Intelligence Officer. Urgentest.' Then I pushed the paper under the glass.

The woman behind read it and said, 'Next floor up. Turn right out of the lift and take the second door on your right. Room B.'

I followed her instructions. In Room B a Scottish woman offered me a chair on the other side of her metal desk. Behind her on the wall there was a picture of the Queen and a map of bus routes of the city. She began asking particulars: name, age, date of birth, height, and so on.

I said, 'It's very urgent that I speak to the head of Intelligence.'

She didn't seem to have heard me, so I repeated the request, on which she looked at me sharply and said, 'We'll see about that later. First I must have all the details.'

'But I can't tell the details except to someone at the top.'

'You must help me before I can help you. Now, are we ready to begin?'

She jotted down in shorthand everything I said. She asked me all kinds of questions about my financial needs, my love life (I had to explain in distasteful detail all the ins and outs of my relationship with Matilda), my mother, my school, and so on.

The interrogation took a little more than an hour in all, and when it was over she said, 'Right, that will be all for now. Don't try to contact us; we'll contact you if the occasion arises.'

My throat was dry with anger.

'Look here,' I said, 'I don't know who you are but I have come here to offer something very valuable, not to tell my life story to a filing clerk. I have a very important invention which will make me more useful to you than a whole squadron of your ordinary agents.'

This announcement had no visible effect on her whatever. I was so bursting with frustration by now that I was willing to tell her my whole invention just to prove her wrong.

'Give me a pencil,' I said, 'and I'll show you how it works in principle.'

I sketched an outline of my new listening device – brilliantly economic in design and significantly ahead of its rivals; but the woman obviously didn't understand a word of it.

When I had finished she picked up the notes I had written and said, 'Thank you. You can leave now.'

I left the embassy dazed, angry, but above all disappointed. I hadn't yet completely surrendered the idea that the Service would contact me in the next few days; but I couldn't help feeling humiliated by this reception. I walked slowly up the rue du Faubourg St Honoré until I came to the house I had lived in as a child, and where I had spied on my father on the morning Daphnée du Barrier left him.

My mother always called her La du Barrier; though a regular guest in our house until that fateful morning, my mama could never bring herself to call her Daphnée. Everyone knew she was my father's lover, just as the buck-toothed ambassador was known to be my mother's. I was often awake in the morning when my father returned from spending the night with her, and I used to watch him through the slats in the shutters as he crossed the courtyard under my window. Generally speaking he strode in purposefully; on happy mornings he would stop to smell the scented geraniums outside the concierge's window; sometimes he would drink from his cupped hand at the tap in the corner. He looked up only once, and always at the same moment: just as he first emerged from the *porte-cochère* into the courtyard. But on that morning when La du Barrier left him my father didn't look up. My instincts told me something was wrong; his halting walk confirmed it. When he got to the front door, instead of taking his key out and letting himself in, he sat down on the steps with his elbows on his knees and put his head in his hands. The morning was fresh and unclouded: later it would be sunny. I knew that my father was crying now and I thought with my childish logic that La du Barrier had left him because he didn't have any big game trophies. How could he not have got himself at least some? I made a promise to myself that when I grew up I would have a houseful.

Chapter 4

The invention which I proposed to the British Secret Service that day in Paris was a listening device which, had they had enough sense to develop it, would have put them three years at least ahead of their enemies in the Warsaw Pact (a vast gap in espionage terms). What I resented most was the smug look on the woman's face when I said I needed their financial assistance. She made me feel as if I was asking for a favour rather than doing them one. For a while I toyed with offering the idea to the French *Deuxième*. I felt sure they wouldn't be as stupid and patronising as their British counterparts. Wasn't I partly French on my mother's side? And hadn't I spent my childhood studying with Dr Fitzer in the rue du Mont Thabor? But I resisted this temptation because I knew that an unflinching patriotism is the *sine qua non* of a good secret agent.

In the end I showed my device to no one, and spent the rest of my university days trying to perfect it myself. The laboratories at the university were not really suitable for the task; but I managed to sell the idea to a French company who put it on the market. All this was unsatisfactory from my point of view: the thing came out four years too late to be really original; however, it had the merit for a few years of providing me with a modest income, and this allowed me to refuse all offers of teaching jobs and concentrate on continuing my research. Now I met Matilda again, coming out of a music shop on the Quai des Grands Augustins, clutching a sheaf of scores to her chest, only a block from where we had said goodbye five years earlier. She had just the same mischievous smile, but she had put on weight. She was wearing a coat of imitation fox and held on a long lead a tiny Pekinese of almost exactly the same colour, so that for a moment one had the impression it was a shag that had moulted off her coat. She kissed me and the dog began to sneeze.

27

Thrusting her scores into my arms she picked up the peke and said, 'The poor little thing has a cold. Snuggle down here *et je te porte chez toi.*'

Apparently not content with her execrable French, Matilda had seen fit to develop a French accent in English, so that she now spoke no language. In addition, she was a master of that supremely infuriating trick of the would-be cosmopolitan: the language mix. It seemed she was incapable of beginning and ending a sentence in the same tongue.

As we walked along the *quai* towards her flat in the rue de Lille I realised that the little Matilda I had known was gone for ever and that what I couldn't help feeling was mere affectation was in fact Matilda as she really was and would remain at forty, at fifty, for the rest of her life: vulgar, dotty, but not without charm. The dogs might come and go and probably the husbands, but she would visit the same *coiffeur* and *pâtissier* as long as she lived. She told me she played in a chamber orchestra now.

'Darling, will you promise to come this evening?'

There was no getting out of it. Impelled by the nagging vanity of Matilda, I took my seat that evening for a concert which changed my life. It was in a gloomy church with scraping chairs and an ill-lit chancel. Matilda's orchestra played through a couple of Brandenburg concertos in a performance that was lazy, even for a charity concert.

The second part of the concert was an organ recital by a young Venezuelan called Pilar Buendia. A spotlight fell on the organ loft at the back of the church and everybody started craning their heads around to see. I was sitting in the transept where the seats faced inwards so I had a good view of the woman who walked in. Young and dark, a girl almost, she looked down and waved to someone she knew in the audience. It was an intimate gesture which jarred with the formality of the rest of the proceedings, something which lasted only long enough for me to take in her face; and then she sat down and immediately began to play Bach's Chromatic Fantasy and Fugue. Unlike the rest of the audience who now turned again to face the altar, I watched her all the way through the recital. Her hair was cut straight across her neck in a way that reminded me of a wig hanging on a stand. You might think it is impossible to fall in love with somebody's back, yet Sterne did with the Flemish lady at the *remise* door in Calais; and hadn't I all the more reason, who had not only caught a glimpse of her, but could hear the excellence of her playing as well?

Later on, after we were married, I made her pose for a portrait in exactly this position. Now it lies in the attic, where a more jealous mind than hers has consigned it: up the dusty, uncarpeted steps in a room filled with old lamps and leather boxes stuffed with wads of ribbon-bound correspondence; yes, I know under exactly which dust sheet and between exactly which two cloying landscapes (English School, nineteenth century) it lies. But far better than this is the huge cinema-screen version in my head, replete with original spotlight and organ-pipes, on to which are projected other images of her which I couldn't possibly have seen during the concert: her brown-skinned face with dark eyes set far apart; the gold ear-rings; the chin held down and lower lip thrust out as she inspects her little breasts; the stride; the head thrown back in laughter. All these are imposed on the back of her head in the same way that in old films we see on the face of Napoleon the marching armies of France equipped with cannon, wagons, outriders; and in the same proleptic way that Doris, on the first evening I saw her, picks a chocolate from the dish and wears a pink sweater which in fact she didn't buy until a year later.

Pilar. My mother said if I was so jealous of her I would drive her to infidelity; but who wouldn't have been jealous? She was everything I ever wanted and it seemed logical that others would want her too. And they did. Not just Arachne who took her from me, but others, everywhere we went. It was an agony for me to go to dinner. And her concerts with their receptions afterwards and the congratulations and the invitations ... Was it my fault if I lost my temper and tried to hit someone? I mustn't make it sound as though we were unhappy together. On the contrary, the years of our marriage made me happier than I had thought possible. I only mention my jealousy because of what my mother said, and because it angers me that she said it.

We met Arachne at the house of Pilar's agent and fellow countryman, Ricardo Menón; and from the first she made no secret of her admiration for Pilar. I never thought, like so many others, that Arachne was beautiful. She had conventionally pretty features of the Greek kind, but without distinction. What made you notice her was the way she skulked about the place. Menón used to say she reminded him of a caged lion, at the same time pitiable and magnificent. And of course this was exactly the impression she was trying to create. When she wasn't the centre of attention she moved right to the edge of the picture, as though she was too wild and alone for mere drawing-room chit-chat. But actually she was addicted to people. She wore kohl on her eyes, and smoked cigarettes through a holder.

I'll say one thing about Arachne. She had extraordinary instincts. My first taste of it came when Pilar and I stayed at her house just outside Paris. I say her house: in fact she had borrowed it from a Swiss sculptor and it had somehow stuck to her web, like so many things she coveted. It was a small Templar castle in serious disrepair, whose circling walls which had once kept out hostile men-at-arms now sheltered it from the crowding *pavillons* of week-ending Parisians. Built like a loaf of bread, the house itself was simply stone wall and ivy with a few tiny windows and a terrace built on by the sculptor round the front door. From here, where we sat round a marble slab to eat, one could see above the walls the tops of three yew trees rising from the graveyard next door; tufts of grass and weeds softened the line of the wall itself, and on this side of it the garden was a jungle of unpruned fruit trees and nettlebeds, rising out of which, like dinosaurs from the marshes, came the rusting metallic spokes and wheels of the owner's art.

The day was hot and I had picked some cherries in the garden. I wanted a bowl of water to wash them in: Pilar said there was one in her bathroom. Inside the house, I remember a series of vast rooms leading one into the other by way of tiny doors. Rare windows were set at random in the massive walls; my eyes had to adjust to the dark when I came in. There were Moroccan rugs on the floor whose faint odour lingered in the air, big low beds covered in Syrian cloths, and plenty of metallic pterodactyls.

In the bathroom I found the bowl I was looking for lying on the floor; it had a puddle of soapy water in the bottom and a long dark hair crawling up the side: Arachne's ablutions. I swilled these out and rinsed the bowl two or three times; there was something repulsive to me in the sight of that hair which doubtless others would be quite happy to stroke and even kiss. At the top of the stairs I had to set the bowl down on a window-sill while I changed my grip, and I noticed Pilar in the garden by the buddleia, intent on an invisible butterfly. Arachne was lying below on the terrace, her skirt hoicked up to the top of her rather plump thighs, the short sleeves of her T-shirt rolled up on to her shoulders and her eyes shut against the sun. I was just thinking how awful it would be if the bowl fell on her head, when the bowl did slip, and though I managed to catch it before it fell, its entire contents slopped over the edge. I shut my eyes and waited for the splash; and when I looked again, there was Arachne, standing quite untouched at the other end of the terrace. Warned at the last minute by her sixth sense, she had sprung to safety as surely as a cat.

She seldom failed to tell this story in company, always making it sound as though I had done it on purpose, but that even at such a disadvantage, she had been too clever for me. Later, when she had stolen Pilar away, she told another one as well: about how I had tried to run her over in the street with my car, and been foiled by the same catlike agility. This was a monstrous lie, totally unfounded, but it was typical of her deceitful nature that even when she had stolen Pilar she had to fabricate these stories to make it seem that I had got what I deserved.

True to her name, she began weaving her horrible webs around us from the very first. If Pilar gave a recital, Arachne would be there in the front row; when Pilar came out of our apartment she would find Arachne sitting in her car or leaning against a lamp-post on the opposite side of the street. If I tried to say anything to her she drove off without replying, but when we went into a café later that evening, she would reappear, and sit alone at a table in the corner. At first Pilar was frightened; later she came to expect it, and if Arachne wasn't there during a whole evening, she became uneasy, as though something was wrong. I pointed out to her what I thought was obvious: that Arachne was in love with her, and was trying to win by these wretched games of power what she could not win by affection. Pilar assented doubtfully, but I could see that she was deeply troubled. When the opportunity arose for me to go and work with Professor Bown in New York I persuaded Pilar to cancel her engagements and come with me. In New York we were happy for six months, and I thought it was all over; but as soon as we returned to Paris it began again. Sometimes Arachne stood for days outside our apartment, even in the pouring rain. Eventually one would ask her in out of pity, but when she did come in she wouldn't say anything. She was devilishly clever though, and every now and then – usually when I met her alone – she would be quite forthcoming and even laugh at her behaviour, always insinuating somehow that I ought to feel sorry for her. So always just when I was about to take some really desperate action to get rid of her, she managed to sense this and defuse it. Later, when she attached herself to us so closely that she practically lived in our flat, she would talk in front of other people as though she was really my friend, not Pilar's – people even talked of my second wife. Don't imagine I put up with all this willingly: by this time if I had thrown her out Pilar would have left with her. And in the end, that was what happened.

When she and Pilar went off to live in London I became completely impotent. A profound gloom settled over my life, in which everything about me seemed to refer to my disability: I couldn't open a paper without seeing an article on the subject; I couldn't go to dinner without the discussion turning that way. If I switched on the TV it was a medical programme about sexual problems, and when I went to the cinema the film was about a man who spent his whole life building a very tall tower which inevitably, in a spectacular slow-motion final sequence, tumbled in a thousand pieces to the ground. Now too, the advertising industry seemed like a conspiracy of evil jinn from an Arabian tale. From everywhere they came to me with wonderful promises of love, knowing all the time in their fiendish cruelty that for me it could be nothing but humiliation.

These are the most thirsty, cruel memories I have: of women encountered for a moment talking with some acquaintance in a café, women whom it was useless to know without the possibility of love: a hat with a black spotted veil, a stockinged ankle, a dark blue leather shoe, a painted umbrella on a slender white wrist, an amber necklace, a flower, a perfume, rose-pink lipstick on the teeth, on the end of a cigarette. How I longed to hold even an ugly duckling, even a paid girl, just to feel once again the manoeuvring of strange legs in the dark and the arms about me of another mortal being. I began to be wracked by appalling headaches in the day, and fits of cramp which woke me at night. My left leg developed a crippling pain of obscure origin which came and went unpredictably and which the doctor told me was a rare and incurable form of rheumatism.

As if my sexual problem wasn't enough I was struck by a business disaster as well. Appropriately enough, Arachne was the cause of it all. Through her introduction I had become involved with a company called FBQ who were financing the development of my latest listening device; but once my work was complete FBQ simply marketed my product and refused to pay me. For the first time in my life I was in the humiliating position of having to borrow money from my mother to live. At this rather desperate juncture I received the letter from Major Shark, which explained that he had known my father and if I was ever in London would I like to discuss a business matter with him over tea? And so, as I have already said, I met Doris for the first time, and became a researcher for the British Intelligence Service.

Chapter 5

Impotence. Like a bird blinded to make it sing more sweetly, I began making a series of breathtaking discoveries in my work. Only this time I kept them secret. It was professionally dishonest, it was probably even some sort of crime against the state; but I didn't care. I had been robbed too long and I wasn't going to let anyone take this secret from me – least of all the ambitious and talent-bereft Codrington. I knew he would take all the credit for it himself. I think right at the beginning he may have got an inkling of what I was up to, but from that time on I worked on vital pieces of the jigsaw at home so that even a snooper wouldn't understand what I was doing. Slowly, with thrilling certainty of touch, I brought the thing to life: a listening device which was so small and transparent that it was effectively invisible; but better than this, undetectable by any known system of electronic detection – what in the trade is known as 'sweeping'. Its only minimal disadvantage was that it wouldn't work when in direct contact with copper or silver: when affixed to a silver candlestick, for instance, or the copper wristband I wore for my 'rheumatism'. All in all, I was probably ten years ahead of the field.

To allay Codrington's suspicions I told him I had begun work on a new bug, and got nowhere; and I let him read my reports for some of the jigsaw pieces I had worked on in the laboratory. But he, with his clodhopping earthbound imagination, was unable to see for himself the silvery path of the river which had led me to the heart of a new continent. In any case his schoolboy mind was far too obsessed by my latest series of experiments with aphrodisiacs. I had started this research when I first became impotent. At the beginning I was mainly interested in curing myself but as I progressed I realised I had stumbled on something far wider and more important; the real question wasn't about impotence but about falling in love.

Since the beginning of time man has had three dreams: to fly; to transform one element into another (the alchemist's quest to create gold); and to make a fellow human being fall in love. Of these the first two have been realised in the last hundred years: airplanes gave us flight; nuclear physics brought the possibility of changing one element into another. So, I began to consider, why shouldn't science also bring us the love potion, the arrows of Cupid, the flower which when rubbed on Titania's eyes made her fall in love with Bottom?

Naturally, Codrington was spellbound by this new line of inquiry. It diverted his attention completely away from the secret new listening device which I had affectionately nicknamed my 'ear'.

In the meantime my relations with Pilar and Arachne had deteriorated even further, if that was possible. It was at this time that Arachne invented the story about my trying to run her over in the street (a pathetic slur, copied from Matilda's schoolmarm husband); and when this failed to gain credence she started telling everybody that I was here in London with the sole purpose of making trouble for her and Pilar. When I told her I had come for my job she laughed contemptuously and said it was just a pretext; and alas, it sounded like one: in order to conceal the true purpose of my work for them, Intelligence had given me the title of radio instructor, and this was all I was allowed to claim. So it looked as though I'd given up the life of an independent researcher for that of a radio instructor, and I knew that my friends must find it odd, to say the least.

The final straw came when Pilar was at my flat one day. Arachne came round to take her to the theatre and as luck would have it Pilar was helping me prepare dinner when she arrived. I went to the door carrying, quite by chance, the meat axe I'd been chopping the cutlets with; and this was enough for the serpent-tongued Arachne to put it all over London that I'd gone after her with a hatchet.

Now the Major rang up.

'Is that you Newton? ... Yes. I was wondering if you'd be free to join me for lunch on Sunday. Quite informal ... Yes. I

35

haven't seen much of you and I wondered how you're getting on ... Good. I'll see you on Sunday then, about one o'clock.'

It was almost exactly a year since I had gone to tea and met the Major and Doris for the first time.

I was greeted by the cook who told me that the Major and Miss Shark were late back from church. She showed me upstairs to the sitting-room (it was one of those tall, thin, London houses with a room on every floor), pointed to a drinks tray and disappeared. I helped myself from a cut-glass decanter. It had a metal sign on a chain round its neck which proclaimed the word 'Jerez' in cursive script. On the floor by the fireplace one of the Sunday papers was open at the women's fashion page. Another pile of newspapers and magazines lay raggedly on the sofa. The armchairs were covered in matching ivy-leaf chintz, rather faded. On the far wall, a break-front bookcase; in the middle of the room, a round table with books in piles: I noticed among them one on communist infiltration in Britain, called *Half Marx*, another about the cocaine trade in Bolivia and a pamphlet called *The Case for Hanging*. On the walls there were a number of modern paintings and drawings, some of which looked to be of the same Spanish village. I finished my sherry and went to the window. Across the square, through the bare winter branches, I could just make out the Major and Doris, both in dark grey coats, getting out of the Major's plum-coloured Jaguar.

We dined on the ground floor at the back of the house. The windows of the dining-room gave on to a small garden of sodden grass and dark wet paving stones. The Major wore a dark suit and a navy-blue silk bow-tie over which he tucked his napkin. He tipped his second glass of sherry into his soup and stirred briskly, holding his spoon like a pen between his pudgy black-haired fingers. He talked about his house in Spain, and then about Spain in general; he talked of 'the Spanish' as though the fact of living in Spain gave everyone an identical set of likes and dislikes, abilities and shortcomings. Then he talked about my cousin, whom he still insisted on calling my uncle, and whom he had actually met since our last conversation, once, and as far as I could make out, in the lavatory of some club.

Doris took little notice of either of us. Refusing the soup, she

36

filed her nails and stared aimlessly out of the window, an expression of total vacuity in her cowlike eyes. I could see now that she was beautiful. Not that she had changed in any particular way since I had first seen her; but suddenly all the rag doll pieces had come together and the puppet had turned into a ballerina. Sometimes I have thought that the key to Doris's beauty was its bounty, as her name implied: her skin rather than milk-white was actually creamy, her eyes impossibly large and yet perfectly almond-shaped, her hair was enough for three women ... but there is no way to pin down the secret of that girl's attractiveness. I remember saying to the Major for the second time, 'No, as a matter of fact, I haven't been to Hawtree since I was six', and wondering if I ever regained my virility would I take that hand in mine and, extracting the nailfile from its grip, lean forward and kiss those oddly tapering fingers? And my imagination rushed upstairs to where she already lay asleep with her hair all over the sheets and her cheeks flushed with the effort of love; while in my mind I hear again and again like pealing church-bells the cries that filled the room only moments ago.

The cook brought in a roast. The Major carved. Doris refused.

'Come on darling, you must have something.'

'All right then,' Doris said sulkily, 'just one slice.'

The Major didn't try to draw her into the conversation. He treated her more or less like a child, and Doris put on a childish voice when she talked to him, even in front of me. As I saw them sitting at either end of the table like husband and wife, I wondered if he was in love with her, or she with him, or both. They had that sort of family conversation which depends on key words which mean nothing to an outsider. The Major would say something like 'Baby Brock, Doris', and Doris's eyes would shine with amusement at something which I didn't comprehend. In fact I began to think that family talk might be the only language she understood: when I asked her questions she would blush and stammer, and the Major would step in and speak for her. I had seldom met a girl who had so little to say for herself.

After lunch, we drank our coffee in the sitting-room and Doris began to eat chocolates. I noticed a pack of tarot cards

37

on the table and asked if she could tell fortunes. This brought out the conversationalist in her.

'Oh yes,' she said, 'I'm amazingly psychic. I can always tell someone's personality the first time I meet them. I write it in my diary and it always turns out right. It's outrageous.' And her eyes shone with enthusiasm. The Major was making grunting sounds behind a cigar smokescreen. 'I'm studying tarot too,' she went on, 'and I Ching. I have an occult teacher. But Daddy doesn't like him. He's in a group,' she added with evident delight.

'Lot of rubbish,' said the Major.

'Don't be cross, Daddy!' said Doris petulantly.

At that moment the telephone rang and the Major picked it up. He said sharply to Doris, 'It's for you,' and then turned his back on her and limped over to the window. Doris simply said, 'Oh, all right, I'll take it upstairs,' and left the room. For a minute the Major went on staring out into the square; his anger showed only in a series of involuntary little snorts which forced out jets of cigar smoke through his nostrils. When these died down he shook his head as if breaking a reverie and returned to the mantelpiece where he crushed out his cigar in a glass ashtray.

'I don't like it,' he said. 'There's some fellow pestering her.' And he shook his head sadly.

I said, 'Perhaps he's in love with her.'

The Major ignored me and went on shaking his head.

When I thought of Doris I was haunted by the impression of the soul of a very beautiful woman gone out to lunch, leaving behind only its envelope, as lovely and lifeless as a ball-gown on a hanger. I know that people always talk as though one could fall in love with beauty alone, but I knew I could no sooner have done it than love a dead woman. I tried to picture the sort of silly young man who might lose his head over Doris. Someone with as few ideas in his head as she – an occult teacher with an electric guitar? Or perhaps a vain, older man who wanted to hear everyone say he had a pretty girlfriend? In my mind's eye Doris's lover was a composite moronic Englishman: chinless, wearing a striped shirt and suede shoes and carrying an electric guitar in his hand like a teddy-bear, for ever on his way to some old school reunion where he and his ilk drank beer and behaved reasonably towards each other.

The Major started talking about the Knights of St Expeth and how they believed in upholding western values against subversion of all kinds. He obviously took the Knights business terribly seriously: his face, which was in any case the same grey colour as the marble of the fireplace, had moulded itself into a marmoreal intensity, and the frown lines on his forehead seemed to be growing as permanent as those on a recumbent crusader. In his absorption a piece of ash had fallen from his cigar on to his trouser leg, where it now lay undisturbed.

Doris came back and collected the coffee cups and the tray. I remember noticing the way she opened the door only a fraction and slipped in through the gap – a way of entering the room which was typical of her. It was the same reticence which kept her face habitually pointed downwards, so that when she looked at you she was quite naturally in that position (face down, eyes up) which is supposed to be so flattering to a woman.

When she had gone the Major said, 'Newton, have you been doing research which you haven't disclosed to us?'

The bluntness of the question, so typical of him, might have taken me by surprise had it come six months earlier, but by now I was so practised in concealment and so inured to the deception, that I was able to give an immediate negative reply.

'I just wondered,' he went on coolly, 'because you know that such a course of action would be an infringement of your terms of employment. We hold exclusive rights on all your work: there is no room for freelancing.'

'Of course. It would put me in an impossible position.'

'Good. Just so long as you know.'

He appeared to be quite satisfied, and went on to question me about my work in general.

'Codrington tells me you're involved with some kind of aphrodisiac at the moment. Is that so?'

'What I'm looking for is something much more than the ordinary aphrodisiac,' I said. 'Codrington sometimes finds me hard to follow.'

'Gifted fellow, Codrington,' said the Major. I gave what I hoped was a condescending smile.

'What I am trying to isolate is the electrochemical mechanism in the brain which corresponds to our falling in love. I want, by means of simple electrodes or the introduction of a chemical into the body, to be able to produce love, full sexual love. I believe such a mechanism exists and was identified by the ancients as Aphrodite's Girdle. In the myths whoever wore the girdle became the object of such love. I want to find this, or else its converse, Cupid's arrow. Again, according to the story, whoever was shot by Cupid's arrow fell immediately in love. The idea is common to practically every culture, every age. There is always a witch or shaman proposing a love drug, something that will conjure an instant passion in the recipient, but until now all this has been no more convincing or successful than the equally perennial search of the alchemists for the philosopher's stone. Does this mean that the existence of a love potion is a chimera? I am not convinced of it – after all, men have tried and failed for millennia to fly, and yet only yesterday we were suddenly able to do it; today of course everyone takes it for granted. And I think aphrodisiacs are a similar case. The witches who administered love potions throughout history were no more capable of producing the real thing than they were of designing jet aircraft. In this sense, history waits on technology. Today the picture is different. In my research I'm using the most up-to-date equipment and the most recent research into the libido. I am convinced that Aphrodite's Girdle is within our reach now; and I believe that such a discovery, if I make it, will not only be of benefit to science, but more particularly to the Secret Service.'

I didn't say anything about the effect of such a drug on impotence because I wasn't sure what it would be. Personally I had a scientist's hunch that its discovery would also be my cure; but my condition made me loathe to dwell on the question. Instead I fell silent as the Major took from a box beside him a cigar which dwarfed his fat little fingers; there followed a click of the cutter and then his match struck a reflecting flame in the corner of the Spanish village, and volutes of smoke began to move out into the drawing-room. Outside the window the burnt husk of a piece of paper floated slowly across the stormwater sky and into the trees where it caught on a branch and hung for a minute like a wig on a stand; then a gust tore it off and tumbled it past the back of the sofa; and I remembered the back of Pilar's head with the black hair cut halfway down her neck, and the portrait of her which has now gone under the dustsheet.

Chapter 6

That day the rats were refusing to copulate. It was as though instead of goading the sex drive like a picador, my latest aphrodisiac concoction had done a matador's work. The little fornicative arena I had constructed in my laboratory was as peaceful and slow-moving as a cricket match: the rats stood about looking slightly bored in their different corners, changing their positions from time to time like fielders at the end of an over. In ironic contrast to this was the control experiment where two rats in perfectly normal condition were making a good-humoured attempt to sodomise a third. I was just considering whether or not it was worth continuing the experiment when the Major said, 'Hello.'

He had come in without knocking, on those soft crêpe-soled shoes of his and was standing just behind me, looking over my left shoulder. His dark grey coat was glistening with the damp of the streets and droplets clustered on his eyebrows; the asphalt-coloured eyes with their rings of grey lard observed my surprise with that utterly matter of fact expression which he loved to adopt when announcing something particularly impressive or astonishing.

'Am I interrupting something?' he asked, and then without waiting for a reply went on, 'I'd like to have a few words with you.'

'Have a seat.'

The Major walked back to the door and shut it. He undid the buttons of his overcoat and thrust both hands into his trouser pockets and stood facing me.

He said, 'I want you to work for me as a secret agent.'

As though it was infectious, I found myself adopting the same matter of fact manner as him. It felt as though we were re-enacting the famous scene where Stanley, having searched for years through uncharted jungles and at last stumbling on the elusive doctor, can show no more emotion than if he's arrived before his host at luncheon and found Livingstone also early, waiting with a glass of sherry in the sitting-room.

'Ah, yes. When do you want me to start?'

'Tomorrow, I suppose,' said the Major, in the tones which Stanley might have used if he'd been asked exactly when his supply of fresh water was going to run out.

'That's fine by me,' I said, 'I'm getting nowhere with this lot,' and I gestured towards the rat-arena on the table. 'Do you have any particular mission in mind?'

'As a matter of fact, yes,' said the Major. 'There's a chap in Barcelona who's supposed to have developed your ... how do you call it? Your Aphrodite's Girdle; and if it's true we want to know about it fast. It seemed to me you'd be particularly well-qualified for the job.'

He paused and peered over the arena. One of the rats, apparently bowled out, was passing with perfect indifference the incoming batsman on the way to the pavilion.

'The scientist in question is a certain Dr Fitzer,' the Major continued. 'For the past twelve years he has run a centre for sexual research which he calls the Fitzer Institute, and where he conducts his experiments.'

Somewhere in my mind the door of a Paris apartment opened on a jumble of leather-upholstered chairs and harpsichords.

'Is this Dr Fitzer a mathematician?' I asked.

'Apparently so. No one knows quite what his origins are; Jewish East Europe, one supposes. But we know that he was attached to the University of Paris for a while. It seems he was defrocked or whatever you call it in universities; left under a bit of a cloud.'

'I think I knew him there.'

He looked at me sideways. 'Before your time Newton, I should think.'

'If it's the same man, he was my tutor when I was a child. I was a child prodigy – perhaps you remember?'

The Major turned his back on me again and walked towards the computer.

'So you were, of course. I was forgetting. So you knew this Fitzer then, did you?'

43

'If it's the same one, yes.'

'That could complicate things. On the other hand it could be useful.' He turned to face me. 'You must begin training immediately. Because this is a special mission I'm going to prepare you for it myself. Can you report to my house tomorrow morning at nine?'

And so the training sessions began. How well I remember my elation as I arrived at the Major's house on that first frosty morning! A delicious smell of coffee pervaded the hall while I took off my coat and my gloves; on the table lay a faded green canvas guncase and beside it a woollen cap in the Rastafarian colours. I assumed the cap was Doris's, and that the gun was to be mine; however, it turned out to be the Major's shotgun which he had taken shooting at the week-end.

'No,' said the Major when I asked him, 'you won't be having a gun.'

'I see. So I'm not to be licensed to kill.'

The Major looked at me so oddly I felt I must have committed a *faux pas* even to speak of such a thing; obviously even within the trade a certain discretion was expected of one. Nevertheless I couldn't entirely hide my disappointment.

The Major didn't offer me coffee; instead we descended immediately to the study for a preliminary briefing. It was dark as midnight down here. The Major switched on all the lamps and the gas-fire under the mantelpiece and I shifted along the sofa towards the flame now turning from blue to an orange glow. Opposite me the Major was indifferent to the cold; he was one of those men to whom the time of day means nothing, who are equally active and awake at six in the morning or midnight. Now he knocked out an old pipe into a big marble ashtray and began stuffing it from a tartan pouch; the match flared and clouds of smoke enveloped the room and my bowels contracted unpleasantly. He took a sheaf of papers from the table beside him, glanced through them and then tapped them down on his knee.

'Dr Fitzer first came to Barcelona in 1966,' he began, 'when he was invited by the University to lecture on computer analysis in sexual pathology. Four years later, in 1970, he left the University to set up the Institute which is named after him. From the outset, the Institute enjoyed a certain notoriety

44

because of the deviants who flocked there. These people were encouraged to come by Dr Fitzer who appears to have used them as raw material for his research, guinea-pigs really, although at the Institute they are always referred to as collaborators. The high proportion of these collaborators, probably as many as seventy per cent, are foreigners, mainly Germans and Americans. However, the Institute is easily accessible to everyone – except for the part that interests us: the top floor which comprises the laboratory of Dr Fitzer himself. This part of the building is kept rigorously separated; security is very strict. As far as we can determine, access is by a private lift which is always kept locked and is fitted with an alarm. It's going to be a tough nut to crack, and I think that the way to do it will be by intensive use of listening devices in the uncontrolled area of the building. It's a common spying technique which could be very useful to us: one deduces the secret one is after from information which isn't classified. There's plenty of scope for this sort of thing at the Institute: on the ground floor there's even a small shop where the various products of the Fitzer laboratory are offered for sale to the public. It's worth noting that in marked contrast to the rest of the retail sex trade, the prices are invariably low. The shop is advertised as non-profit making – to this day the funding of the Institute remains obscure. Contrary to what one might expect, the Institute is tolerated by the authorities. Even during the Franquist era, Dr Fitzer seems to have experienced little or no police harassment, though on two occasions privately organised right-wing groups have raided the premises. Once a bomb was left there, though it was later defused by a disposal squad. In neither instance did the trouble-makers manage to get as far as the laboratory. In view of these two raids I am disinclined to think that the Institute enjoys the active protection of the authorities. Rather, I believe it has profited from the long-established laxity of morals in the Old City particularly as regards sexual deviation.'

The Major spoke with evident disgust whenever he touched on 'deviation' of any kind; and with the vulgar insensitivity common to all bigots he assumed that I didn't disagree. He made no concession to the fact that this Dr Fitzer was in all probability the same man who was my old friend and teacher.

Listening to him talk, I experienced the same stifling feeling which I get in cabs where the driver, leaning back and half turning his head towards the slit in the glass partition, makes some remark, which begins, 'It's not that I'm prejudiced but . . .' In taxis it's easy to rap on the glass and get out, but on this occasion I had no choice except to sit and listen to the Major's insinuations. What was the man talking about? Didn't he know my wife was a lesbian? Did he think that made me agree with him? Sweat broke out on my forehead and I tried to remember Dr Fitzer's long-suffering dictum, 'My tear, it were the world that were small, not Mozart.'

It was an odd and exciting period in my life, looming far larger in my memory than the actual time it occupied. That I was jealous of Dr Fitzer there was no doubt. Because we had always been intellectual equals I couldn't help looking on him as a rival; it might seem ungenerous, but in my heart I hoped that he hadn't found Cupid's arrow.

Once I actually dreamed of uncovering his drug as a hoax: it existed in my imagination as a bottle of heart-shaped lozenges of livid green colour and I was standing at the counter of an imaginary shop in an imaginary Institute. 'Look at this,' I was saying to a crowd of customers, and pumping an inflatable woman so that her head jerked backwards and forwards ridiculously, 'It's no more like a real woman than a bunch of balloons. And these are the same.' And here I shook the pills on to the counter like pepper from a pot and the people in the shop began to curry the Fitzer of my childhood with plastic vibrators. I was ashamed of these jealous feelings. But it is interesting that even in my great namesake, Sir Isaac Newton, who was so dispassionate about what he had discovered that he didn't bother to publish it until many years later, even Newton was swept up in a fury of jealousy when Leibniz claimed to have discovered the calculus first. But whatever my mixed feelings as a scientist, above all I was elated by my new-found role in the Secret Service; and naturally in the back of my mind there was also the hope that Dr Fitzer's aphrodisiac might prove to be my cure . . .

When the preliminary briefing sessions were over, I began an intensive course of espionage technique. The Major was a mine of fascinating information – as he said himself, he'd been beating the Russians for forty-odd years now. And he in turn was pleased by my proficiency in what he himself obviously found a difficult and taxing subject: codes. We began on a clear winter day – I remember it well, because we were in the sitting-room instead of the subterranean study and I could see the white sun through the filigree of branches in the square, right down almost on the rooftops in the winter-blue sky, and turning the sugary rime on the pavement to a black wetness as it swung the long blocks of shadow across the square. The Major was irritated by a navy-blue shoelace which he must have thought was a black one the night before under artificial light; he kept cocking his foot and peering round his knee as he lectured me (our sessions always had something of the lecture about them – it was the Major's style), telling me about different sorts of codes and how to use them, then explaining – and getting slightly wrong – the various methods of code-breaking. I pointed out that it was really quite easy to make an unbreakable code and explained how it was done. I could tell the Major was impressed by the way that I suddenly had his full attention; for a moment he even seemed to have forgotten his shoelace.

When I had finished he said, 'Good, I can see you really understand these things. Have you ever thought of working in codes?'

'Not really,' I said. 'I feel spying is more my thing.'

'Yes. Of course you do.'

He taught me about communications. 'The single most important ingredient in any mission. If communications are good, almost any obstacle can be dealt with, but without proper communications it's a bloody mess. I can tell you because I've worked on that kind of mission, and it's been a disaster from the word go.'

So I learnt how to pass or 'drop' information by means of a 'brush drop' when the hand-over takes place on a bus, or in a church, or even better, in the darkness of a theatre, coming in late and picking up the ticket that's been left for one; or by a 'drop' in some secluded 'post-box' in the country, where it's easy to see if you're followed; or else by a city 'post-box' – usually a trusted and conveniently-placed intermediary like a hotel reception clerk or a café waiter. He showed me how to use various invisible inks, pointing out as he did so that this popular schoolboy game was really very useful in the real spy world. 'It's actually almost foolproof,' he said. 'You see there's almost no chance that your enemy will hit on the right developing agent straight away and, of course, to use the wrong one would destroy the message altogether.' I learnt about microdots which condense a whole page of information into something the size of a full-stop. 'This might fool an unsuspecting customs officer,' the Major said, 'but unfortunately even a microdot is quite easily detectable by someone who's looking for it. A much safer method is the screech message. In this case you condense a two-minute message into a five-second burst of "screech". The person at the other end picks it up and expands the screech back to its original length. The beauty of this method is that no one knows which wavelength you are going to use, or when you're going to use it, and the broadcast is too short to be found by simple scanning. Technically it's so simple you could buy the equipment at a corner shop.'

As far as locks were concerned, the Major insisted I wouldn't have any problem. 'Most locks in Barcelona are of such an elementary old-fashioned kind,' he said, producing from a drawer in the desk a set of seven skeleton keys, 'that with these you should be able to open any door in the city.' And he showed me how to operate them, demonstrating on various doors about the house. Copying his procedure I was surprised how easy it was, when I had always imagined it to be a special art known only to practised burglars and spies. In fact I was beginning to feel a certain professional confidence about my new role.

The most tedious part of the training was the days we spent on listening devices. If anything was my domain this should have been, yet unlike with codes the Major seemed incapable of leaving me to it. Again and again we went through such matters as bugging technology, how to place bugs, and how to detect them. The odd thing was that it was I who was giving the lessons here, not the Major. At times I grew so bored I was tempted to tell the old buffer about my newest device which made most of this stuff obsolete; but I resisted. Instead I patiently explained for the fourth or fifth time how one set about positioning bugs in a room, in a corridor, in a car; how to listen to street conversations; how to sabotage venetian blinds. ('Why do you want to do that?' the Major asked. 'Because it scrambles any reflector system and the monitor picks up nothing intelligible,' I explained. We were really on our ABCs.)

He was almost insatiably inquisitive. We wasted hours, even whole days, on aspects of bugging which I had mastered in the days of my sorties to Matilda: such things as could hardly be expected to give one the edge over an enemy spy. I think it was principally out of exasperation that in the end I placed bugs in his house − naturally not the kind I was teaching him about, but my very latest babies, my undetectable darlings, my ears. So when I was alone in the evening I could turn on the tape-recorders and play back the life of the Major's house. There were sounds of typing from the study, or long silences punctuated by the turning of a page and the occasional click of the cigar cutter; or else the tapping of his pipe on an ashtray or on the grate of the fireplace − the latter had a metallic ring which distinguished it; and an occasional telephone conversation. From Doris's room came the rustle of chocolate papers in the box, the flick of tarot cards and magazine pages, the record player which played the same song again and again, 'I Heard It Through The Grapevine' in a punk version; I later discovered this was a record made by her boyfriend and his friends, their only one, but which had never been released. It was all trivial enough, but then I wasn't trying to discover anything in particular. I think the irony of it appealed to me: while I explained the crudest type of bug to the Major I was at the same time using the most sophisticated one on him. It was a kind of specialist's revenge on the pedantic beginner ...

As my experience and skill developed, so I began to see the Major's limitations more clearly. Although a complete professional, he had grown up with the modern bureaucratic Intelligence Service and therefore lacked the real imagination, the flair, which has been the secret of success for all the great classical spies; and since he had no knowledge of the history of espionage he was blissfully unaware of it. Where in the Major's tidy British mind was the cruel psychology which had allowed Mata Hari to play on men's passions? And where the mastery of language and disguise which enabled Sir Richard Burton to penetrate the bazaars of Sind and the mosques of Mecca? Such matters were fairyland to his plodding *modus operandi*: he lacked the imaginative leap which would have taken him from the ranks of the efficient bureaucrats into the pantheon of master spies. Sometimes he would say rather pathetically, 'We must use our imagination, Newton.' To which I could only reply, 'We must indeed.'

Another example of his pedestrian approach was his refusal to look at the great issues. He was fixed on the details of the mission in hand whereas I, while equally able to concentrate on details, always kept the broader picture at the back of my mind. It seemed clear to me that one shouldn't forget the ideologies and political alliances which formed the background of a particular mission: to ignore them was to invite misunderstanding. But if ever I asked him about the structure and organisation of the KGB for example, he would say, 'The KGB doesn't come into it,' or more annoyingly, 'You just concentrate on not stubbing your toe and the KGB will take care of itself.' This was a footling joke which referred to the time when, without my glasses and in the semi-darkness, I'd stubbed my toe on the step down to his study. The Major had that sort of sense of humour which regards as the height of drollery physical pain in others, and dog-messes.

He taught me nothing about the art of disguise. Indeed, as far as I could make out he knew nothing about it either; but I knew from my reading of *Kim* that disguise was essential and in my spare time I studied the principles of it from an actor's manual. I chose a variety of types which I thought would be useful: an old lady in a camelhair coat, an Orthodox priest (false beard), a balding labourer, and – inspired by Burton – a Sikh. This last was in many ways my best one but I recognised that in Barcelona it would be less useful to me than in London.

The Major now took it into his head that I should join the Knights. This was a great mark of confidence, even favour, and I had the utmost difficulty in dissuading him. When I said I didn't think I would agree with their aims he became furious and demanded to know what aims? I really didn't know, besides an obsession with chastity, and he was so touchy about anything to do with honour that it was difficult to gauge how explicit to be. Luckily he came to my rescue by telling me in glowering and snapping terms that I didn't know what the ideas of the Knights were.

'In that case,' I said, 'how do I know if I want to join them or not?'

'Oh you'll agree with them all right,' he told me. 'I'll get the papers for your application.'

One week-end the Major left me a coding and decoding exercise and went to stay with Lord de Witt in the country. This particular week-end had been alluded to almost daily over the past two weeks. Cousin of General de Witt whom the Major had served under in the war, Lord de Witt was one of the rather grand acquaintances that the Major talked about so much. His snobbishness was of an old-world kind, which must have had its origins in his early youth: I remember thinking that the plum-coloured Jaguar was acting as a time-machine to his spirit, taking him not merely down to the woods of Gloucestershire but back through time to the world of his boyhood in the age of European empires; so that by the time he reached his destination the great houses of England would be once again lavishly maintained by armies of white-capped maids, the Land Rovers metamorphosed into shooting-brakes, the light, modern suitcases into heavy trunks and black hat boxes with hotel labels on them. This was the attraction of my cousin and his country house where I had been sick in the lavatory as a boy. Sometimes I wondered if the Major hadn't taken me on merely to strengthen this connection; but I knew this was ridiculous: we were far too distantly related.

I didn't really blame the Major for his snobbery. I grant that at times it made him appear in a bad light but on the whole it was such a quixotic affair, maintained so much in the teeth of reality, that it was hard to take it as anything other than a sort of boyish wish he'd never quite grown out of. This should have been touching, but wasn't. There was something too grim about the Major for him ever to be touching.

That Saturday Doris let me into the house. I had obviously got her out of bed – she was clad in a dirty bathrobe – and she went back to bed immediately afterwards. Around lunchtime she re-emerged in the kitchen, wearing a tight, black leather skirt and a leopardskin T-shirt and she had very heavy black make-up on her eyes: not the sort of get-up one would have expected the Major to approve.

'Oh Daddy's very old-fashioned,' she explained, 'he'd do his nut if he saw me wearing this stuff round the house.' She smiled and added, 'I put it on to go out at night though.'

'Doesn't he mind at night?'

'He doesn't see. I put on a long overcoat over the top when I go out. When I get home he's always in bed anyway.'

My lunch and her breakfast coincided. Doris made the coffee, smoked, answered the phone, played the radio, read her stars and mine out of *Fashion*, the magazine where she worked as a typist. In all this I felt a certain shyness; for twenty-five she was unusually girlish. She told me about a special sort of belt she was going to buy that afternoon and which she described as being 'very tech'. The belt had four rows of studs and you wore it crosswise 'like a gunbelt' but it didn't hold up your trousers. Doris was very excited about it. Her boyfriend Mungo already had one: he was in a pop group who all 'played computers'.

'It's tech,' said Doris. 'Don't you love computers?'

Unable to match her enthusiasm I pointed out that I'd nevertheless worked with them for twenty-odd years.

'Wow, you must be a real star at Space Invaders.'

'Space Invaders?' I said, 'What's that exactly?'

'Computer game,' said Doris. 'Incredible. And what do you think of computer music?'

'Computer music?' I asked, thinking of Xenakis and Kagel.

'Yes,' said Doris. 'Like the Dancettes.'

She took me upstairs to her room and put on one of their records. I thought it was pretty awful but I didn't say anything because I gathered Doris and her boyfriend knew some members of the band.

'They're not very well-known yet,' she said, 'that's the only trouble.'

She showed me her pets: a caged gerbil and some worms which she kept in a glass-sided box. The worms were in earth but you could see their tracks where they coincided with the edge of the box. She had a budgerigar too which she fed with seeds and cuttlefish.

'I wanted to have a dog and a cat too,' she said, 'but Daddy only lets me have animals which you can keep in a cage. He says he doesn't want the house turned into a zoo. He won't even let me have rabbits in the garden. Don't you think it's unfair?'

'I suppose he has his reasons.'

'I have a dog in Spain called Screw-screw. I got him for my birthday when I was little. But I can't bring him back here because of the quarantine.'

She opened the gerbil's cage and put her slender forearm in through the door. The gerbil let her pick it up without showing any sign of fear, and she held it up for me to see, its head poking out between her tapered fingers.

'His name's Minos but I call him Minipin-pin-pin.'

She looked at it with the same sort of loving admiration as she looked at her father. I remember thinking there was something incredibly pure about this, and about the freshness of her complexion and her big chestnut eyes and their immaculate scleras. While she held the little animal I cleaned out the cage under her instructions.

'Do you like animals?' she asked.

'Not much.'

'Not even dogs?'

'I don't much like any pets.'

'How horrible.'

'It's not horrible. I just like wild animals better.'

'It's horrible to hate any animals. I always mistrust anyone who doesn't love animals and children.'

She told me to stay absolutely still and then put the gerbil down on the floor. It walked slowly away from us, across a patch of sunlight on the grey carpet by the brass bed, stopping now and then and sniffing the air unhurriedly.

Doris's room was clearly the same room as she'd had in her childhood. On the wall was a faded wallpaper of small red dots on a white ground, the white now gone yellow and the red turned darker, almost to brown, like the colour of her mouth. The curtains, even more faded, bore a balloon pattern in primary colours which had since turned a rather nostalgic pastel shade. On the bed a great heap of animals made out of cloth were propped up on the pillow; the dressing-table bore a framed photograph of a very beautiful young man whom I took to be her boyfriend, and another of her mother and father, the Major looking handsome, even romantic, in a double-breasted suit. The mother had clearly been a great beauty and one could see that while Doris had inherited many of her features, her mother seemed to have more grace, more elegance. On the floor, just where the gerbil had got to, was an old box-type record player with the lid open and a lot of records lying out of their covers beside it.

'Is that a crystal ball?'

'Yes. Actually I'm meant to cover it up when it's not being used.'

She picked up the crystal ball from where it lay on the floor and put it on the dressing-table next to the picture of the beautiful young man. Then she covered it with a blue silk handkerchief from the drawer. I noticed that she only looked awkward when she moved; if one could have frozen her now, say, with one hand resting on the shrouded ball and her reddy-gold hair spread around her shoulders and her brown eyes contemplating the gerbil, she would have had all the beauty of the mother in the photograph.

Chapter 7

The Fitzer Institute was a large grey building in the Gracia district of Barcelona, just off the Plaça del Diamant. Its identity was proclaimed by a single brass plate, attached inconspicuously to the doorpost just beneath the bell. I pushed the bell, a buzzer sounded and I walked into a dark hallway with a staircase going up. Through a door to the right was the shop of the Institute where the Fitzer merchandise was sold; a sign on the wall indicated that Reception was on the first floor. The impracticality of this arrangement was soon apparent to anyone who ventured upwards: in a Spanish house, the first floor is usually several floors up, the intervening storeys belonging to that multifold species *entresuelo*. In the Fitzer Institute the first floor was really the third.

'Reception' was in fact more like a common-room for the people who worked at the Institute. It was a large room, very modern in design, with a prevailing atmosphere of quiet opulence. Double-glazing had been fitted to the windows on the street side of the house, and the air was cool and conditioned. Low, leather sofas and armchairs were grouped round shiny black tables, alongside which reading lamps arched their long stainless steel necks. The walls were hung with framed prints whose protective glass threw back the light from the long windows. Opposite the door at a desk surrounded by plants sat the receptionist, a little fair-haired man from Nebraska who had tinted eyelashes and wore colourless lipstick and pale-coloured, immaculately pressed suits. Behind him was an American-style filter machine for making coffee. In its outward appearance all this was not very different from, say, the reception-room of a large company. It was only the occupants who were likely to strike the newcomer as unusual: in the lavatory it was a common sight to see a man adjusting his make-up; and the arrival at Reception of a woman wearing a dog's collar and held on a lead by her companion, would not have caused so much as a raised eyebrow. To the uninitiated, it might seem that the *habitués* of the Institute dressed as men or women more or less indifferently; in either case, there was a marked preference among their *couturières* for leather and rubber and plastic.

The Nebraskan receptionist asked me who I was. 'I'm doing research into aphrodisiacs,' I said. 'I have an appointment to see Dr Fitzer.'

Beneath their tinted lashes the man's eyes bore a look of cautious mistrust. 'Dr Fitzer only communicates with the press in written statements.'

'I'm not a journalist,' I said. 'I'm a scientist.'

The man pressed a button on an intercom and told somebody I had arrived; I took a seat. Sunk deep in the broad leather armchair I noticed the prints on the wall were all of mythic sexual heroes: Pasiphae, Onan, Sappho.

A dark-haired woman came up to me and said in Spanish, 'Are you Herman Newton?'

'Yes.'

'Will you come with me please?'

It was not the sing-song Spanish of my Mexican childhood but it wasn't the lisping Castilian, or the heavy-vowelled Catalan of the city either. I followed her out on to the landing, where she took from her handbag a key-ring attached to a small silver phallus, selected a key and inserted it in a steel door. The door opened on a lift, which I knew from my briefings with the Major must lead up to Dr Fitzer's laboratory. It was a very small lift so I had to stand close to the woman. She was in her twenties, strong looking, though not above medium height. All her movements were powerful and her voice was strong and deep; there was some sort of force, too, about the severity with which the planes of her face were defined. She had dark hair and dark lips and a squint which seemed to accentuate the strength of her black eyes. She was not conventionally good looking, but there was something sensual about her mouth and about the whole force of her personality.

I said, 'Where do you come from?'

'Skopje,' she said, and then seeing I hadn't understood, added, 'In Macedonia.'

'Ah, a Yugoslav.'

'Of origin. Now I have a Spanish passport.'

She opened the door, once again using her phallus-attached key, and we stepped out into a room which brought on a rush of that sensation called in English *déjà-vu*: suites of leather furniture, ranks of chessmen, Indian gods, a harpsichord. Only now the gods were on posters and the chessmen which had been so tall and splendidly carved were quite diminished and not unlike a set I myself had purchased a few years previously on a rainy weekend in Massachusetts. When I had been a child Dr Fitzer's chessmen and his gods had seemed practically real, rather in the same way that I remember pantomimes of breathtaking splendour replete with treasure chests rich beyond dreams and the women pure, incredibly embellished in spangles and silk, flying through the air; pantomimes which as a grown-up are no more than paste jewellery, a repertory actress and badly-concealed ropes.

Signalling me to wait where I was, Myrna went into the next room, where I could see part of a massy kneehole desk bearing the display screen and keyboard of a computer, with a grey plastic belt looping away from it across the room to a printer that must lie concealed by the angle of the door. All round the desk papers and scientific periodicals lay in snowdrifts: I recognised immediately the peach-coloured covers of the French quarterly LIMP (*Lectures sur l'impotence et le malfonctionnement du pénis*) which I subscribed to myself, as well as the journals of the aphrodisiac association. I wondered with a tinge of professional pride if Dr Fitzer had read my article in last November's issue, volume CCCXV, with the cunning pun in the title, *Restoration of sexually utile penile erection among impotent males:a reappraisal.*

'But I told you never!' A voice that came across a quarter of a century and the greater part of my life was raised irritably in the next room. 'How many times do I have to tell you that nobody, but nobody comes up here? Well? What are you waiting for? Take him down to my sitting-room and have him wait for me there.'

And I remembered now this tetchiness of Dr Fitzer's: when I forgot my homework he would click his tongue irritably in just the way I could hear him doing next door. Myrna re-emerged pouting sulkily, her dark complexion turned a shade deeper than usual. She looked at me briefly and jerked her head towards the door as she strode out. In the lift I said I had known Dr Fitzer a long time ago in Paris and she muttered something I didn't quite catch about senility.

The room where I waited for the Doctor was clearly designed for receiving outsiders: there were various pamphlets about his researches on a side-table as well as some pornographic magazines published by the Institute. Myrna offered me a drink from a dumb waiter in the corner but I took a coffee instead. Perhaps because there were so many Americans here, there seemed to be one of those filter machines making watery coffee everywhere you went: the whole Institute reeked of it.

When Dr Fitzer arrived he didn't recognise me at all. No longer clicking, in fact in quite good spirits, he advanced stoopingly to shake my hand, tall even to an adult, and thin as ever, though now his cheeks were hollow and his eye sockets had deepened so that each olive-coloured eye looked out like a beast from its lair. His hair was a rich brown, of a very slightly redder hue than its natural colour had been.

'How do you do?' he said, 'Have a seat.' His eyes automatically checked the clock on the mantelpiece: behind his attentive gaze he was already making up his mind how many minutes he would give me. I suppose I had imagined that he would know me immediately, that his long frame would unwind out of its chair as it had in the past, and that he would start to pace the room excitedly, the way I always remembered him, saying, 'Tear boy! Tear boy!' As it was I had to remind him of our connection and for a moment he seemed to have difficulty recalling which in a long line of precocious pupils I was.

Finally he said, 'Herman Newton? Yes, I remember. Ah, you were such a beautiful child . . .'

His voice trailed off and for a minute the olive green eyes seemed to lose their focus . . . then he was back in the present and asking me what brought me to Barcelona. I began to talk about aphrodisiacs, explaining that I had been doing research in the field for two years and that, quite by accident, I had heard about his work from a colleague.

'You certainly keep yourself to yourself,' I said.

'In a field like ours you have to. Nowadays scientists find it

58

easier to steal discoveries than to make them. One must be very careful. And as for the press – well, I don't need to tell you how they look on anything to do with sex. All in all I've found that it's better to be circumspect.'

This wasn't very encouraging. In order to put him at his ease, I told him about my own research. When I described the setbacks I'd encountered he assented dismissively, as though he'd found them out long ago or else (more crushingly still) could have predicted the result without bothering with the experiment. This attitude reminded me very much of the lessons I'd had with him as a child: it wasn't that he was condescending, it was more the way he moved the conversation on from time to time when something didn't interest him.

'Cast a few flies on the water,' the Major had said, 'see what you can tease him into telling you outright. There's no point in pretending that you aren't an expert.' I cast flies, but Fitzer was lurking in the depths. And I could understand why. Oh yes, I knew only too well what makes us inventors so secretive: hadn't FBQ stolen my first listening device? And back in London I knew that Codrington, like a sort of bureaucratic lightning conductor, was ready to appropriate the least flash of my genius. No, it didn't surprise me that Fitzer stayed mum. I was impressed, however, by the coolness of his act. Even when I began describing Aphrodite's Girdle he showed no special interest and merely remarked in an off-hand way, 'Come, come, you surely don't imagine something as complex and personal as falling in love could be induced by anything as simple as a drug?'

'But Dr Fitzer, you yourself sell Spanish Fly downstairs. What's that meant to be if not an aphrodisiac?'

'Ah, aphrodisiacs, yes. I've always thought it a terrible swindle myself, but people will have what they want; and it seems people want them. You've no idea how much rhino horn costs these days . . .'

'But Spanish Fly and rhino horn have been around for centuries and we know they have no aphrodisiac effect whatever. Surely as men of science we can do better than that. After all, our age is the first in history that has taught man to fly . . .'

'So why not make him horny you mean? Well yes, I suppose there's a certain logic in the idea.'

Then I asked him straight out, 'Does the Institute have any

research on the subject? I'd be very flattered if you'd let me see what you've done.'

'Tear me no. I don't have time for such things. But tell me about your own work. You want a drug that actually makes you fall in love, you say, *s'amouracher, plutôt que bander*. That's very interesting.'

I detected a note of satisfaction in his voice, as though we had gone back three decades and I had obligingly put my finger on just the problem in mathematics which he wanted to explore; but apart from this inflection, almost indiscernible to anyone who wasn't looking out for it, there was no clue that we were speaking of a breakthrough he himself had already made. I cast another fly.

'I believe that a chemical could very easily be a sufficient catalyst to make somebody fall in love,' I said. 'Consider first of all the reasons we might normally give for loving someone: well, we might say it's the beauty of the person: their eyes; the way they stick out their lip and look at their breast; that particularly hairy belly, and so on. But does an impartial observer believe this? Of course not. He smiles to himself and turns the whole chain of reasoning around: the lover's causes are effects, and love itself is the cause: after all, nobody else thinks her eyes are uniquely beautiful and nobody else finds that stomach so special. To me this suggests very strongly that something very simple happens when we fall in love and when it happens everything else vibrates in sympathy like those extra strings on a cymbalum. That's why I think the real aphrodisiac will be a sort of Aphrodite's Girdle.'

I was feeling my way, trying to pass off as my own work what must in fact be his discoveries in the hope that he would be stung into putting me in my place with a show of really original knowledge. But nothing gave in his defences. He let me run on, only commenting at the end with the remark, 'Ah yes, most interesting. I had always assumed love would be more complicated than that.'

'Why should it be?' I asked. 'After all, the great things of life aren't always complicated – often it's only a case of uncomplicating things. For instance, religious truth is very simple and many people believe its perception can be induced by mescalin and related molecules.'

'My tear Herman, religious truth may or may not be simple. But say we assume it is, your argument about drugs doesn't hold any better. Under the influence of lysergic acid you might think you were God ... Well, perhaps that's impossible to disprove with certainty, let's take another example ... you might imagine you were, say, Napoleon. Does that mean you really are Napoleon? Drugs only give the illusion of religious insight and similarly, a chemical aphrodisiac could only give an illusion of being in love. I used to argue the point with Huxley.'

'But Dr Fitzer, if the drug made you fall in love the illusion would be indistinguishable from reality. So you would have to call it real. Let's take a simple example. You have a dream that you are making love to Marilyn Monroe. Of course you are merely asleep in your bed, but even so you have an orgasm in the dream. And you wake up and find the orgasm was a real one. But you know that making love to the actress was an illusion because you're all alone in the bed, and besides, she died a long time ago. Now imagine you are actually making love with an ugly woman and you are under the illusion that she is Marilyn Monroe. This time you can say it is an illusion because the girl isn't Monroe – perhaps she is offended and slaps you when you call her Marilyn. But now imagine you are with a woman you don't love. A real dolt, say, a regular rag doll of a girl. You don't see her as anything other than herself this time; but you are under an illusion, as you take her into your arms and look into her eyes, that you're madly in love with her. To you these are the most beautiful eyes in the world, the most luscious, softest brown hair, the prettiest mouth, whatever. Now what difference would there be between this and actually being in love? Couldn't you say then that a drug had made you really fall in love?'

We argued on in this way, me putting what must have been his own views, and he elegantly parrying them. But any attempt to annoy or bore someone into betraying himself inevitably depends on having plenty of time; and mine was limited. Punctual to the precise time he had allotted me, Dr Fitzer rose as the clock struck, and shaking my hand, invited me to make what use I would of the Institute during my stay. I was to take him at his word.

Chapter 8

Wasn't it de Gaulle who once said, 'de Gaulle is above the parties'? So was Dr Fitzer above the details of Institute life. Many of its activities, in fact whole departments, had been started up by people who appointed themselves in charge of a particular operation: the shop, for example, was run by a pair of energetic lesbians from California who quite by the way adhered to some kind of sect whose nature I never quite fathomed, and which involved giving all your money away and taking an Indian name. It was in this spirit that Kolowski had made himself the Institute's official photographer. Beginning with some rather flattering pictures for Dr Fitzer's press releases, he'd worked his way in the space of only six months into the catalogue and magazine departments, so that now everyone knew where to go if they wanted a good photo, not too expensive. He was gregarious and popular, falling somewhere in between the kinky regulars and the serious graduate students. His conversation was amusing – which was lucky, because he talked incessantly.

Wild black hair, red cheeks and nose, flashing white teeth – Kolowski was a cherub crossed with a satyr, having the ugliness of one, the beauty of the other, the vivacity of both. Most of all it was his eyes that one noticed. When he looked at you felt he was interested in no one else; and when he looked away you saw it was the same for everybody. He had that kind of personality which can't sit still for a moment. Brilliant otherwise, he lacked the concentration he would have needed in any sustained piece of work; in this his vocation was a fortunate one. Although he would never be very rich or successful as a photographer, his portfolio contained flashes of genius, totally unworked-on, lying like gold flecks in an ironstone shelf. I remember the way he would move round a room rather like a child does when the grown-ups are talking, picking a plug out of the record player and inspecting the wires, opening an address book, turning over an envelope and casting a quick look round to check if he was being watched. As with a child, the arduous drinking bouts and sleepless nights left no trace on him; even his red cheeks and nose could pass for the painted health of a *puttino*; perhaps like the satyrs he was blessed with an eternal and goatishly lecherous youth.

One evening I was having a drink in a cocktail bar near the Plaça de Catalunya when he and Myrna came in. It was a small place with no more than half a dozen stools at the bar so they had no choice but to sit down next to me. We shook hands, I offered them a drink.

'Straight vodka,' said Kolowski, 'Russian.'

The barman took a frosted bottle from the ice-box under the bar and poured the clear, syrupy liquid into two tiny glasses. Before he could put the bottle away Kolowski had drunk his and put it back on the bar with a practised gesture of his little finger which in some mysterious and inevitable way communicated a request for an immediate refill to barmen everywhere; and when this was accomplished he shut one eye and raised the brimming glass up to the other.

'This,' he said, observing me across the rim, 'is the only thing I really miss about my goddamn mother country. You know what? I've got to drink a toast to freedom. Raise your glass!' He smacked his lips. 'May vodka always be free!'

He roared with laughter at his rather feeble joke, but Myrna, not knowing English well enough to see the pun, said, 'The West isn't free, the West is enslaved. No one will be free until sex itself is liberated.'

There was something rather touching about her seriousness. Kolowski gave me a knowing look.

'Another vodka,' he said, 'I'm all for sexual liberation. Heavens I try hard enough don't I?'

'You're very good,' said Myrna soothingly.

'Sometimes,' said Kolowski, 'I think that real liberation would be no sex at all. I'm sure that's why God doesn't have it in Paradise — think how relaxing life would be.'

'In Paradise there would be sex all the time,' said Myrna.

'I don't agree,' said Kolowski, gobbling an olive, 'I don't agree at all. Just tell me what conception of Paradise out of all the religions of the world has a place for it? Even in Communism I'm sure there won't be any sex. There won't, I swear, everyone will be wedded to his tractor instead. We'll all be drivers, not swivers. All this copulation is just a ghastly sort of purgatory that we have to struggle through.'

'He's joking,' said Myrna.

'Joking apart,' Kolowski continued, 'if I have it much more I'll drop dead from exhaustion. You see,' he said turning to me, 'I'm an old-fashioned fellow who toes the party line. It's my Soviet upbringing, I suppose. As far as I'm concerned, fucking is like revolution: an uprising leads on to a triumphant climax which is in turn followed by the withering away of the state. That's the traditional view. But Myrna here goes in for some deviationist theory of permanent revolution.'

Myrna giggled and lit a cigarette. I said to her, 'Have you worked for a long time with Dr Fitzer?'

She shook her head. 'About five months, since his old assistant died. I applied immediately I knew the post was vacant. You see, I have a passionate interest in the field,' she added, somewhat ingenuously.

'Myrna knows all about chemistry,' said Kolowski, rolling his eyes. 'That's what makes her so formidable.'

'I believe our bodies are like machines,' Myrna went on, 'only for the most part they have gone rusty because of inhibition or lack of use. Dr Fitzer's chemistry is like oil. I believe that a well-oiled machine can last practically for ever. Having sex makes us younger. If only we could have more of it, I think we would be immortal.'

'The hankering after immortality,' said Kolowski, 'is one of the legacies of poor literary criticism. Nobody in his right mind would want to live for ever, least of all if he had to spend his whole time screwing. Personally I always believed my mother when she said it took a day off your life each time you did it.'

'The Taoists thought the opposite,' said Myrna.

'They couldn't help it, they were Chinese. The Chinese are deviationist by nature.'

I said to Myrna, 'Tell me about Dr Fitzer's chemistry.'

'Oh, we do all sorts of things. Dr Fitzer's great obsession is infertility. He's discovered some incredible things to help you

64

get pregnant. Then there's the ointment I gave to Konstantin here: it's a new one but it seems to be effective.'

'Surely you haven't made him pregnant?'

Myrna laughed. 'No, no, the ointment's for ... you tell him,' she said to Kolowski.

'Don't try it,' said Kolowski. 'It's the most damnable thing I ever had in my life.' And then, leaning closer he said in a low voice, 'You put it on your wanger and it burns like hell. Apparently that's supposed to make it stand up for longer; all I can say is it almost killed me.'

'What nonsense,' said Myrna, 'you know you loved it really.'

Everything Kolowski had said about permanent revolution was beginning to make sense to me now.

I said to Myrna, 'I'm very interested in this sort of thing.'

'Are you?'

'Yes.'

'Then I think I could tell you a lot – that is, if you'd like me to.'

She touched my knee with her hand where Kolowski couldn't see.

I said 'I'd like it very much.'

'Well, so would I.'

'Myrna, stop talking shop,' Kolowski intervened. 'Come on you two, another round – or we'll all be dead. This one's on me. Myrna, drink that down! You should do it at one go. In Russia you'd be lynched for sipping it like that.'

'Fucking Russians,' said Myrna, with a smile that suggested that this was something she wasn't averse to.

'There's nothing wrong with Russia,' said Kolowski, 'that vodka can't cure. Do you know why no one in the Soviet Union does any work? Because they think that Communism's just one big party!'

He roared with laughter again and his hand flapped helplessly up and down on the bar. Myrna had obviously heard this joke before. She sucked in her bottom lip and let it out again. Her young face was slightly flushed with the vodka and I thought she looked very attractive with her black eyes and her squint.

'In particular I'm interested in aphrodisiacs,' I said to her.

'Do you have anything of that kind at the Institute? The sort of thing, I mean, which could make a person fall madly in love.'

Myrna thought for a moment. 'The ointment works on the blood vessels of the male genitals ...'

She began, with all the dogmatic enthusiasm of the specialist to explain the mechanism and statistics of the ointment's success; her eager brows came slightly together and her brown hair fell forward on each cheek as she leaned towards me.

I let her run on for a while, before gently interrupting, 'I was really thinking of something that would make you actually fall in love, like Titania with Bottom.'

'Bottom? You mean, *algo del culo*?'

'No, a character in a play. It's not important. What I mean is a drug that can make us fall in love, you know, give us that itch of the spirit which can drive one to get up and cross town in the middle of the night, or else sit at home all day by the phone. An obsession in other words. Do you understand what I mean?'

'I think so.'

'Do you have anything that can bring it on?'

'Not really.'

'*Midsummer Night's Dream*,' said Kolowski, and he began to recite, describing histrionic loops with his empty glass:

> 'Yet mark'd I where the bolt of Cupid fell:
> It fell upon a little western flower,
> Before milk-white, now purple with love's wound,
> And maidens call it, Love-in-idleness.
> Fetch me that flower; the herb I show'd thee once:
> The juice of it on sleeping eyelids laid
> Will make or man or woman madly dote
> Upon the next live creature that it sees.'

'What are you talking about?' said Myrna.

'A drug that brings on love,' Kolowski replied. 'It made Titania fall in love with Bottom dressed as a donkey.'

I said, 'Hasn't Dr Fitzer got anything like that?'

'Donkey?' said Myrna incredulously, 'No, I don't think he has.'

'It's too bad,' said Kolowski. 'What a havoc you could create with it!'

I didn't press my inquiries any further for the moment and the conversation drifted to a discussion of other more sinister and sadly more common drugs – apparently Barcelona was a major port of arrival for South American cocaine and Myrna said the underworld was full of it. One of the Barrio Gótico bars had been raided the night before and two men were being held by the *Guardia* for questioning.

'Apparently,' said Myrna, 'they're quite small-time and it wasn't really them the police were after.'

'It's always the same,' said Kolowski, 'they never catch the big guys. It's always the poor dealer who cops it. The big guys always know when it's coming because they're in with the police; so they clear out in time. Cops and robbers, they're all the same when it comes down to it.'

'That can't always be true,' I said. 'Because every now and then some of them end up in gaol.'

'That's when they're double-crossed. Or else when they don't pay up on time. The Guardia's very particular about their accounts.'

Certainly they were more particular than Kolowski, who left without paying for any of the drinks. As I got to know him better I learnt that he always called for more drink, saying it was on him, but when the bill came he never paid a penny.

None of my attempts to glean information from Myrna was more successful than this first interview. She would willingly talk about the ointment she'd applied to poor Kolowski, or about any of the other products of the Institute, but whenever it came to Aphrodite's Girdle she shut up like a clam. Obviously she'd been better drilled in secrecy than I'd thought. She acted as though Aphrodite's Girdle didn't exist, and whenever I mentioned it she asked me questions about its composition and side effects as though it was I who knew all about it. But then even with Kolowski's charm one couldn't have expected to obtain such important and valuable secrets for nothing.

Chapter 9

Here's how it happens: I am fingering the ear in the cash pocket of my jacket, Kolowski gets off his barstool and takes Myrna by the arm, placing himself between us; I lean across him to say goodbye to Myrna; my hand darts out surreptitiously and as I bump him with my shoulder I simultaneously slip the ear under his collar at the nape of his neck. He has felt nothing: it is exactly the same manoeuvre as I will use to retrieve it later, one I have used so often I have a pickpocket's confidence in my act.

I wish I could lose this bad habit of placing bugs quite frivolously. When I was bored with the Major's discussions of bugging during my training I had done the same thing. Even an irritating shop assistant can sometimes provoke me into leaving an ear on them. It's stupid, because each one costs a small fortune; but Kolowski had annoyed me by getting in the way of my cross-questioning Myrna, and the thing was done almost before I knew I was doing it.

Oddly enough, this banal little bugging turned out to be extraordinarily fruitful.

That evening after dinner I went back to my hotel and finished reading Burton's *Pilgrimage to Al-Madinah and Meccah*; and then, as it was still too early to go to sleep, I got out the photographer's metal case which contains my recorder. Kolowski's bug was on tape number six. I switched on and turned up the volume. From the echoing roar of traffic it was clear that he and Myrna were on the street. Their voices were punctuated by the clacking rhythm of their shoes on the pavement. Despite all this irritating background noise I could hear Kolowski saying he wanted to drop by the Institute on their way home. Myrna protested that the Institute was closed.

'But you have the keys don't you?' Kolowski said.

'I'm not allowed to open it up outside hours,' said Myrna. 'It's against the rules.'

'Rules? People like you and me don't obey rules.'

This piece of bravado, so typical of Kolowski, had the effect of silencing her. He hailed a cab and they got in. Now there was less background noise from the street and it was easier to hear what they were saying. Myrna clearly disliked being forced to open up the Institute and began nagging him to tell her what he wanted in there.

'I have to change some chemicals in my dark-room. Otherwise the pictures I'm developing will be spoiled.'

Evidently no expert on photography, Myrna let herself be persuaded by this.

When they reached the Institute Kolowski said, 'Give me the keys, Myrna, and I'll let myself in. I won't be a minute.'

'Why are you so secretive? You never let me in your dark-room do you? In fact ever since you set it up I don't think anyone's set foot in the place. What are you hiding in there?'

'You wouldn't be able to see anything anyway: that's what a dark-room's for, to be dark.'

He gets out of the cab and I hear him let himself in and go upstairs. My mind's eye takes me up behind him, invisibly stretched out on my hotel bed. It is quite dark in the Institute: only the dim emergency light is burning by the stairs on each corridor. It gathers his dim shadow into focus as he passes, shrinking it down to life size and then throwing it on ahead of him into the murkiness of the next flight. Entresuelo 1, Entresuelo 2, Primer Piso, Segundo Piso: I can hear Kolowski puffing as he goes up, but for me, spying is effortless. I glide behind him on my back, a glass of old rioja wine in one hand, a piece of goat's cheese in the other. There! He has reached the door of the dark-room and unlocks it; under my shoulder I readjust the bolster with bated breath.

The conditions for listening are perfect in here: no echo, no background disturbance, just the sound of a slightly wheezy breath, interrupted by Kolowski's cigarette lighter. I suppose I'm expecting the trickle of poured liquid to follow, or the splash of a stirred chemical bath: instead comes the familiar sound of paper being ripped across, a sound I recognise instantly as a telex message being torn from the roll. So we are not in the dark-room at all! I hear the sound of paper rustling and then Kolowski goes out into the passage, and I follow behind, sipping my wine and wriggling my toes at the end of the bed. Now this door must surely be the dark-room. Kolowski sits down and there begins the ratchet-whirr of the telephone dialling, dialling: it must be an international call to dial for so long. Then a long pause.

'Hello?'

'...'

'Yes, don't worry, I've spoken to the Dove and he says that it'll soon be Christmas.'

'...'

'Yes, but by that time I have to lay my hands on Venus ... I've got it all set up but I have to get confirmation from the Hawk as well.'

'...'

'O.K. Till then, *Adiós*.'

Something about the whole tone of this conversation told the spy in me that all this talk of hawks and doves had more to it than ornithology. The clue lay in 'Venus' which Kolowski had to lay his hands on. Venus, the goddess of love whom the Greeks had called Aphrodite! Was it possible that Kolowski was after Aphrodite's Girdle as well? If 'Venus' meant what I thought it meant, then Kolowski was not only looking for the same secrets as I was, he was also a step ahead of me in the game. It was a lead I was going to have to overtake.

Kolowski went back downstairs and rejoined Myrna in the taxi. Myrna gave an address to the driver which I scribbled into my notebook, unfortunately spilling my wine on the bed as I did so. I could hear the recurrent click of the taximeter and later the all-obliterating sound of something brushing across the ear itself: presumably Myrna's arm around Kolowski's neck.

On their arrival they went up to bed straightaway. I had turned the volume-control right down and was thinking about Venus and the Hawk and the Dove when very faintly yet quite distinctly I heard my name.

Myrna was saying, 'That Herman Newton's a funny person. D'you think he's really a scientist?'

'I dunno,' said Kolowski, 'he looks a bit thick to me.'

'D'you know what Dr Fitzer told me? Apparently he was a child prodigy. Dr Fitzer actually gave him lessons when he was a boy. In Paris.'

'Really? Well, you wouldn't think it to look at him now.'

'I think he's quite sweet, actually.'

'That's a nice way of saying he's a terrible wimp.'

'Not really. I think he's sweet because he's so old-fashioned. Haven't you noticed? When Lucy put her hand on his thigh at lunch he almost fell off his chair.' Myrna giggled, 'I suppose all the English are like that.'

'I suppose so.'

'It's a funny thing though: sometimes I get the feeling he's not really prudish, just afraid of something. Perhaps he has something to hide; perhaps he's come to the Institute because he has some kind of sexual problem which he's too shy to air, and not for any scientific reason at all.'

'And I suppose you think you could come to the rescue.'

'Konstantin darling, don't be silly. I'm not the least bit keen on him. I just think he's sweet – in spite of the buck teeth and those awful black spectacles.'

Their talk drifted to other things and before long they were asleep. I turned off the volume and reset the recording mechanism to begin automatically at the sound of the human voice.

This conversation had given me an idea which began to turn into a plan of action. It was clear that the key to the Institute was Myrna. If she could let Kolowski in to 'change his chemicals', then I would get her to let me in too. And she could also supply me with information: important details of the burglar alarms, for instance, and of the files where Dr Fitzer's secret formulas were kept. My first step would have to be seduction, Mata Hari style. Despite what she had told Kolowski I knew she was attracted to me by the way she had put her hand on my knee and called me sweet.

In the days that followed I spent a good deal of time listening to Kolowski. I ought to explain here that when you're in the business of bugging people, time is an absolutely vital ingredient. You see, in general the better your information-gathering system is, the more information you have to process; and this takes time. Of course, we buggers have devices that 'save tape' as we call it: the original machines switched themselves on whenever there was a noise in the room; later ones could be set to activate to the human voice only; nowadays we can select the particular voice or voices which we want to hear. All these 'savers' cut down the time needed to process the data, most of which is uninteresting and unimportant. You can see why when I plant a bug on a whim I seldom bother to record the information received – in fact I hardly ever listen to it. Sometimes, for example, out of exasperation and pique, I have left an ear on Codrington, but the idea of spending an evening listening to what he says! No, the pleasure I get from bugging Codrington is simply the pleasure of outwitting him in our common field ...

In the event, bugging Kolowski led to more discoveries. A day or two after the original Dove-and-Hawk conversation I received a conversation in Russian. Now I don't speak Russian, so I couldn't understand what they were saying, but it got me thinking about the broader implications of Kolowski's role. Didn't it seem likely if the British were interested in Aphrodite's Girdle, that the Russians would be as well? When I had tried to raise questions of ideology and world strategy in training the Major had always told me not to bother about that, almost as though my mission was too small to be concerned with wider issues. Now it seemed that my concern was justified and the Major's approach to spying was simply too bureaucratic: had I adhered rigidly to his precepts I would be blind to the cold war implications of a Russian presence at the Institute. A lucky thing I'd read my Burton!

But if it was clear that the Russians must be interested in Aphrodite's Girdle, and must therefore have a spy at the Institute, what was much less clear was why on earth they should choose a man like Kolowski. Wasn't he Barcelona's most notorious dissident? And wouldn't such a dissipated character be more of a liability than an asset? Spies are warned against sexual entanglements for security reasons; yet it was an open secret in the Institute that quite apart from his affair with Myrna he went to bed with many women and – people gave me to understand – some men too. How could such a person be doing a serious espionage job for the Soviets?

Over the next few days I observed Kolowski scrupulously, and a new conviction dawned on me which seemed to explain everything: Kolowski's bohemianism must be a disguise. To a spy with imagination what could be more natural than to choose a persona which is the very opposite of one's own? All the straggling curls, the battered leather jacket, the constant boozing and womanising, the loose talk full of anti-Soviet jokes, clearly this was no less than a piece of sublime camouflage on the part of someone whose real qualities were the very contrary. The debauchery must be assumed, the anti-Communism false, even the curly hair was very likely a wig. In fact now that I thought about it I could imagine quite easily the Russian crewcut underneath it. Clearly the Russians took the art of disguise more seriously than the Major. In terms of spying they were the true heirs of Burton and Mata Hari, while Western intelligence had degenerated into bureaucracy. While deploring his allegiance, one couldn't help admiring the professionalism of Kolowski. It made me wish I'd come here in disguise myself. No wonder people like Burgess and MacLean were on their side.

There were several Russian conversations in the days that followed. I had no idea where these conversations occurred but I imagined it was in a 'safe house' – one of those places which are so complicated to set up and which spies use as a base to meet each other and from which they run their operations. In *Tinker, Tailor, Soldier, Spy* this is a two-room flat in Lexham Gardens. I could imagine the equivalent in Barcelona: the dark *piano nobile* in a nineteenth-century backstreet, with intricate iron balconies, and tall, curtain-darkened windows; and within, a dilapidated drawing-room with art nouveau tiling on the floor, a grimy chandelier of an earlier period converted to electricity, a large table with a radio transmitter and two pairs of headphones and next to it a big Calor gas heater. Here sit Kolowski and the crewcut Russian with bottles of beer in front of them. Kolowski is smoking. As he makes his point he stabs his finger at his interlocutor in much the same way he would at the Institute, in a discussion of Reich's orgone box (an obsession of his dissident *alter persona*), except now there is something cool and measured in the gesture, which gives a chilling sense of ruthlessness. Crewcut replies icily. Kolowski takes up from the floor his old leather briefcase with his initials KK embossed in cracked and half worn-off gold, and searches through a sheaf of paper work. At last he finds what he is looking for: three or four typewritten pages. Crewcut accepts them and, putting on a pair of wire-rimmed spectacles rather like the kind Lenin wore in *Dr Zhivago*, he peruses the documents. There is a long pause on the tape. I put out my cigarette in the ashtray and watch the reels turning in my photographer's case on the bed beside me. It seems that the conversation is over. The sound of Kolowski putting his briefcase on the floor must in reality have been the door shutting as his companion left the room. If only the Major had given me a crash course in Russian! As it was I had to be content with keeping a record of these conversations for translation later on when I got back to London.

Chapter 10

I have always regarded sex shops with a certain trepidation. Before my stay at the Fitzer Institute I had certainly never set foot in one; I always imagined though, that they would be exotic in a rather oriental way – an impression deduced no doubt from the way the doorways to these places always seem to be screened with a curtain of beads such as those I have seen in shops in Turkey and the Middle East to keep out the flies, and which I somehow associate in my mind with all oriental doorways as far back as the Palaces of the Arabian nights. So when I first went into the Fitzer shop I was surprised by the tawdriness of the place. Its drab display of goods, barely laid out on shelves and tables round the room, hardly seemed destined for commercial success; the somewhat naked effect of this lay-out was heightened by the strip lighting, to whose stark and uniform illumination was added a very slight tinge of blue which emanated from a necklace of fairy lights strung up above the counter. A curious smell of indeterminate origin, which was smooth like oil and vaguely reminiscent of rubber, gave one the less than agreeable feeling of having come slightly too close to something that had better been kept private. I was so nervous at first that for no reason at all I slipped an ear under a rack of magazines. Most of the magazines were sealed in plastic wrappers of a very faintly opaque kind which gave the colours of their covers a muted, milky quality. Above each pile, however, a well-thumbed copy hung from a string so that customers could inspect their contents: mainly pictures of obese models with blonde wigs and bosoms like waterfilled balloons administering excruciating sexual tortures with a fixed grin; or else with their fat bodies trussed into revealing clothes, standing expectantly in front of swine or swinish men. If, as the man standing next to me now did, you bought one of these publications, the girl at the counter (the self-styled

Parvati) put it in a brown paper bag so that you could carry it away unobserved. A note on the counter instructed you to make your cheque payable to 'Ramakrishna S.A.' – presumably in order that even your banker wouldn't know you had shopped at the Fitzer Institute.

I was astonished by the nonchalant way the man had strolled over to the counter and paid for his magazine as though he'd been purchasing a newspaper or a packet of cigarettes. For my part I felt rather as I had when I mounted the stage at school prize-giving: every step I took, every time I turned my head to look one side or another, it felt as though my joints were full of rapidly congealing glue which would soon bring me to a halt. It was the thought of my mission that kept me going: I knew I could afford to leave nothing to chance so I began to inspect the wares and layout of the shop in a methodical way, taking mental notes as I'd learned to do in training with the Major: approximate size of the room; exits and break-in points; conceivable places of concealment; nature of locks employed, and so on. I also made a mental inventory of the principal wares on sale. The size of some of the dildos amazed me: even in my days of potency I could never have measured even half what they did. Some were bright pink and some bottle green, many had little wartlike bumps all over them; one was two-headed; one of them had a special chamber from which a liquid might be expelled at a propitious moment. Making a mental note of all this I went on to the clothing display. There were no mannequins like you see in ordinary clothes shops so that the rubber underwear, for example, was simply tacked to the wall on pins at an odd angle which was perhaps intended to add an artistic effect. There were some leather odds and ends similarly disposed, and a number of heavily-studded belts and bracelets which reminded me of the one Doris had bought. I wondered if Doris bought her clothes in shops like these or if the sort of things displayed here were regularly on sale in fashionable boutiques. I had an idea I'd seen a mannequin holding a whip in a shop window in the King's Road. Was that possible? There were whips in abundance here, at any rate, and plenty of handcuffs too. What interested me most among the garments was the underwear which, even among the rubber and wet-look pieces, but much more obviously in the imitation satin, appeared to have become caught in a time-warp circa 1950. Why this date should be particularly pornographic I couldn't guess, but there was no mistaking the vintage of those frilly garters, the lace panties, the style of the stockings and the beribboned belts with their black suspenders hanging off them.

If the underwear dated back thirty-odd years, the patent medicine shelves were positively medieval. Many of them bore the Institute's label – something which did not, I felt, redound to Dr Fitzer's credit. There were aphrodisiacs galore, some of which had been taken in vain for centuries, others which I knew from my own investigations were failed modern attempts, and still others which I had read about in LIMP as being unashamed and intended frauds. Apart from the aphrodisiacs there were pills to assure all kinds of wonderful potency and stamina as well as a plethora of Dr Fitzer's homeopathic inventions for assuaging the possible after-effects of a sex change.

I had completed my inventory and memorised all the important dimensions of the room. Now it was time to act: I picked up two sets of handcuffs. As soon as I touched them the glue thickened again in my joints and I could hardly walk to the counter. Californian Parvati put the handcuffs in a bag, thoughtfully removing the price from the box as she did so.

I said, 'I'd like some chains too.'

I was so nervous my voice came out in a squeak. Parvati unlocked the cupboard and asked me which sort of chains I wanted. I chose some with ankle-locks attached and another set that were plain. Then I asked for a gag. All the time I was choosing these things I was painfully aware I was being watched but I was too nervous to look around me. I just kept my gaze fixed on the things I was buying. Parvati gave me my change and handed me the two brown bags and said, 'Have a nice day.' It was only as I left that I realised nobody had been paying me any attention at all. In those days I was still a little unused to the ways of the Fitzer Institute.

I managed to see Myrna alone for a drink one evening in a bar off the Via Augusta, and got her talking about the latest drugs and devices that had been developed at the Institute. Her enthusiasm for the subject was that of a convert.

'Dr Fitzer's experiments have proved it time and time again,' she told me. 'All the range of human passions can be aroused by the right mechanical and chemical stimuli.'

She told me about electrode-induced erections and potions which could make you homosexual or heterosexual just by drinking them, and special harnesses which could radically alter the size of your sexual organs in a matter of days. There was no service, it appeared, that the cornucopia of the Fitzer Institute couldn't provide. At one time she herself had used a kind of hair oil which meant that she could satisfy ten men in a night. I didn't believe very much of this. There was an obsessive quality in her conviction which struck me as slightly deranged; for all I knew she could satisfy ten men without the hair oil.

But in spite of her enthusiasm for his ideas it was clear that she was having problems with the Doctor. She said he was impossible to work with, that he didn't trust her and that he treated her like an office boy. I encouraged her to speak against him and by working on these grudges I managed to make her tell me invaluable things: for instance, that the formulas of his medicines were kept in the computer memory; that copies of them existed in the blue filing cabinet in the laboratory, along with most of his laboratory reports; and that the new medicines which weren't yet on the market were kept in pyramid-shaped bottles. She even gave me information about the burglar alarm system which protected them: it struck me that Dr Fitzer would have been better off if he *had* mistrusted her as she accused him of doing.

'By the way,' I said, 'that ointment which you and Konstantin were talking about the other day – I couldn't find it anywhere in the shop.'

'It's not on sale in the shop,' said Myrna. 'But I can get it for you.'

I said weakly, 'Yes, please do.'

'What about tomorrow?'

'Yes. Or perhaps the day after.'

'Friday then,' she said, and smiled, and squeezed my hand.

That evening, lying on my hotel bed I dialled the Major's number, and after the familiar double ring of an English phone I was greeted by the flat tones of Doris's voice.

'Hello Doris,' I said.

'Who's there?'

'It's Herman.'

'Who?'

'Herman Newton.'

'Who?'

'Herman Newton. I helped you clean the cage for Minipin-pin-pin.'

'Oh, yes. How are you?'

'I'm fine. What are you up to these days?'

'I've got some leopardskin tights and this friend lent me a leopardskin jacket.'

'Oh, yes.'

'And I have some glitter nail varnish. And glitter eye shadow. We're seeing the big cats you see.'

'At the zoo?'

'No; at the circus. The zoo's been closed down.'

This really took me by surprise. Knowing Doris's fondness for animals and not knowing much about the clubs where live bands played, I supposed that London Zoo had shut down and that Doris was going to a circus to see lions and tigers. (But why was the zoo closed? I'd never heard of it happening before.)

'I hope you like them,' I said.

'Oh, I think they're amazing. Mungo knows the lead guitarist. He's really good-looking and he's been to prison.'

'What for?'

'Oh, I don't know. Listen, I've got to get ready. D'you want to speak to Daddy? Oh, by the way, don't tell him about the Circus, you know how he is about groups. I said I was going to a movie, OK?'

'OK Doris.'

The Major was not in the best of moods. He demanded rather curtly why I hadn't damn well rung him before. I excused myself on the grounds that I'd been afraid of being overheard if I spoke on the phone.

'Well you're on the phone now aren't you?' he said angrily.

'That's why I can't tell you any details. I just wanted to say that I'll have your information the day after tomorrow around midnight or one in the morning.'

'Have you bugged the Institute?'

I wished the Major wouldn't talk so wildly on the phone. If the Russians were listening to this I was the one who'd be taking a long look at an angle-poise.

Doing my best to be circumspect I said, 'I'm getting the information by a much better and surer method than the plan you propose.'

'Newton, how many times do I have to tell you? Bug the damned Institute! Didn't I make myself clear last time?'

'But Sir, I've a much better way of finding out what you have to know, believe me. I can't say exactly what on the phone . . . '

'Newton, are you listening to me? I want you to bug the Institute, do you hear? And then I want you to ring me back and tell me you've done it; and where each bug is, d'you understand? And until you've done that I want you to do nothing else. Is that clear?'

At the moment the only ear I had in the Fitzer Institute was under the dirty magazine rack in the shop, but I told the Major I'd got the whole place wired, just to shut him up. He sounded suspicious and asked me lots of questions about where I'd put them and so on and I told him some story about how I'd put a bug on Dr Fitzer's computer monitor – this was the only thing I'd actually seen in the laboratory. Then, remembering what Myrna had told me about the place, I elaborated a bit and said I'd stuck one in the blue filing cabinet where he kept his secret documents and another on the door of the cupboard where the control was for the burglar alarm. All this talk of bugging had a calming effect on the Major. I asked him if he wanted me to bring the information back to London or if I was to do a 'drop' like we'd practised in training. He told me he was going to be at his house in Spain that week-end and I could bring it there. Before he rang off he said again that bugging was the only way to get what he wanted and expressly forbade me to do anything else. I decided that it must be because the Major understood so little about bugging technology that he put such faith in it. Sometimes I am astonished by how out of touch the older generation of British spies are. No wonder they were all so easily fooled by Philby and company.

Chapter 11

That day was one of those freakishly hot days that come at the end of a Catalan winter. I dawdled slowly up the Ramblas, my jacket slung over my shoulder, thinking about Sir Richard Burton and rather regretting that I didn't need a disguise to put my plan into action. From a newspaper stand I bought a copy of *La Vanguardia* and a little further on I sat down at a café table to glance through the day's news. I started reading an article about a Catalan man of letters who had written a history of his Pyrenean village in the last century but somehow my gaze kept straying from the paper. From the café where I was sitting I had a good view of the people going by, all looking somehow unready for the new season. Aetiolated and blinking, they emerged from the mouth of the Metro like subterranean creatures into the light of day, still wrapped up in all kinds of unnecessary overcoats and hats and scarves. Not far from here, at a street stall, a woman in a green felt hat was purchasing a canary in a cage. Just beyond lay the Canaletas Fountain where football enthusiasts gather to discuss their sport. There must have been a match the night before, because this morning the pavement was thronging with men engaged in urgent conversation. On the other side of the fountain lay the great square where last month some terrorists had seized a bank and paraded their hostages round; now the traffic was back and the crowds of people and it was business as usual at the bank. Cars poured out of the square down the Ramblas in the direction of the port, passing the iron-shuttered door of the cocktail bar where I had met Kolowski and planted an ear on him last week. I was just reflecting on how valuable that ear had proved to be when something caught my eye in the window of a black and yellow cab at that moment passing the cocktail bar. It was one of those things that happen so quickly that one doesn't have time to look; there is only the original impression, and then it is gone: a back window, with a curved hypotenuse, and in the corner, curiously disembodied so that it seemed to hang there like a turnip lantern, the pale grey, bag-eyed face of Major Shark. The window flashed in the sun and then went dark; the cars shuffled themselves; I was no longer sure which cab it had been. Was it really him? I knew the Major was coming to Spain and it occurred to me that he might have come to see me. But when I asked at my hotel there were no messages. Had he been on his way from the airport to catch a train to Caldeya at the French station? Or had it not been him after all, but some similar grey stranger?

I had lunch at the Institute and then coffee with Kolowski in Reception. He invited me to come over to his flat one day and try out the orgone box he'd built for himself.

When he'd gone I went and got myself another cup of coffee. It was always a busy time in Reception after lunch and I had to wait my turn at the machine. Two Dutch boys in front of me were just off to Morocco. They were dressed all in leather and had both shaved off all their hair which gave them the curious look of being twins although they were not at all related. One said it made them feel like convicts and was very bad for hitch-hiking. 'But it'll grow again soon,' said the other. I wished them luck. When I sat down again I noticed that Kolowski had left his briefcase on the floor beside his chair. It was made of pigskin which had gone a very dark brown with age. Between the two clips which fastened it the sunlight caught a few remaining flecks of gold on the worn K.K. embossed in the leather. Clearly there is no time to lose. I put down my coffee unfinished and pick up the briefcase. Nobody notices anything. With perfect nonchalance I stroll across the room, briefcase in one hand, the other thrust deep in my trouser pocket. The Dutch boys say goodbye. I shake them by the hand as I go past, as though I had all the time in the world, and then make my way down the stairs – murky even at this time of the day – and out into the street. At the corner of Calle de Asturias and the Mayor de Gracia I lose myself in the mouth of the Metro.

Back at my hotel a surprise awaited me. While I'd been away I'd had a visitor, and he hadn't been the polite kind who believes in leaving a card with the concierge. I don't know how he'd got into my room in the first place, but once he was in there he'd certainly got restless waiting for me: the drawers of the commode were on the floor and my clothes lay higgledy-piggledy all around them. The closet had aroused his curiosity too: my best grey flannel suit lay on the floor with its lining ripped out and my suitcase and shoes were flung across the room. The bed was stripped, the bedside table had been turned over, my papers were crumpled and tossed about everywhere. On the floor by the window lay the photographer's metal case which contained my tapes, its top slashed crudely open like the top of a tin can. The tapes themselves were lying on the window-sill, half-spilling off their reels in a tangle of brown ribbon. The recorder was smashed and the receiver appeared to have been tampered with. I started to move towards it and then something hit me on the back of the head.

I came to about ten minutes later, still lying on the floor where I had fallen. At first I thought I was at home in London. An excruciating pain filled my head. I put my hand up to it and found it surprisingly the same as ever, except for a little trickle of blood on my fingers. I was sweating coldly. I wanted to go back to sleep, but the pain in my head wouldn't let me. Slowly it dawned on me that I was in a hotel in Barcelona, on a secret mission. I got to my feet and began to grope about for my spectacles; when I found them I staggered to the bathroom and was sick in the lavatory. I was shaking all over. I sat down on the bidet. In the mirror my face was the colour of dirty paper and there was blood on my suit and my shirt collar. Moving slowly and holding my head as still as I could, I poured some whisky into a glass and took a big gulp. Then I took some aspirin and some more whisky and got undressed. The shower hurt my head but it did the rest of me a lot of good, cleaning off the horrible clinging sweat and putting some warmth back into my shivering body. I got into a bathrobe and cleaned my teeth, and then I drank some more of the whisky. For some reason the pain was less bad if I held my head slightly to one side with my mouth half open.

I did my best to clean up the room because I didn't want Myrna to see it looking that way. The recorder was a write-off so I slid it under the bed along with the tangled-up magnetic tape, but the receiver looked repairable. I packed it in my case along with the rest of my belongings. I left out my shaving things and put Burton's *Pilgrimage* beside the bed: I didn't want it to look as if I was about to leave. Fortunately Kolowski's briefcase was still lying on the floor where I had fallen.

After checking carefully for false bottom and sides and finding none, I went through its contents. There were several sheets in Cyrillic script, handwritten presumably by Kolowski himself; then there was a letter to Parvati from the printers of the Institute mail-order catalogue about some technical changes in the reproduction of photographs; several invitations to art shows; a copy of *Cambio 16* magazine; the catalogue of a Russian bookseller in Madrid; a street map of the city; yesterday's *Vanguardia* with half-completed crossword; two folders of his own photographs; a spiral-bound notebook; several rolls of film to be developed, some lens filters and a lens brush with a grey plastic bellows; and then I found something which really interested me: several mimeographed sheets showing diagrams of machine pistols and a rocket-launcher, labelled in Spanish. Each sheet showed a different weapon, and there were nine sheets in all. There was no explanatory text, no address and no date. The quality of the reproduction was poor.

A second and more thorough study of all this brought another clue to light: in the spiral-bound notebook, among a host of trivial personal memoranda I found a page with the following entry:

- Call Dove re UB Suisses
- time of Xmas
- 15 kg.

This clearly referred to the operation I'd overheard him planning on the phone: his plan to steal the secret of Aphrodite's Girdle, code-named Venus. Christmas, I had already deduced, was the date of the operation. The 'Dove' had been mentioned before by Kolowski in his telephone conversation. 'UB Suisses' was almost certainly the Union des Banques Suisses: perhaps a financial transaction was involved – or did Kolowski and the Dove intend to bank the information itself to prevent anyone else getting hold of it? '15 kg.' looked like

15 kilograms. Could that be the quantity of the drug which they intended to steal? It sounded like an awful lot. Possibly the pages in Russian would throw some light on the matter when I had them translated. I put everything back in the briefcase and hid it in the cupboard. Then I thought that Myrna might want to hang a dress in there so I took it out and slid it into the space between the floor and the bottom of the chest of drawers.

Head cocked and mouth half-open: apart from the fact that I was only comfortable in this slightly ridiculous posture I thought I'd escaped quite lightly. What the intruder had been after I couldn't guess. I deduced that when he had heard me come in he must have slipped into the bathroom and then, when I had my back to him, seen his opportunity and sapped me from behind. It seemed a cowardly way to dispose of someone, but I knew that in the real spy world one didn't pull any punches. Probably I was lucky not to have been shot: it's well-known that these people count life pretty cheap. Whoever it was he had certainly known his business. The blow had caught me on the crown, exactly where the Major had shown me in training. It was a really professional wound, so I felt a certain pride in it.

Later that afternoon I hired a car.

Myrna met me at the restaurant I'd suggested. As soon as she arrived she said, 'Why are you sitting in that extraordinary position? You look quite half-witted.'

I straightened myself up and shut my mouth and my head began to ache dully.

'I need a drink,' I said. We ordered some whisky. The restaurant had seemed a quiet enough little place when I'd been here before at lunchtime, but now a guitarist arrived with a piercing voice, accompanied by a gypsy man with a tambourine. I suppose I must have stood out as a foreigner in that place, because they immediately came up and played at our table, the gypsy banging his tambourine beside my right ear. By the time they left us, my head was throbbing wildly and I must have gone so pale that Myrna noticed and asked me what the matter was.

'I banged my head on a low doorway,' I said, 'when I was out shopping this afternoon. I'm afraid it's given me rather a headache. You wouldn't have an aspirin would you?'

She gave me two aspirins from her handbag and also three small yellow tablets which she produced from a little unlabelled phial.

'Take these now,' she said, with a meaningful look. 'They will make it good for later on.'

The little pills were sulphurous on the tongue: my first taste of chemical love was washed down hurriedly with a mouthful of Catalan wine.

'What exactly do they do?' I asked.

'You'll see.'

I was beginning to feel very nervous about the night's business.

After dinner I wanted to go to a few bars but Myrna pouted and said she was tired. I realised that I couldn't put it off any longer so I hailed a cab and we set off for my hotel. I took advantage of the darkness inside the taxi to open my mouth and lean my head over, but Myrna, who was sitting that side of me, thought I was trying to kiss her and put her mouth up to mine. Even here in the taxi she seemed quite unusually excited.

Up in my hotel room I locked the door and poured us each a glass of whisky.

'How long do the pills take to work?' I said.

'Oh, they're just to help our stamina. But I've brought you some ointment as well which we can put on now.'

'Is it the ointment you gave Konstantin?' Now that my time had come I was feeling less and less brave about it.

'Yes,' said Myrna, 'that's the one. It's very strong.'

She came over and took me in her arms and began to kiss me on the mouth and neck, her hands moving voluptuously up and down my back.

'You're hurting my head,' I exclaimed.

'Oh you poor thing. I'm sorry, I forgot. Don't worry, I promise I'll make it up to you.' She gave me a peck on the cheek and said, 'Go and lie down on the bed.'

She disappeared into the bathroom. When she came back she drank down the whisky at a gulp and then took off her blouse, unzipped her skirt and folded it on the chair. Now that I saw her undressing I realised how young she was. She was heavily built, but with beautiful proportions and lovely brown skin; it made me feel a little ashamed of my own puny physique. Myrna pulled down her pants and stepped out of them, casting me as she did so a shy cross-eyed glance. For the first time I caught sight of a vulnerable side in her; it made her seem terribly attractive all of a sudden and it also made me feel doubly ashamed to be playing a trick like the one I was about to play. I took another gulp of the scotch. Spying is a cruel business. Myrna switched off the overhead light. She came over to the bed and knelt beside me and began to unbutton my shirt. After two years' hibernation, a whole hive of sensual longings swarmed into my body and I gave an involuntary moan. Myrna tossed her head prettily and giggled. Unzipping my fly, she opened my trousers at the top and put her hand down my pants.

'Heavens!' she exclaimed in surprise. 'Is that a prick you've got down there or a piece of old leather?' And she pulled down my pants to have a look.

'I'm afraid it's been rather a problem for me lately,' I said nervously. 'Whoever I go with, it doesn't seem to make any difference. I hoped perhaps you might cure me with some of that ointment you gave to Kolowski.'

'Ointment?' she said. 'You're going to need a bit more than that. I've seldom met a man with so little to say for himself.'

'D'you think I'm a hopeless case?' I asked.

'Don't be silly. We'll soon have you fixed up.'

She wasn't in a hurry. There was something of the meticulous craftsman about her as she carefully made up her lips in the mirror and then put on a black garter belt like those in the Institute shop, and a pair of stockings; next she divested me of my clothes. Then she unpacked from her bag an exotic assortment of articles: bottles and jars, leather thongs, a small dildo, a lemon. One of the jars was of the pyramid-shaped type which she'd told me contained the new unmarketed drugs. From this one she took some pale green ointment with her fingers and rubbed it all over my lifeless member.

'That will bring you to life,' she said with satisfaction. 'We have to wait about ten minutes for it to take its effect.'

Despite this assurance, a feverish itching set in almost immediately which I pleaded with her to abate.

'I'll soothe it in good time, don't worry,' she said.

Nevertheless, it seemed she was going to leave nothing to chance.

She had got hold of the dildo and rubbed it with olive oil and now she was shaking a pepper pot all over it. My protests went unheeded.

'Don't make a fuss, boy,' she told me, 'just wait till the ointment takes effect and then you'll see.'

And she began inserting it in my anus. As if this wasn't enough, she tied a leather thong round the base of my prick. All these extra decorations were making me feel more and more like a Christmas tree.

We waited and waited, but not a flicker of life stirred in my afflicted member. Myrna rolled and kneaded it with her strong hands but in spite of all her efforts the thing was still flopping around like a dog's tongue. After what seemed like an eternity, Myrna was forced to concede defeat. She untied the leather thong and removed the dildo, which eased my more immediate pains a little though my whole genital region still felt like it had gone through a nettlebed.

'*No lo entiendo*' she was saying, shaking her dark head slowly from side to side. 'I just don't understand it.'

She couldn't even look me in the eye – the poor girl seemed to regard it as her failure as much as my own. The moment was ripe. Odysseus-like, I produced my Trojan Horse.

'Myrna,' I said, 'There is one way that I know I can make love to you.'

She looked sadly at my genitals and shook her head.

'I promise,' I said, 'even this can be put right if you'll let me ...' I let my voice trail off hesitantly.

'If I let you what?'

I wanted to sound embarrassed about it so I said it quickly and quietly as if I was ashamed.

'Will you let me tie you up?'

'Tie me up?' said Myrna, laughing incredulously, 'you want to tie me up? Why didn't you ask me before? Good gracious, do you mean we've gone to all this trouble when all along you only wanted to tie me up?'

She was so excited she leaned down and kissed me on the head and I let out a howl of pain.

'My head!'

'I'm sorry!'

'It's all right. Please lie down on the bed.'

She could hardly believe her luck now. She lay on the bed and wriggled with excitement when I produced from the bottom drawer of my wardrobe the chains and handcuffs which I'd bought from Parvati. Giggling and tossing her head, she helped me to get them on to her, encouraging me in a sexy voice to pull the chains tighter. I handcuffed her wrists to each side of the bedhead and did the same thing at the bottom with her ankles. Then I tried to look sheepish again and asked her if she would mind if I gagged her as well.

'Silly boy, of course not.'

The words were hardly out of her mouth before the gag was in it. Once I had this properly knotted up I bound her eyes too for good measure. She didn't offer the least resistance. Then I went to work. I tipped out her handbag on the floor and sifted through the contents till I found her keys. Then I quickly got dressed and threw the rest of my things into my suitcase. At the door, I glanced back and caught sight of Burton's *Pilgrimage* which I'd left on the bedside table. Not wanting to leave this behind, I crossed the room and slipped it into my suitcase. As I did so Myrna, who must have thought I was approaching with other things in mind, let out a low moan and stirred expectantly on the bed.

'I'm going to leave you now for a few minutes,' I said. 'I want you to stay very still where you are and when I come back you'll be really pleased.'

Then I switched off the light. Downstairs I paid my bill and checked out of the hotel.

Chapter 12

I drove off immediately towards the harbour where the tall cranes stood out blackly in the night sky, bending their reflex-angled tops down to the masts of the yachting beneath them. Circling the Columbus monument I ran between the palm trees and the jetties in the direction of the French Station and the Barceloneta, then went left up the Via Layetana. Now I plunged into the maze of little streets in the neighbourhood of the old Cathedral; I took the most roundabout route imaginable, weaving in and out in the way you have to if you want to lose someone on your tail. Not that I was exactly sure there was someone following me; but after having my room searched I thought it was a wise precaution in keeping with the high standards of professionalism I had set myself. Unfortunately, because I was a comparative newcomer to the city I actually got lost myself so it was some time before I got to the Institute.

I parked the car round the corner in a side-street and examined Myrna's keys by the light of the dashboard. You couldn't mistake the key to the Fitzer laboratory: it was one of that sophisticated kind which are pitted all over with tiny indentations and are supposed to be uncopyable. There was one which I guessed would be for the front door; there were also two small ones which looked as though they might be for turning off the alarm. I switched off the dashboard light, locked the car and walked round the corner to the door of the Institute. Although it was late there were still a number of people on the street and any of them could see exactly what I was doing now: I just had to act very cool and trust to my luck that nobody from the Institute would happen to pass by. The big key gave me access to the hall. I shut the door behind me and found myself in pitch darkness. This shouldn't have been a surprise: there are no windows in the hallway apart from the tiny slit over the door, and naturally after the light of the streets I couldn't see anything by this. Unfortunately I'd left my torch in the car and stupidly, in the heat of this first moment of my first-ever break-in, I didn't think of waiting for my eyes to get used to the dark, but blundered across the hall in the direction of what I thought would be the lift, crashed into one of the heavy wooden chairs which stood by the shop and fell heavily on my left elbow. My spectacles came off and the blow to my arm sent the keys flying from my hand: I spent the next minutes on all fours, feeling my way across the marble flags.

By the time I found my glasses my eyes were used to the dark so I spotted the keys quite easily; I let myself into the lift and pressed the button to go up. In the daytime I had never noticed it making any noise at all, but in the stillness of the night its motors wailed dismally and the mechanisms cranked and thudded somewhere in the basement of the building. On the fifth floor it ground to a halt and I fitted the little indented key into the door of the laboratory. It was a three-way lock, heavy to turn, but the door opened easily. I was now in the ante-chamber of the laboratory – no windows here. I found the light and crossed to the door of the laboratory itself. I had never been in here: in my mind it existed only as a blank space on the end of a looping computer ribbon, and in this blank space I had stored the various cabinets and files which Myrna had described as containing important information. Among these was the double-doored wall cupboard where the burglar alarm was. I got ready the two little keys which I thought would be the ones and pushed open the door.

There was no buzzer. Most burglar alarms have a buzz which sounds when you break the circuit, and if you don't turn it off within a certain time the alarm rings. Instead, there was silence. I looked around me. It was a long room with windows down the whole length of it on one side with their shutters open and the light of the streetlamps outside throwing the shadows of their glazing bars on to the ceiling above. The reflections of this light brought a ghostly illumination to the scene before me.

It was immediately obvious that the laboratory had just been searched. Drawers of papers and smashed bottles were scattered on the floor; a long workbench lay on its side with mounds of wiring and electric points exposed on its underneath. Particular attention seemed to have been paid to Dr Fitzer's desk which was surrounded by drifts of paperwork. First my hotel bedroom and now this: I was beginning to feel that the mere fact of my wanting to go into a room was a sufficient condition for its being thoroughly ransacked. My heart sank as I realised I would have to sort through it all to find the documents I wanted. Certainly the job was going to take much longer than I had initially calculated. Who the devil could have been here before me? Kolowski? The person who had hit me on the head? At the far end of the room was a cupboard with its doors open: inside this I found the burglar alarm already switched off. One advantage of arriving second on the job was that all the locks had already been picked or broken. It had been very professionally done, just the way the Major had taught me.

My first target was the blue filing cabinet. All the files had been dumped on the floor and the cabinet itself had been overturned. I gathered all the papers into a pile by the window where a pool of light made it just possible to read and began to go through them. I already had a headache and the strain of reading in poor light made it even worse. There were plenty of lab reports on the ointment Kolowski and I had been subjected to as well as files on other new products. Among these was a collection of notes on an aphrodisiac of the conventional kind which I put on one side, but there was nothing which referred to Aphrodite's Girdle itself. I turned my attention to the computer. Whoever had searched the room before me hadn't known much about computers. In this, the richest of all storehouses of information, the extent of their search had been to turn the monitor upside down and prise open the casings of the hard disc unit and the processor. As a way of finding out what was stored on the computer it was about as sophisticated as breaking up a gramophone to find the orchestra inside, or looking under the altar cloth for God. Unfortunately for me the efforts of this vandal had disrupted the working of the machine, so I was unable to look in the memories according to the principles I'd wheedled out of Myrna. I began scouting the other drawers and files.

It happened after I'd been searching for about half an hour. I suppose I might have seen it earlier if I'd been able to put the lights on, but by the reflected glow of the streetlamps objects such as this didn't stand out clearly. It lay on the shelf half-hidden behind a box of laboratory syringes. It was only when by chance I shifted these that I saw what it was: a pyramid-shaped bottle! I picked it up in both hands. There was no label or other mark to identify it. The stopper was cemented into place to make doubly sure that none of its precious contents escaped. The liquid was black and, as far as I could tell from the movement of the tiny bubble of air when I picked it up, of high viscosity. It seemed very probable indeed that this was Aphrodite's Girdle: the pyramid shape meant it was still being tested in the laboratory, and as a top secret drug it certainly wouldn't be labelled. I realised that even without the documents containing the formula, our laboratories in London would soon be able to work it out, once they had the liquid in their possession. With this phial, my mission was accomplished. I couldn't help laughing to myself as I took hold of it, knowing that I had so easily discovered what the bureaucratic Major would never have found out by following his spies' rule book. In the most unconventional and original manner, I had beaten the professional at his own game. Still laughing, I stepped back to examine the bottle in the light of the window and – alas! – the wound on my head came into sharp contact with a metal lamp which stuck out from the wall on a heavy iron bracket. I uttered a stifled groan, my hand flew to my head and the bottle slipped from my fingers and sailed across the room where it broke with a delicate tinkle by the desk.

Still clutching my head and with tears of pain in my eyes, I leapt across the room to the scene of the disaster. On the floor a few broken pieces of glass lay in a patch of liquid which evaporated even as I watched. The chemical was too volatile for me to be able to save any of it. Nevertheless, as I knelt beside it the fumes stung the inside of my nose and throat and my heart began to race. I struggled to my feet but the room began to lurch and reel like a ship. I've taken plenty of drugs in the course of my experiments, usually to test their aphrodisiac potential. But the effect of this vapour I had accidentally inhaled was really very strange indeed: the walls begin to billow in and out like curtains in a draught; racks of test-tubes turn into glittering chandeliers; on the floor are scattered not pieces of broken glass but necklaces of diamonds which grow like crystals as you watch; Fitzer's desk covered in papers is transformed beneath my eyes into an altar strewn with the petals of a gigantic white flower. The angle-poise laboratory lamps turn their heads this way and that, strutting and ducking like flamingos. I stagger, a thick rain begins to fall, I black out for a minute. Then my sight returned and everything went back into its old shape and the lamps were lamps again, and the test-tubes were glass and the movement of the walls was reduced to a vague flicker.

I searched everywhere now, and with increasing desperation, for another pyramidal bottle of that chemical. I worked methodically, in the way the Major had taught me, dividing the room into sections and taking each one in turn. Alas, method failed where intuition had so brilliantly succeeded. There was no bottle, no document, no clue of any kind which might have given me a lead to Aphrodite's Girdle. It is a curious fact, as well as a tribute to Dr Fitzer's security arrangements, that apart from the black bottle I had broken, there was nothing in the laboratory to suggest that it existed at all.

Chapter 13

Clutching the file which was my only booty, I took the lift down to the hall and let myself out of the front door. In the street a couple were passing with their arms about each other but they took no notice of me. I walked slowly to the corner and turned into the street where I had left the car.

I got in and started the engine and had a good look in the mirror. No sign of anyone so far as I could see. I drove south on Calle de Menéndez Pelayo and turned on to the Diagonal. Still no sign of anyone following. I drove slowly down the Diagonal towards the Plaza de las Glorias, letting the cars overtake me as they came and keeping an eye on the mirror all the time. Once I reached the *autopista* I relaxed and sped on northwards in the direction of Gerona and Perpignan.

At Figueras I turned off and crossed the plain of Ampurdán to the coastal hills. A pitted, winding road threaded its way between these, climbing above the olive groves to the open hillside with its patches of stunted woodland where even in the cold night the smell of pine hung in the air. Every now and then a car coming towards me in the distance jigged this way and that like a firefly flaring up and then suddenly disappearing as it followed the invisible twists of the road, until eventually some magic force drew us together, we passed, and I watched its red tail lights wobbling away behind me in the mirror. At the pass, I glimpsed for the first time the lights of Caldeya, stretching raggedly down the slope towards the little crescent-shaped harbour. There, at the waterfront, I could make out the umbrella pines and tamarisks under the streetlamps of the Paseo and the headlights of a car crawling between them. The road zig-zagged down the hillside, my headlights sweeping the *maquis* round its switchback corners. Eventually, just before I got to the village, I saw the hand-painted sign which indicated the Mas dels Cavallers. A long drive full of potholes led me back up the hill to the Mas itself: an old stone building which sat comfortably under a number of long tiled roofs set at different heights and angles in the typical style of the province. Its big ashlar stones gave to the building a feeling of rustic strength, but there was also something thoughful about the size and placing of each window, something in the sweep of the wide arch above the barn doors and the particular lengths and angles of its roofs which gave to the whole a lean and unstudied elegance. By the door a mimosa, already in flower, looked startlingly yellow in the headlamps. There was a light on downstairs: the Major was waiting for me. I switched off the car headlights and got my bags out of the boot. At this time of year there were no crickets or cicadas and the night seemed incredibly still. I walked over to the door and rang the bell.

I waited several minutes but no one came so I rang again. Still no one came. I went round to the window where the light was and tried to look in, but a white blind drawn down on the inside prevented me from seeing anything. I walked back and rang the bell vigorously several times. After this I heard the sound of a door closing and then footsteps coming towards me. A bolt went back and then a key turned in the lock – and there was Doris.

I said, 'Hello.'

'Hello,' said Doris, blinking and peering at me. 'I'm afraid I dropped off to sleep. Had you been there for long? I heard the bell ring in my dream.'

She yawned and put her hand up to her mouth. 'Daddy rang this afternoon. I'm afraid he's been delayed. But won't you come in?'

This last question had to be repeated several times. The fact was that I was completely disorientated by a sudden and very surprising conviction: namely, that this Doris Shark was not the same one that I had met before. In this confused state of mind, I followed her into the sitting-room, still carrying my suitcase.

'Would you like a drink?' she said.

'I'd love some whisky.'

She went into the kitchen to get some ice and I was just warming my back in front of the fire when out of the kitchen a white blob shot across the room and fastened itself on to my ankle. My first idea was that it was a rat, but when it let go of my foot and began barking in a maddened, high-pitched way, I realised that by some monstrous trick of nature this bloated and boil-covered creature was a small and incredibly diseased dog. Enraged and revolted, I gave it a good kick while Doris, alarmed by all the yelping and commotion, sallied out of the kitchen ice-bucket in hand, and clasping the loathsome creature to her bosom, said to it, 'There, there Scwew-scwew!' and kissed it on the face. When she spoke to it she used the same baby voice as she used to speak to her father. Screw-screw (as the dog was called) stopped its yapping and sneezed into the ice-bucket. I inspected my ankle, and was surprised to find that no blood was drawn. There were plenty of tooth-marks though, in two well-defined semi-circles.

'He's not naughty really, he just gets frightened of people he doesn't know,' she explained. Then to the dog, 'Don't we Scwew-scwew? Now say hello nicely to Hellman, he's a fwiend.'

'The name's Herman,' I said.

'Herman.'

She approached the white blob to my face. I wanted to recoil in horror but found myself spellbound – hardly ever had I beheld such a repulsive creature. Its nostrils were horribly distended, red on the inside and dripping with snot; one of its eyes was closed up by an infection, the other had a great clot of blood in it. Its whole face was covered in warts and boils, some of which had pus seeping out of them. Doris kissed it again.

'You can stroke him, it's all right,' she said, 'he only bites people when he's afraid.'

To make my escape I went and filled my glass from the whisky bottle.

'D'you know, Doris, I don't think I'll have any ice after all.'

Doris sat down on the sofa with the dog in her lap; I took an armchair by the fire. Now that Screw-screw had calmed down I began to relax a bit and got myself accustomed to the idea that this Doris was the same one I had met in London. What I saw now, which I had never recognised before, was that something seemed to be radiating from her, as though the reddy-gold of her hair and perfect whiteness of her skin were in some way reflected in the simple objects of the room, giving everything a richer, more saturated appearance. Was it to do with the drug I had inhaled in the laboratory? I was muddled. Yet my senses were so alert to everything that I fancied I could even anticipate things happening. When, for instance, a log shifted in the grate, I knew it a split second before, so that instead of being surprised by the sound, I knew it was going to come, like the beat at the beginning of a musical bar. And in addition I felt very elated: how marvellous it was to be drinking whisky in this old farmhouse sitting-room! The shape of the room, the wooden table, the shaded reading lamps, the fire, the uneven tiled floor – everything seemed as clean and resonant as a well-cast bell.

We decided that she should read my tarot. Doris untied the silk handkerchief which contained the cards and which she claimed had been given by a Hopi Indian to Mark Rafftrap, a friend of hers who was a singer. She shuffled the pack and told me to cut.

'The cut card,' she said, 'is the one that sets the tone of the whole reading, a sort of general influence over the whole spread. This card is the one that dominates your present existence.'

I cut The Moon.

'The card of illusion,' said Doris. 'This card is deceived by the way things seem. It represents somebody who bases their life on an error.'

I wondered if this was to do with my mission and asked, 'What sort of error is it?'

Doris looked at me and put her head a little on one side.

'It's a card for people who are interested in the surface of things. Socialites and that sort of type. After all, you live in rather a grand world.'

'Do I?'

'People like that uncle of yours whom my father knows. He's very grand.'

'But he's not my uncle. And I don't even know him.'

'Oh, well,' Doris said. 'That's what the card says anyway.'

I realised that because the Major always spoke of me as the nephew of this rich and influential man, Doris assumed that I too was rich and influential in some way.

I picked out eight more cards from the deck and Doris laid

them out in three rows to form a square with The Moon in the middle.

'Now,' she said, pointing to the top row, 'this is your past: The Lovers, The Tower of Destruction and The Magician. That's quite straightforward. You were married, it broke up and now you're alone.'

Doris knew I was divorced so there was nothing in this to impress me with her powers of divination. However, it did make me feel slightly uneasy to see how accurately the three pictures told the story of my past. The Magician with his objects on the table made me think of myself in the laboratory with my experimental apparatus. And The Tower of Destruction with its picture of a tower falling down naturally made me think of my impotence, proved once again by Myrna only this evening.

'The middle line is your present,' said Doris. 'What have we got here? The Knave of Swords.' She had to resort to the book to see what this meant. ' "This is the card of the spy," ' she read. ' "It symbolises a person adept at perceiving, discerning and uncovering the unknown and less obvious. Someone who has the quality of perception and vigilance. A crafty person." I wonder what that means?'

The card of the spy! She picked it up in her hand and looked perplexedly at it, and like ski-tracks in the snow, two little furrows of thought appeared on her white forehead. I remember looking at the card in her hand and thinking how like a tarot card she was herself: the big empty eyes with their ancient symbolism, the oddly tapering fingers holding the card with its back covered in gold and russet whorls, the stone flags of the floor and the heraldic flames jumping in the chimney. Suddenly I longed to tell her that I was a real spy, not a radio instructor, and not just to impress her, but because I wanted her to know who I really was, without any pretence. Then she would have realised that far from being some sort of socialite I was actually engaged on a dangerous mission in the course of which I'd already been knocked on the head.

'Now,' said Doris, 'what's next? The Moon. Yes, superficial character, we've dealt with that. Ah yes, The Seven of Cups. I know this card. This is the one that Mungo calls the "drugs card". It means the influence of drugs or drink. A card of artificial fantasy. Mark Rafftrap always gets it because he takes so much smack. You don't take drugs do you? Or drink?'

'Not a lot.'

'Then in your case it must mean daydreams or foolish whims. It looks as though your present character is rather frivolous.'

She was quite unembarrassed to tell me unpleasant things about myself. I knew she was meant to be only interpreting the cards, but it seemed a bit abrupt, almost rude, the way she put it. For my part, when I heard her say that this was the drugs card my mind flew immediately to the little fragments of glass like diamonds on the floor of the laboratory, and the curious prickling sensation in my nostrils. Did it simply mean that I had found the drug or did it mean I was actually, because I had inhaled its vapours, ever so slightly under its influence? Unquestionably it had had an effect when I first breathed it. And didn't I feel more attracted to Doris now than I had before?

Doris swung her legs up on to the sofa and picked a chocolate from the box on the table in front of her. She nibbled, decided she didn't like it and put it away in the ashtray. There was something in the way she leaned forward, in the way that her face came clear of those long, thick coils of hair which was immensely elegant and graceful in a way I hadn't noticed before. Was it possible that I should fall in love with her? Surely not, I told myself. I felt quite alarmed at the notion that I could ever be in love with someone with as few ideas in her head as Doris. Yet it did seem that I was attracted to her, and perhaps the fumes I had inhaled were responsible for this: it wasn't so long ago, after all, that I had thought of her physical appearance as resembling a rag doll. Was this why I had picked the drugs card – The Seven of Cups? I knew that the cards were merely superstition, yet it was tantalising that they seemed to come so near the mark. Surely to have picked The Falling Tower, The Spy and the drugs card was an uncanny coincidence.

'And what about my future?' I asked.

'The Devil, The Fool and The Five of Cups,' said Doris. 'That's interesting. The Devil is the card of sensuality. It suggests lack of control and a tendency to bad impulses. In an extreme case, it represents enslavement to the flesh. The Fool is the card of the playboy as far as I remember. Let's see.' She picked up the book and flicked through it to find the page. 'Ah yes, here it is. "Folly and frivolity. In the extreme case delirium and unrestrained excess. Infatuation, passion, obsession, mania, craze." You know it's funny, these cards really suggest a mad love affair, a great sensual passion.'

She talked about me as though I was completely out of the running as far as anything romantic was concerned. I suppose I am a bit conservative in the way I dress, and maybe I seem a little bookish to someone whose sum total of mental effort could be fully engaged by a Space Invaders machine; all the same I found her attitude galling.

I said, 'What about The Five of Cups?'

'That one can mean two things,' said Doris, 'It can be marriage without love or it can be inheritance.'

'I think we can discount marriage without love,' I said. 'I couldn't bear life with someone I didn't really love.'

'You might really love them,' said Doris, 'but they might not love you.'

I decided it was going to be inheritance. Doris got me to cut a card to see from whom I would inherit, or what sort of girl I would marry, whichever it was. ('It doesn't make any difference which – the cards are always right.') I cut The Queen of Cups, the card of someone who modifies their character according to whom they're with at the time.

'I wonder who that could be,' I said.

'Why are you doing that?' said Doris.

'Doing what?'

'Sitting with your mouth open and your head bent over.'

'Just a wound I received today,' I said. 'I was picking something up off the floor and I hit my head on a bracket.'

'Picking up what?'

'Oh, nothing important.'

But I was beginning to wonder if it was.

Chapter 14

The next morning after breakfast Doris still wasn't up so I planted a few of my ears about the house. I suppose this shows how obsessed an inventor can become with his invention because I still hadn't mended my briefcase with the recorder in it, without which the ears themselves were useless. Nevertheless I planted them conscientiously and strategically; the operation of doing so always made me feel better.

Several hours later, Doris appeared stretching and yawning in a dirty little nightdress and took up her position of last night on the sofa. She drank a bowl of milk coffee, dipping her bread into it and leaning forward so that the drips would fall back in the bowl. Then she ate a few chocolates. It was always a mystery to me how on her sort of diet she could have such a perfect complexion. Even now, when she had just got out of bed, she looked as fresh as the morning itself; and this was always the case, even in London after long nights of drinking and taking drugs.

Doris put on a record. She gave me the impression of somebody who, having got as far forward in their day as having breakfast, has no real intention of going any further. Time seemed to stand still. I made some fresh coffee and Doris took some varnish from her bag and began to paint her nails a lurid green. After this she periodically waved her fingers in the air to aid the process of drying the varnish as if she was playing an invisible piano. All this languid activity threw me into a state of turmoil. I tried hard not to stare, but my troubles were not helped by the way her nightdress rode up her long white thighs.

The Major had still not arrived, so I asked her what her plans were for the day.

'Me? I think I might do some sunbathing.'

'Is it really warm enough for sunbathing?'

'Oh yes, there's plenty of sunshine if you can get out of the wind.' I must have looked less than enthusiastic at the prospect because she added, 'I know you don't like the sun. That's because you're a water sign.'

I said, 'I'm Sagittarius. That's Fire.'

'Oh really? I thought you said you were Aquarius.'

'My birthday's the 10th of December.'

'Then you're right. That is Sagittarius. Still, I always think of you as being water. Mungo says one's first impression of someone determines the way you see them always. For example, if I meet you wearing a suit and tie at a boring social function then I'll always think of you as a boring conventional person. But if you're shouting at someone in a really great bar then I'll think of you as angry and interesting. Do you see what I mean?'

I thought this was extraordinarily superficial, but I didn't say anything – confronted by such a heavenly countenance as hers, one felt bound to pay at least formal obeisance to the notion that beauty is truth.

Doris was quite right about sunbathing. There was a stiff breeze blowing off the sea which kept the air chilly, but where there was shelter from this the sun was hot. In the village the old men were sitting out on a bench on the plaza and in front of the café a boy was putting out tables and wiping them off with a sponge. Above him, in the next door house an old woman brought her budgerigar on to the balcony and leaned on the balustrade, looking down. At the shop Doris bought some almond chocolates and a new type of sun lotion which was supposed to make you go brown fast even in weak winter sunlight. Then we went to the newsagent and bought newspapers and magazines. We were now equipped for sunbathing. At the first sheltered spot outside the village we lay down and plastered ourselves in the new lotion. We ate some chocolates and read our newspapers and soon Doris fell asleep.

While she slept I lay on the grass beside her and watched the gentle rise and fall of her breathing. She was lying prone with her arms forward and her face hidden in the crook of her elbow. She had twisted her hair into a pony tail and stuffed it under her shoulder so as to expose the whole of her back to the sun; but her hair was so abundant that a thick coiling lock had escaped and was lying across her shoulder, the colour of a golden peach. Under her armpit a bikini string curled on the ground like a green worm. Her skin glistened with the quick tanning lotion we had put on. What was happening to me? Already I could remember only as in a dream the time when I had found Doris awkward and dull. I found myself imagining a scene that would take place that evening when we returned to the Mas: Doris is lying on the sheepskin rug in front of the fire in the sitting-room; her right foot flexes idly in the air as she turns the pages of her magazine; from my place on the sofa I get down beside her, and kiss her where the fire plays with the gold highlights in her hair. Timidly she turns her lovely face up to me; I kiss her again and begin to take off her clothes. How smoothly they come off, falling as easily as coils of peel from an apple on to the floor around us! Now she is completely naked, lying on the white sheepskin rug like a long dollop of cream, her tresses of hair spilling round her like strings of golden toffee. Doris!

When I woke up the sun was low down in the sky, and the air, even in our sheltered corner, was definitely chilly. I put my shirt on, noticing as I did so that Doris's tanning lotion had lived up to its reputation. My back felt uncomfortably burned and I saw that Doris had turned a pink colour. I thought I'd better wake her.

'Don't worry,' she said, 'I've got some ointment we can put on that'll take out the sting.' But when we got home, she had a better idea. 'I seem to remember seeing a recipe for a herbal remedy for sunburn in some magazine. Perhaps we should try that instead.'

We found the recipe in one of the women's magazines that she kept in piles under her bed. Called 'French Mixture' it proved to be harder to concoct than we'd imagined, involving such diverse ingredients as muskrose in bud, powdered root of Florentine iris, and hamamelis leaf. For these we substituted what Doris judged their nearest equivalents, choosing from a number of powders in unlabelled boxes in the kitchen. Apparently no one was absolutely sure what these were, dating as they did from Doris's mother's day. At all events, I followed Doris's instructions to the letter, grinding to powder all the ingredients with a pestle and mortar.

Doris, out of last-minute nerves I think – or was it some premonitory instinct? – suggested I take the first turn. I ran the bathtub full of water, threw in a handful of powder and got in. The water smelt mildly of curry which made me wonder if Doris hadn't got the powders mixed up by mistake; also it made my skin tingle faintly. As far as I could make out in the failing daylight the colour of the water was lavender blue but I couldn't be sure of this and before long I was lying in almost complete darkness. According to the recipe, I had to stay submerged continuously for half an hour. When the time came I got out of the bath and switched on the light at the door and it was only then that I caught sight of myself in the mirror and I realised I had been turned a royal navy blue from the neck downwards.

No amount of scrubbing – particularly painful in view of my tender condition – could restore my original colour. I called Doris and showed her what had happened.

'Your father's going to get a shock,' I said, 'if he finds me like this when he arrives.' This idea brought a peal of laughter from Doris.

I suppose I expected that, as a woman, Doris would know all about how to remove stains and that kind of thing. Unfortunately the opposite was the case: she seemed to have even less idea than I did. In the end I had to make do with trying to cover up the stains with clothes; but although I buttoned up my shirt to the collar, a blue tide mark still ran up behind my ears, cutting across my hair at the back of my head, and my hands looked as though I was wearing blue gloves. I awaited the Major's return apprehensively.

The French Mixture had had the same indelible effect on the bathtub. While Doris was having a shower next door I set to work with bleach and ammonia but no amount of scrubbing could make it come clean. In the course of this I banged my head on the towel rail and my old wound began to bleed again; but now Doris appeared at the doorway, dressed only in her panties and with a towel clutched across her breast.

'You couldn't possibly rub some of this on my back could you?' she said, handing me a bottle of after-sun lotion. And then seeing my expression, added, 'you look really gross when you do that.'

I straightened myself up and shut my mouth.

'I banged my head,' I said, 'where it was sore already. But it's fine, really. Here, let me have the bottle.'

She handed it to me, and as she turned round I couldn't help giving a gasp of admiration at the perfection of her back and waistline. With infinite care, I began to rub on a little of the lotion. I did it as delicately as I could, to protect her sunburnt skin but also out of a sense of awe. The feel of her warm body under my fingers excited me so much that my breathing became painfully rapid. When she went back to her bedroom to get dressed I felt almost nauseous, my head filled with pain, my body with desire I was incapable of satisfying.

I went to my own room and lay down on the bed, but immediately jumped up again. 'Heavens,' I thought, 'why am I breathing so fast? Am I really falling in love with Doris?' I thought of the pyramid-shaped bottle lying smashed on the floor and the acrid vapour rising from the stained carpet. 'But surely not,' I told myself. 'If I was in love with her, I would think she was a wonderful person, whereas in fact I can see quite clearly she is the same silly, rather spoilt girl that I knew before.'

But however much I tried to think of her as dull and babyish, my imagination kept reconstructing the scene I had imagined that afternoon, where Doris and I lay on the sheepskin rug tasting the cream-and-sugar sweetness of the flesh.

I went downstairs and had a drink. Soon Doris joined me, dressed in black: a thick, man's suit which didn't fit her, suede shoes with inch-thick soles and her hair in a beret. Some people seem to know what suits them, others can make even the plainest things look dashing; but Doris had absolutely no sense of how to dress. Paradoxically this very ignorance gave her a wonderful natural quality: the less her clothes suited her and the worse her make-up, the more her true beauty stood out, like a saint surrounded by sinners; so that when, as tonight, she came down after changing, dressed worse than before, the effect was to make her even lovelier.

Nine o'clock came and the Major still hadn't arrived, so the two of us sat down at the table. We ate omelettes and anchovies and tomatoes and drank the black wine you get in that region, which comes in huge pitchers and is so heavy it has to be drunk watered down.

Doris began to talk in glowing terms about her boyfriend Mungo. She told me he had just gone to New York but that he was going to send for her as soon as he had made enough money. It appeared that he was involved in the making of some film which might quite probably earn him a fortune.

'Only please promise not to tell Daddy,' she said. 'It's got to be a secret from him.'

'Why's that?'

Doris became worried.

'Daddy doesn't like Mungo, because he's in a group,' she said. 'He's really not meant to know that we're still together.'

'How long is Mungo going to be away?'

'I don't know. Maybe six months.'

'Isn't that rather hard for you?'

'It is: but we both decided to do it. He has to go to New York to make the film. We still speak on the phone. I think if you love someone very much, it doesn't matter being away from them.'

'You love him very much?' I said uncertainly.

'Oh yes, very much. We've been together for three years.'

'And you're completely faithful to each other?'

'Completely,' said Doris.

'And you've never wanted to be married?'

'Not really ... Yes, in a way. What I mean is, one day I would like to be married and have children but I don't want to be married now.' And then, 'Daddy wouldn't like it with Mungo.'

After dinner the Major telephoned to say he would definitely be arriving the next morning.

Doris said, 'It's Saturday night. Let's go down and see what's happening in the village.'

Caldeya was a resort, so winter was the quiet season. All the same, at the week-end quite a lot of people came out to their seaside villas from Barcelona, and there were several restaurants and bars open. Doris knew which were the right ones to go to. She said the others were 'naff' and screwed up her nose. The one she chose was called La Fonda. It was owned by a Canadian she knew and it was full of people, young for the most part and with an abundance of good looks. Even without my new half-blue hairdo, courtesy 'French Mixture', I would probably have felt shabby and staid among this *jeunesse dorée* of the Costa Brava. The gathering had a distinctly international flavour: you could hear just about every European language being spoken. I noticed that Doris's Spanish was quite good: while her mother had been alive, she had spent all her vacations down here.

Doris seemed to know everybody. We were plagued by young men coming up to embrace her with what I thought was unnecessary effusiveness. A girl dressed in leather who had the complexion of a gypsy tried to sell us drugs; it appeared that her father was a millionaire who owned one of the villas on the hillside. A godlike Italian offered to drive us to the Casino nearby; when I told him we'd rather stay here, he looked at me sharply and said, 'Who asked you to come anyway?'

Doris was beginning to get tipsy. The musicians struck up and I took her to dance. A number of the beautiful young things around us were dancing about in a provocative manner. Taking my cue from them, I clasped Doris to me and covered her lovely cheeks with kisses. In a minute she was kissing me incredibly strongly on the mouth without the least sign of resistance. It must have been about four when we left. We walked up the tarmac road into the hills and turned on to a footpath which was a short cut to the house. The air was cold and very clear up here and the hillside looked flattened under a moon that was bright enough to see your breath in. Olive trees were grey metal, the sea invisibly black. Above the village the old church sat hunched like a crab on its rock.

'When we get back,' I said, 'let's smoke some grass by the fire in the sitting-room.'

'OK,' Doris said cheerfully.

When we got home we found Screw-screw lying on the sheepskin rug so I sat down on the sofa instead, and Doris sat beside me and rolled a joint. We kissed as we smoked it and I began to unbutton her shirt. Doris huddled up to me and took a chocolate from the box by my side. For a long time we both stared into the fire. I remember thinking I would probably never hold another such woman as this. Doris too seemed overwhelmed by the strength of what was happening, her gaze fixed on the flames and a particular distant look in her eyes which I felt must speak of interior rapture.

At length she started and said, 'What have you done to my shirt?' and began to do up her buttons. I stopped her, kissing once again those nectar lips.

'What are you doing?' said Doris.

I murmured into her ear that I loved her, that I wanted to hold her all night close to me.

'Oh no!' she said.

'Please don't say no. I really couldn't bear it if you said no.'

'Well all right then. But not down here anyway. And I've got to put Screw-screw out first.'

Not only did we have to put Screw-screw out, we had to have him in the bedroom with us. While Doris was taking off her make-up I tried to push him off the bed but he gave my hand a nasty nip. It wouldn't have been so bad having him on the bed if he hadn't begun barking in my ear when Doris and I started to make love; but Doris said, 'Don't worry about him – he always does that.'

We let him bark. Caught in a storm of mutual ecstasy so sweet that even my blistered back was forgotten, we plunged on in the darkness. And then at last everything inside me that had been for years in the desert meditating on a diet of water and biscuits and living in a rock cave, suddenly found God.

That night, after Doris had fallen asleep I got up in the darkness and opened one of the shutters. For a moment I stood in the freezing air and looked on the universe as it stood on the night of my healing: the white moon, now with a ring of vapour round it, the cold stars, the wide blackness of the sea with a great highway of moonlight going across it. Everything was very vast and old and cold, and none of this was the least bit awe-inspiring, but on the contrary it seemed a great joke to frolic in such an arena. I could almost believe that perhaps I'd been mistaken these past four years and that all the time I'd been full of sexual potency, a power coiled up inside me like the kundalini serpent, waiting only for Doris's touch to unwind.

Chapter 15

To those of us who are ugly, there is something cruel about beauty: our love of it is always shot through with a certain pain. How could a beautiful man understand what I felt when I woke up for the first time with Doris? I was pretending to be asleep so she took no notice of me and went to the mirror to brush out her masses of golden curls. From between the shutters the pale morning sun lit her face from the side, showing me in the mirror her creamy white skin and the deep reddy-brown of her lips and nipples. Her tall legs and long neck gave an overall impression of slenderness which her clothes always disguised, an impression that was accentuated by the smallness of her breasts, which stood rather high up. All this, together with her way of standing with her stomach forward and her head slightly bowed, reminded me of the white-skinned *châtelaines* of the Books of Hours whose marvellous deep eyes seem to reflect the waters of their moats, guarding with discreet silence the secrets they enclose.

We were so late getting up that we were barely dressed when the Major arrived. As soon as we heard his car draw up outside, Doris ran downstairs to greet him. I could hear her chattering excitedly, her high voice punctuated from time to time by his gruff tones. In a few more minutes I heard Doris run up the stairs and shout, 'Herman, are you up yet?'

Sunlight flooded into the hall through the open front door. Outside the Major was bustling round the boot of the car, pulling out a suitcase and some parcels. He was still wearing his dark grey London town coat open at the front over a pin-striped suit. He seemed to bring a breath of the grey businesslike city with him; the farmhouse looked almost physically diminished by his presence. Like that of the empire of shopkeepers from which he sprang, one felt the Major's brusque disregard for the spirit of the place he had taken over.

'Morning Newton,' he cried over his shoulder as he leant into the boot of the car. 'Could you give me a hand with some of this?'

I went up and shook his hand.

'I say,' said the Major, 'what's happened to your hands?'

'I took a bath in a special mixture for curing sunburn, only I think we got the recipe wrong.'

Doris let out a peal of delightful laughter.

'Good Lord,' said the Major, 'and the back of your head too I see.'

'I was lying in the bath.'

'Damn silly thing to do,' he said.

We got his bags into the house and Doris made coffee. An open doorway linked the sitting-room with the kitchen so that the Major and I were never really alone. Accordingly, neither of us mentioned my raid on the Fitzer Institute.

The Major simply said, 'You look very pleased with life.'

'I am,' I said; and of course I was, pleased beyond measure by my new-found virility and by divine Doris in the kitchen with her curls down the back of her blue-striped shirt.

'I think the sea air has done me a lot of good. What a wonderful place you have here.'

'Yes, it *is* pleasant. Originally I bought it for my wife – she was Spanish you know – but now I keep it mainly for Doris, I suppose.'

'He said he was going to give it to me when I was twenty-five,' said Doris, emerging from the kitchen with coffee, 'but when I was twenty-five he changed his mind and said I'd have to wait.' She turned and shook her finger at the Major. 'You're a vewy naughty man,' she said, mispronouncing her 'r'.

The Major laughed. 'You shall have it when you're grown up.'

'I'm vewy gwown up,' said Doris.

This sort of babyish act which one might have found ridiculous in a woman of twenty-five was oddly captivating. When she pouted like that I thought she was the prettiest thing I'd ever seen.

'You'll be grown up when you're properly married,' said the Major. 'If I give it to you now, some rogue might marry you and get his hands on it. Isn't that right Newton?'

'I don't think you give enough credit to your daughter's judgment,' I said. 'I'm sure Doris would have more good sense than to become involved with anyone whose intentions weren't absolutely the best kind.'

'Are you really? I'm not so damn sure about that.'

I looked at Doris and wondered if she was thinking of myself or Mungo. Apparently neither: she was telling the Major about a bathing suit she'd seen for sale in the village which she wanted him to buy for her. It was clear that he would buy it; but it was equally clear that he was enjoying being persuaded. He rubbed his hairy fat hands and laughed, showing his big, perfect teeth.

'But I've just bought you a pair of boots in London,' he said.

'But that was *weeks* ago, *months* ago!' said Doris.

'It was last week. However, if you want, I'll come and look at the bathing suit with you. That isn't a promise to buy it, mind you, just to come and look. I'm not feeling rich at the moment. Sunny Day came in fourth at Epsom on Saturday.' He winked at me as he said this.

When we had drunk coffee, he and Doris went down to the village and came back with three bathing suits. Doris put them on one after the other and came down to show us each in turn.

I was just wondering whether there was any possible way I could get rid of the Major and be alone with Doris, when he said, 'Run along Doris. Mr Newton and I have things to discuss,' and Doris went outside in her swimsuit and lay on a deckchair in the garden and read a magazine.

When she had gone the Major laid his briefcase on the sofa, snapped back its locks and withdrew a new box of Havana cigars. Crumpling the plastic wrapper in his plump hand he ran his nail across the paper seal and took one out and laid it carefully on the sofa table. I watched him in silence as he went through the ritual of clipping, warming, lighting it up. He wore a slate-coloured suit with a very faint stripe and a gold watch chain across his waistcoat which described a flat 'W' where it went through a buttonhole at his solar plexus. Once he had lit the cigar he took out the watch, which was a half-hunter, and flicked open the top for a second, then shut it again with a tiny click and dropped it back in his waistcoat pocket.

'Did you come from Barcelona today?' I asked.

'No, London. Why?'

'Oh nothing. It's just that I could have sworn I saw you on the Ramblas the other day. You were going towards the harbour in a taxi.'

'Must have been someone else,' the Major said shortly. 'Now what about your mission? Tell me about that.'

I began to give him a full account of myself, starting at the beginning. I spoke confidently because I had prepared the speech already, being a little nervous of his reaction. I told him how I'd begun by trying to get Dr Fitzer himself to confide in me.

'He wasn't giving anything away though. I think he has become mistrustful of everyone in his old age; he seemed to think people were after him in some way or other. Apparently he won't talk to the press at all and only does interviews in writing. He denied all knowledge of a drug that could make you fall in love and even pretended to find it theoretically incoherent. Well, I pushed him as far as I dared in the way you told me, trying to tempt him with arguments he must have used himself a hundred times. But he wasn't giving anything away.'

I went on with my story, telling how I'd met Kolowski and heard him talking about the Hawk and the Dove and the time of Christmas; and later heard him talk Russian in bugged conversations.

'Why on earth should it make him a spy to speak Russian?' interjected the Major. 'He *is* Russian, after all.'

'Quite so,' I said. 'I thought that was suspicious from the start. But then I found something even more damning. Have a look at this.'

I went over to the side-table and picked up Kolowski's briefcase which was lying there. 'In this, I not only found notes relating to Dr Fitzer's secret, but diagrams of guns too. Now that certainly suggests a political involvement.'

The look on the Major's face at this moment is the nearest thing to utter astonishment I ever saw on that boiled-grey unruffled exterior. The fat-lined eyes blink, the hand bearing a cigar to his mouth is frozen in mid-air with the lips still fractionally parted to receive it.

'Is that Kolowski's?' he said.

I indicated the initials on the front.

'Exactly where these guns fit in I can't work out. Obviously they aren't connected to the attempt to discover Dr Fitzer's secrets. Possibly it's some gun-running affair. Who knows? Barcelona's an important jumping-off place for South America.'

'Let me have a look at that.'

The Major was waving a hand at the briefcase. I gave it to him and he opened it on his knee. He looked through the papers till he found the diagram of the guns; then with only the briefest glance at it, accompanied by several low snorts which shot cigar smoke from his nostrils, he put them back and shut the case again saying, 'I'll keep this.'

Silence. I could see my discovery had made an impression on him. Perhaps it would do something to make up for my failure with the main part of the mission.

I went on with my story, explaining how I'd returned to my hotel room to find it had been searched, and how I'd been struck on the head from behind.

'A clean knock, perfectly positioned,' I said. 'In a way one has to admire the professionalism of these people, painful though it is.' I put a blue hand gingerly to the swelling and the Major gave a snort of laughter: blows to the head appealed to his banana-skin sense of humour.

'Personally I think Kolowski did it ... First, he was the only person who had a motive: as a rival spy he was bound to be interested in what I was up to. Second, whoever hit me was a professional and Kolowski is the only spy I've come across in Barcelona. These two reasons, while not being absolutely conclusive, point to Kolowski. It's a lucky thing that he was in too much of a hurry to notice I had his briefcase.'

'And what about the Institute?' the Major said. 'Why didn't you bug that?'

'I did. Like I told you.'

'In the microcomputer and the burglar alarm and the blue filing cabinet?'

'That's right.'

'And where are the recordings you took from those bugs?'

This was my weakest point. I had told the Major I'd bugged

the laboratory to shut him up, but of course I hadn't really bugged it at all. My plan of seducing Myrna and then doing a burglary had seemed so much cleverer. Of course if I hadn't broken the little pyramidal bottle everything would have been well; instead I found myself without the aphrodisiac and without even any tapes with which to pacify the Major. Improvising as best I could I told him that when Kolowski broke into my room and knocked me out he had automatically erased the tapes by breaking open the little photographer's case which contained them: a safety device of my own invention.

'The only ones that were spared,' I said, 'were those of Kolowski talking Russian. I had already transferred those to my suitcase. But you see, none of this mattered, or at least it didn't seem to at the time. There was nothing on the tapes which I hadn't learnt already from Myrna. And in any case, I had a much better and more daring plan.'

I described my clever seduction of Myrna and the burglary of the Institute. When I got to the part where I discovered somebody else had been there before I had to admit I was baffled.

'You'd think it would be Kolowski,' I said, 'because he's the only person we know for certain wanted the same thing as we did. On the other hand it's almost incredible that Kolowski could have bungled it so badly. With the computer, for example, he had behaved like a complete ignoramus. Can you believe he actually broke it open physically? What did he think a computer memory was? Some sort of piggybank? At any rate, it prevented me from getting any data out. Instead I searched the rest of the room – or at least what remained in the wake of that blundering idiot. It was almost as if he'd been trying to make it hard for me; instead of looking at the files where they were in the blue cabinet he'd ripped them out and thrown them higgledy-piggledy on the floor, like a jewel thief going through a chest of drawers. It took me ages to sort through them and there was only one that was really interesting. But even that wasn't about the sort of love potion we're interested in. In the end I found what I was looking for lying in pieces on the floor. The cretin had picked it off the shelf and dropped it. I assume he struck his head on a light bracket which stuck out from the wall just there and let the bottle slip in his surprise. At any rate it was smashed to pieces and the vital liquid had all evaporated.'

'If it was evaporated,' said the Major, 'how do you know it was the one we were after?'

'It was labelled Venus,' I said. 'That was the laboratory code-name for the love potion, and the name by which Kolowski knew it.'

This was a lie because the bottle hadn't been labelled at all. But I had to convince the Major somehow that I had really found Aphrodite's Girdle: how could I tell him I was in love with his daughter? He seemed to exist in another world from the one where Doris and I had met and loved; another world where spying shaded away into bureaucracy; where sunny day was the name of the horse and love a zero score in tennis; where people in dark grey overcoats moved around from office to office and success was a favourable change in a column on an accounts sheet. How could this mean anything to me, whose tongue was sore from kissing Doris? What I saw was the copy of ¡Hola! over which her face had been bent down so recently; what I saw was the long white neck reaching forward and the big eyes slowly moving as she read the astrological section. I saw a sheepskin rug and a sofa where she had kissed me; I saw the ash drop from the joint on to her black jacket, the dirty nightdress on her long thighs, ten green-painted nails waggling in the air; and hovering in front of all this, pushing the picture back like a station-identification symbol on a TV screen, the saggy-faced Major sat among wreaths of cigar smoke, meticulous, rational, and in some way I find hard to describe, not quite on my side.

'We chose you for this job Newton, because of your expertise in listening devices. I expected you to get me this information by a careful and systematic strategy of listening, not by going to bed with someone who – from your version of events – was probably a recruited Russian agent.'

In retrospect, several things about this conversation puzzled me. First: despite his assurance that he'd come from London, I couldn't dismiss the image of him in the taxi from my mind. Was he hiding from me that he'd been in Barcelona? And if so why? Second: why was he so unreceptive to the idea that

Kolowski was a Russian agent? Was it because in his ignorance of disguises he couldn't imagine a KGB agent behind the bohemian mask? Or was it simply that, bureaucratic to his fingernails, he viewed all issues of global ideology with scepticism? If this was so it was a weakness which amounted to a blind spot. Third: the Major had a touching and persistent faith in listening devices. No matter what I told him, he seemed to think I could find out anything simply by placing a few bugs here and there. Considering he didn't know about my invisible ear his ideas were wildly optimistic. Even with the ear, a job like the one he had given me could be complicated, dangerous and not at all certain of success. But you couldn't say anything against bugs to the Major. At first I thought he liked them because they were a novelty to him: now it was beginning to look more like an obsession.

Chapter 16

I wasn't quick to be convinced that I had fallen in love. I asked myself how I could love a girl whose main interests were eating chocolates, reading magazines and playing pinball in the village café. Without Dr Fitzer's drug I would have gone on thinking of Doris as a rag doll, my employer's daughter, and no more. And in those first days the idea that I loved her because of a drug seemed somehow to detract from that love. This was perverse of me: I knew from my own theories that a real love potion would be able to make you really fall in love. But even scientists have feelings which aren't always logical. Then imperceptibly, as the days went by and I got to know Doris better, my attitude towards her began to change. I saw in her for the first time signs of a deep and mysterious intelligence. It wasn't the sort of intelligence that showed up in quickness of mind or perceptiveness; in fact, I could see why a careless observer might have thought her dull and there was no doubt that on the surface of it, Doris was extremely dull. But underneath that, hidden somewhere inside her, I could sense an immense awareness unable to communicate itself in her conversation or in any ordinary intelligible way, yet there none the less and full of great possibilities.

'Doris's mind speaks its own language,' I told myself. 'An inaudible one, yet comprehensible if one can get close enough to her.' And, as with all secrets, I longed to make it known. Already I entertained notions of bringing her marvellous soul to some sort of articulate expression . . .

The Major's taste was for all that was simple. 'Astringent' was the word he used to describe it. To hear him speak sometimes you would have thought that decoration was immoral. Naturally, much that was Spanish appealed to him. The village itself, a stack of flat, whitewashed planes, answered exactly to his particular idea of beauty. He was impatiently averse to the whole of Baroque art and when referring to Gaudí's cathedral in Barcelona, he would speak of an 'awful over-egged pudding'.

The Mas dels Cavallers reflected this. Doris's bedroom for instance was of an almost Spartan simplicity. It had a tiled floor without a carpet, a bed without a bedhead and windows without curtains, though there were slatted shutters on the outside which she closed at night or during the siesta hour after lunch. The furniture was minimal: a marble-topped table on a wrought-iron stand; wooden chairs; a tall, mahogany wardrobe where she hung her clothes.

In this austere surrounding, Doris herself positively radiated luxuriance. I can see her now, with her hair piled about her, and the sheets pulled up across her breast, smoking a cigarette and watching her reflection in the mirror. In the shuttered half-light of the siesta, her hair is browner than usual and her lips are a dark red, almost brown too; even her skin against the starkness of those white walls and cotton sheets has a richer and softer hue, like that of a silk pillow. It is now as I watch her watching herself that I realise why she fascinates me and why I am perfectly right to be fascinated by her: she is pure intuition, unadulterated by the processes of thought.

I really don't think she had any ideas of her own. She had the sort of adaptive character which her astrological handbooks would have called lunar. The more I got to know her the more I came to realise that every trait was a characteristic not of *her* personality but of somebody else's. The views she expressed on the subject of art or politics were usually her father's, but they were sprinkled with a different and rather contrary assortment of opinions which she had from Mungo – for example, her enthusiasm for almost all forms of drug-taking. Her opinions were so often at odds with each other that when you first knew her you couldn't help being puzzled. They became clear only when you saw where they came from, and how little of them in any case she understood. And in a way this excused her everything: in my lover's mind her clothes reflected not her own tastelessness but the tastelessness of current fashions; her vulgarity was not anything to do with her, but with the magazines she read.

At first I thought of her as wax, receiving and effacing

impressions with placid indifference. Later I felt that her impressionability went even further, that she could be melted down completely, poured into a mould, and reset. She actually longed to take her shape from someone else; and I felt that her instinct would always take her to the strongest shaper, and this infuriated me. I wanted to produce for her like a conjurer out a hat, her own soul.

We stayed in Caldeya two days after the Major arrived. Doris used to sunbathe a lot, and when she wasn't sunbathing we went to a café she knew. On these occasions she always told her father – and the innocence with which she lied was something I would remember later with a dry sort of feeling in my throat – that we were going for a walk on the cliffs. For some reason her father didn't like her going to cafés during the day although he didn't mind if she went out in the evenings. This particular café, called the Galeón, was where she and her friends went in the summer. Perched on stilts above the harbour, it was approached by a gangplank over a thin alley of oily water. From the street and the main square you could see nothing of the interior: the bar was built along this side so as to give all the tables a picture-window view on the harbour, now in its boatless season. Sitting at the wooden table – a coke for Doris, a coffee for me – I looked out across the bay to the other end of the village with its streets worming down the hillside and the white houses dotted all over with yellow mimosa in flower. In the corner by the bar Doris is playing the pinball machine; sometimes I get up to take a turn; and then almost inevitably the ball disappears between the two flippers which I cause to flap their arms hopelessly, as a matter of form really, because the trajectory of that horrible silver projectile seems to be written by fate on the exact path that takes it between Scylla and Charybdis. Doris laughs delightedly whenever this happens; though when we're not playing she looks on my lack of skill – and even more on my lack of enthusiasm – as something terribly old-fashioned and really almost reprehensible.

Like everyone else in Caldeya, Doris professed to believe that there were too many tourists in summer, just as it was universally agreed that Caldeya had been much better in the old days. These are the main articles of faith in any resort, together with the usual preoccupation of a resort community about how many years you have been coming. But in fact it was obvious that Caldeya wasn't really much fun in winter precisely because there were too few people there. Doris used to tell me about the café in summer and the people who sat in it. Never having met them they began to acquire in my mind the status of legends: the French boy who made the record score on the flipper machine, the American girl who had taken lessons in Flamenco dancing, the German and his half-Czech girlfriend who both shaved off their hair at a party. In my mind they were featureless, like figures on a shooting-range, and I used to muddle them up so that the French boy shaved off his hair and the flipper champion had the half-Czech girlfriend and so on. The fact that I kept forgetting their names was also looked upon by Doris as droll and rather stupid.

She used to read magazines here too. I had finished the second volume of Burton's *Pilgrimage* and had begun a book I had got out of the library about the CIA. And when Doris began to flick through *Epoca* and *¡Hola!* I would dip into this extraordinary and, to my mind, wrong-headed book, written by a man who had been a CIA agent himself, called J. P. Lipsky. This Lipsky was a dogged proponent of what I termed the 'bureaucratic' approach: the same old plodding methods which the Major favoured, utterly devoid of imagination and daring. Lipsky even went so far as to say that Intelligence agencies could get their information from newspapermen and scientific journals. It seemed incredible that such a bore could get a job in the CIA. Clearly the Americans were suffering from the British disease and the situation was worse than I had imagined. But even the world crisis couldn't hold my attention for long. Between pages, between paragraphs even, my gaze would wander up the page past the title of the book (*Espionage: How it Really Works*), up over the café table with its ring stains and yellow ashtray with 'Ricard' written round the edge, and the dark green coffee cup with the gold rim; up past Doris's tapering fingers splayed across a picture of the King of Spain and a topless girl in a carnival mask; and on up over the pink sweater with a badge saying '*Syd es inocente*', until I am looking at the picture which will always remain in my memory. The metal edge of the window forms the frame of it and the cloudless sky outside makes an abstract background of pure blue of the kind you sometimes see in early renaissance portraits. On to this is painted the head of Doris, decked in gold ringlets, her long, white neck held forward and her face in half profile looking down at the magazine. Her wide eyes have exactly the same expression as the Virgin Mary, so that everything she brings up into the picture – a filter cigarette, her glass of coke, or whatever – seems to be medievalised by its contiguity with her.

Doris was never very keen on any show of affection in public. She didn't really like me putting my arm round her, and kissing always embarrassed her dreadfully, even if it was another couple doing it. But here in Caldeya we had to be doubly careful because there was always a danger that the Major might appear. I couldn't help feeling I had been terribly unlucky in a village with an almost Europe-wide reputation for its bohemian lifestyle, to fall in love with a girl whose father was a Knight of St Expeth. To make matters worse, the Major seemed to have got it into his head that I wanted to become one myself.

'I was speaking to your uncle the other day at the club,' he said one evening at dinner. 'I told him about your becoming a Knight and he thought it a sound idea. Have you seen him recently?'

'Not for twenty-five years,' I said, a little loath to enter into another discussion about this distant relative.

'Ah well, I'm sure he'll second your application when I put you up.'

Unwelcome as this proposal was, I felt it must signal a certain degree of confidence in me despite my failure in Barcelona. We didn't discuss the Fitzer case any further, but during those few days I began to formulate a new plan for discovering Dr Fitzer's secret. Obviously after what I had done to Myrna I couldn't very well present myself again at the Institute, nor did I think that the Major's idea of bugging the place would help us find out very much. What I decided would be better than either of these would be for me to go in disguise like Burton into Mecca, on a second foray on the Institute: if my disguise was good enough even Myrna and Kolowski wouldn't recognise me, and if the computers had been mended I might have an opportunity to read and even print out some of the secret files. This way I would hope to come away not just with a sample bottle of the drug but with the actual formula itself.

I put my idea to the Major on the morning of our departure for London. I remember the conversation took place on the cliffs by the old lighthouse. The Major had lost some of his usual pallor. He wore a mustard brown jacket and sunglasses which changed colour according to the brightness of the sun. From where we stood I could see the windows of Doris's room at the Mas, flanked by the little grey shutters behind which we had made love for the first time. Looking back from the lighthouse to that secret personal beacon, I explained to the Major my plan for Dr Fitzer's drug. I purposely played down the role which disguise played in it because he had refused to teach me about disguise and I didn't want to look as though I was saying 'I told you so.' When I had finished he took his cigar between his forefinger and his thumb and with a powerful flick, sent it spinning out over the edge of the cliff. Then he struck his boot-toe with his walking stick and turned to me abruptly and said, 'No. I'm taking you off the case. You're too valuable in the laboratory for us to lose.'

Nothing I could say was of any use. I tried to explain how good my plan was; he didn't even want to listen. As we walked back across the hillside to the Mas, I knew I had had my chance and lost it. I felt as my father must have felt the day La du Barrier left him, but I refused to sit down on the steps and weep. As a child I had vowed to have a hundred big-game trophies on my wall; somehow I would make sure that I got them.

Chapter 17

I find it difficult to be level-headed about the time I spent with Doris when we returned to London. Even then I knew it was the happiest moment of my life and usually happiness is something one is aware of only in retrospect. It would be easy for me to paint a picture which left out everything which rankled, like a veteran telling stories about war. Only children believe these stories, rather in the same way they believe their pop-guns can fire bullets. For my part, I only believe in happiness now. When I hear people using the past tense about it I am filled with the same sort of unease I experience when a vague acquaintance, mariner-like, gets hold of my sleeve at a wedding and begins to reminisce about an unrecalled childhood, which little by little turns out to be not mine at all but that of a Spanish cousin. At last you wrest your arm free and, as he turns boozily towards the approaching green bottle swathed in a white napkin, you slip away in the direction of an unclaimed gilt chair in the corner. Unhand me, grey-beard loon! Installed on this gilt chair, then, let me try to tell without sentimentality how my unheroic life with Doris really was.

I begin at the beginning: one minute past midnight usually finds us in a nightclub, or a bar called the Rangoon in South Kensington. I am already quite drunk, or 'out of it' as Doris would say. Doris knows everybody here, and like her, they all work in something connected with fashion. This year black is *de rigueur* in London. You also score points for having your clothes ripped or for wearing a beret or wrap-around sunglasses. Men's suits are all in a style which I can't identify exactly but which reminds me of the ones which iron-curtain diplomats used to wear in my childhood. Almost everybody has a belt with steel studs all over it like those in the Fitzer sex-shop. The overall impression must be shabby: any suggestion of chic would look absurdly out of date. Which is certainly lucky for me. Of course anyone can see at a glance that I'm not really quite correct but I consider it best not even to try; certainly it would take weeks to master the nuances of what can be torn and what can be all in one piece and – most vexing question of all – what can be coloured. Doris said I'd look all right if I put on sunglasses but unfortunately I have already broken them getting off the bus. In any case the girl I am talking to at the moment, a hairdresser, is telling me she loves my hair.

'And your hands too,' she exclaims. 'I'd never thought of doing hands to match.'

At times the disastrous bath in 'French Mixture' has its advantages.

My attention is all on Doris, who is disappearing into the toilets with an impish black boy, probably with the intention of indulging in some drug . . .

'It's a ghastly place,' the hairdresser is saying, 'full of awful hairdressers and people like that.'

She is a tiny thing with a mountain of hair piled up on her head and a very loud, cockney voice. This evening I have talked to her a lot, not just because she is Doris's best girlfriend, but also because she's the only person I can hear above the music. Despite her diminutive size she has absolutely huge breasts which must be held up by one of those half-moon brassières you see in the Fitzer Institute. Her fingernails, like Doris's, are painted green. When Doris comes out of the lavatory she has definitely taken something. I have never seen her so vivacious and we go immediately to the crowded floor.

We dance until we are thirsty, and then drink beer out of bottles and then dance again . . . but now is the Cinderella hour, around half-past two, when Doris decides she has to go home. Once again I ask her to come back with me. Once again she says that she can't because her father would notice. The taxi stops in the deserted square. Doris kisses me with real love and then jumps out saying, 'Cheerio.' I tell the driver my address. As the taxi pulls away the Major's black front door shuts on Doris, and the house returns to anonymity in a row of white porticoes, each with a black number on the pillar, and between them the line of black, spear-headed railings.

One minute past midnight (alternative version). We didn't

go to the club every night. By far my favourite start to the day was to watch TV until closedown and then to slip into bed with Doris. She was always very shy about making love. In order for it to be all right it had to be night, all the lights in the flat had to be out, she had to have taken off her make-up and cleaned her teeth and preferably put on a nightdress. Then, as long as we didn't talk about it she would, as she used to say herself, 'do it'. I am trying to be factual. For me these were moments of heaven.

2 a.m. The alarm rings and Doris gets out of bed. At night my room is always penetrated by the orange light from the sign of the Indian restaurant underneath. (In the old days this used to say 'Baroda Palace' but having lost its two middle 'A's it now bears the more humble title 'Barod. P.lace'. In this faint orange glow, reminiscent of the strange light of a colour negative, moves the largely undecipherable outline of Doris, struggling into T-shirt and studded belt, a writhing form out of which from time to time a crooked elbow detaches itself in profile, or a bunch of fingers on the end of a sleeve. Fully dressed now, the figure crosses the room to kiss me goodbye. For a second, two almond eyes swim out of the orange darkness, and a wonderful mixture of perfume and cigarettes lingers on as her outline slips away across the room and then suddenly disappears into the blackness of the doorway. I lie on my back with my hands behind my head and listen to the door of the flat shutting behind her. Then comes the sound of feet on the stairs and the slamming of the front door. And if I go to the window now I can watch her cross the road, her thick hair bound in at the neck by a black scarf, her hands in her trouser pockets and her rubber-and-studs bag over her shoulder which is hunched up against the cold. If she looked up now she would see me and wave, but instead she turns where the window of the newsagent reflects the ghostly words 'Barod. P.lace' written backwards, and sets off along the avenue, casting glances back over her shoulder for the more welcome orange illuminated sign of a taxi for hire.

10 a.m. I arrive at the lab. When I first got back from Barcelona Codrington was particularly sarcastic. As if it wasn't already humiliating enough to be demoted from spy back to researcher. But I have a new idea for an aphrodisiac

which consoles me: in the Nilotic basin there is a fatal disease, one of whose symptoms is a permanent penile erection. How ironic it would be if I found a cure for impotence now that I no longer need it! Codrington keeps pestering me to go back to my old speciality of listening devices. He can't conceive how boring this would be: having already discovered the device of the next decade, I would now have to pretend to be discovering inferior ones.

12 p.m. Doris arrives at work. Sometimes she's a little late so I usually leave it until 1 p.m. before I phone. Also, at this time her boss is at lunch so we can chat.

6 p.m. Drive back to my flat and have a bath.

8 p.m. Evening begins. If this is one of the days when Doris has to stay in I usually get a takeaway from the Barod. P.lace and listen to an opera. Doris doesn't like opera 'because of the voices'. Other nights I read. Recently I have found an interesting book on hawking in Sind by Sir Richard Burton. Lipsky continues to astonish me.

8 p.m. (alternative version). Released by the Major, Doris arrives flushed and slightly breathless at the top of the stairs with the winter night still clinging to her clothes and her cheeks. Usually we would sit around the flat and watch TV. She didn't much care for films and shows. She used to say it was too passive just to be entertained but the truth was she was too lazy to go. Her real interests lay in social life, and that usually came later on, towards midnight, when the clubs started. If I am to be completely factual about the happiest time of my life I have to record that these evenings we spent together were somehow restless. Perhaps because we had few interests in common we used to talk a lot about our plans, so that we seemed to be perpetually on the point of doing something, yet doing nothing.

To some extent this gap was filled by drugs. Doris loved to take drugs and get drunk every night. Nothing pleased her so much as when I brought her some cocaine. I didn't tell her how easy it was for me to get these things in the laboratories because I didn't want to encourage her. Occasionally I put it to her that merely to take drugs was rather a boring way to spend one's time, but I could tell she thought that, on the contrary, it was rather exciting. In her eyes I suppose I was hopelessly old fashioned. Even the fact that I didn't work in the clothes trade put me right out of line – a heresy from which I was restored only by the fact that I worked with computers. In vain I tried to explain that discovery and invention are the two great forces changing the world. In vain I spoke of Archimedes and Newton or of Stephenson, Bell and Marconi. As far as Doris was concerned my work was a grandiose version of Dungeons and Dragons and therefore eminently 'tech'. Unfortunately even this point in my favour was lost the day Doris met Codrington.

'You mean you work with him?' she asked, screwing up her nose in distaste. 'Did you see his tie?'

This abolished at a stroke whatever traces of modernity had previously clung to me.

'Sometimes,' she said, 'you remind me of someone out of the Middle Ages. You don't seem to belong to this century at all, sitting here at your desk and fiddling with those inventions over and over again. I suppose that's why you like medieval music so much.'

By medieval music she must have meant Bach. Or possibly Verdi. I couldn't say.

The curious thing was that I saw her as being medieval as well. Her deep, mysterious eyes dated her centuries back into an age of religion. It was the reason why I had seen her as the Virgin Mary in the Galeón café at Caldeya, white and gold against a background of uniform blue. And it was why I thought of her now as one of those women in a tall, pointed hat, walled up in a castle. Her real self was the woman, and she was imprisoned in Mungo's fashionable world, or alternatively in the stronghold of her father's protection. Loving her, I longed to get her out.

At this time I believe I had sunk to a new low point in Doris's estimation. Not only my clothes and my apartment but now even my job, bereft of 'tech', put me in the rearguard of everything she considered interesting. Often, she would spend a whole evening attacking my character, bit by bit. I think that this excessively critical tendency stemmed from a curious split in her personality which made her a child at the same time that she was a fully grown woman. Like an adolescent, she was hardest on those whom she loved the most, reserving her praise for what she didn't quite know and understand.

Another adolescent trait was her indecisiveness. Even the simplest decision weighed over her like a labour of Hercules. She could never decide when to meet or where; and when we did meet we often spent whole evenings talking about what we were going to do, until in the end it was too late to do anything. At that time I was convinced that this indecisiveness was a direct result of her sexual frigidity, and there was probably a measure of truth in this. To those without orgasm, are not all pleasures frustrating? So it was with Doris, that free and open enjoyment – the enjoyment that is so well expressed by the French word *jouissance* – was somehow always lacking. Perhaps that was also the attraction of narcotics for her, that they filled a space which would otherwise have been empty.

On the evening I am thinking of Doris is being particularly difficult. To please her I am doing some précis of articles in a Spanish magazine about *la psicología del amor* which her boss needs for the next day. Apparently his company is thinking of buying the series for *Fashion*. Of course the articles are clap-trap of the worst kind. I say so. Doris immediately says she finds them very interesting. A horrible quarrel ensues. When one looks back on quarrels between lovers they often seem to be about extraordinarily trivial things, but I have never had such trivial quarrels as I used to have with Doris. I remember at this time we argued almost every day about a certain pair of shoes which she found in my cupboard. As it happened they didn't fit me very well so I never even wore them; but Doris regarded it as abomination that I even allowed them in the house.

Around ten o'clock I go down to the Barod. P.lace and fetch up that familiar brown bag with the stiff paper handles, between which the top edge of the pappadums can be seen to emerge cocooned in a white paper bag. Delicious smells of onion, garlic and cardomum invade my sitting-room as one by one I lift out the rectangular aluminium tubs. Their white cardboard lids are stained yellow at the edges with seeping saffron-coloured ghee. Doris brings in the plates and forks from the kitchen, suddenly in a much better mood. It seems that whole lifetimes of abominable karma generated by the pair of shoes in my cupboard have been obliterated by the avatars Chicken Jalfrezi and Rhogan Josh. Taking advantage of this truce I begin to prepare the ground for the declaration I am leading up to.

'Doris, I'm not really in computers. I just happen to know about them. What I really do is top secret so I'm not allowed to tell anyone.'

Doris tears off a piece of Nan and dips it thoughtfully in her lentils.

I say, 'Don't you want to know what it is?'

'I suppose so.'

'If I tell you you must promise to keep it a secret. If anybody knew my life would be in danger.'

'I promise I won't tell.'

'All right then, as long as you promise.'

'Cross my heart.'

At last I seem to have struck on something which Doris finds at least as interesting as Space Invaders. It's true that she is always a good listener, but this time, as I divulge my hidden *métier* of secret agent, I see a sparkle of real excitement in her eyes.

She says, 'And do you carry a gun?'

But even the fact that I am going about unarmed doesn't diminish me now. As I had always suspected might happen once I showed Doris a little of my real self, she began to look at me in quite a different light. The only things I didn't tell her were the details of my mission and her father's role as an Intelligence officer. Even though I trusted her discretion absolutely, some instinct made me shirk from giving out such specific bits of information. In any case it wasn't the details which mattered: it was the fact that I was a spy at all.

From this point on my relationship with Doris went from strength to strength. Gone were the arguments about my shoes and gone too was the extremely critical and aggressive attitude towards me. She asked to borrow some Bach recordings I had praised. She started to read a biography of Sir Richard Burton. No longer was I considered boring for not being in a group; in fact she discovered there was a well-known singer who'd invented something. Not the sort of thing which I personally would have considered an invention at all – more a banal piece of household gadgetry – however, I let it go. The point was that Doris trusted me now, so that whereas before everything I did had been suspiciously measured against Mungo, now when I said something she accepted it immediately simply because it came from me.

Whenever she talked about Mungo, Doris had always given the impression that he was immensely talented and strong and independent and dashing. And the photograph of him in her bedroom at the Major's house told the same story. Once, when the Major was away I stayed the night there with her and I hung a towel on the brass end of the bed so that when I lay in bed with her I wouldn't be able to see it. How I hated his confidence, his marvellously fresh and youthful good looks! Whenever I looked in a mirror and saw my own protruding teeth and my thick black glasses I always felt hopelessly inferior. But now that Doris knew me better a very different picture of Mungo began to emerge. Now Doris was telling me how insecure he was and how much he depended on her emotionally. She admitted their affair had become largely a matter of routine, boring and sexually unsatisfying. With Mungo safely away in New York I felt more and more sure that in spite of my physical disadvantages, Doris was coming to see me as the glamorous one.

Chapter 18

Of course it is natural that someone as uniquely beautiful as Doris should have a lot of people who are in love with her. What annoys me is the way this particular fellow called Rod (he pronounces it Vod) keeps putting his arm round her and generally behaving as though I wasn't there at all. Vod has that sort of blond hair which owes more to ICI than the noonday sun of his native Sydney. Although the sleeves of his cut and patched shirt are long and buttoned at the wrist, you can imagine, almost see, the perfect musculature underneath. I am not astonished to learn that Vod is a model. He is telling Doris about his recent trip to Japan in vaguely patronising tones which suggest he has completely failed to see her true worth. Even more than his refusal to acknowledge my presence, this implicit insult to Doris infuriates me. At the first opportunity I suggest to Doris that we go, but now, for the first time that evening, Vod turns to me and says, 'Great idea. Where were you thinking of going?'

'The Blackout's Thursday,' Doris says.

'I don't know the Blackout. Is it any good?' This is addressed to me as though women wouldn't know about such matters.

'I don't know,' I say, getting up from my chair and putting on my jacket. 'Maybe see you there later.'

'Are you people going by car? Can you give me a lift?'

Personally I would have quite happily told him to get lost but Doris says, 'Okay, you can come with us.'

The Blackout was unprepossessing enough on the exterior. On the street there was just a yellow sign over the door saying 'Cabaret'. This was the name of the premises which on various days of the week were transformed into different 'clubs' with more or less distinct personalities. It was the way with any place that was at all fashionable. There was something very *passé* and even ridiculous in the idea of a club which happened every night of the week. The one-night-a-week clubs which we always went to were run by anyone who could fill the house; many of Doris's friends were managers. Usually they lasted about six months – a few dozen nights – after which people were bored with them and anyway the fashion had changed. Some opened for a single night only; this was a kind of pay-your-way replacement for the private party, now too expensive to be given on any sort of scale.

Of all the clubs we went to at this time the Blackout was probably the one which held the most *cachet* for Doris. Run by the son of a jazz musician, it was one of the places where the big stars came to get a glimpse of authentic street fashion. That night when we arrived – Doris and myself and Rod – the place was in full swing. In spite of its fame the Blackout was smaller and dirtier than almost all of the other clubs. Perhaps this was part of its attraction. You went downstairs from the neon-lit entrance to a concrete-floored basement, already swimming in spilt beer, and crunchy underfoot with patches of broken glass. To the right and left there were wooden tables with candles set out under the low vaults of an eighteenth-century coal-cellar. At one of them a white boy with dreadlocks was rolling a cigarette; beside him a fat-faced woman in a leotard appeared to have gone to sleep on his shoulder. At another, two rag-clad boys in pork-pie hats were bent in earnest conversation with an older man wearing a pinstriped suit. One of them nodded to Rod as we walked past, making our way towards the bar. Here it was so full you had to stretch across a crush of people to get your bottles of beer. Everyone was shouting to make themselves heard, Doris was greeted left and right by people who seemed vaguely familiar, someone's beer went over Rod's cut and patched shirt. Up comes Margot the hairdresser with a friend – a fat girl with piggy eyes and a grating voice who designs jewellery for someone whose name I can't quite catch. Why have I changed my hair back from blue? It was so nice before. Someone has just come back from Milan and somebody else is off to Japan. Who? Rod? But hasn't he just come back? I look towards Doris who has drifted a little way off and is talking to a gaunt-looking man in a patched-up T-shirt and a black beret. Then I am imprisoned as Rod comes up and puts his big arms round me and the two girls. His sleeve on my neck is still damp with beer as he introduces us to a friend who seems to have been cast from the same godlike antipodean mould, although actually a Scot by origin. The man thrusts a bottle of amyl nitrate in our faces and my head spins. For a moment I seem to be very far away and the music goes quiet and although I can't move I can feel my heart beating wildly, then the music comes crashing in again, and with great relief I realise I am back where I was – only now I have lost Doris.

Although the club is quite small it is always difficult to find anyone in here because there is no vantage point to look from. Eventually I come upon Doris sitting at one of the tables under the arches with a young couple: Mark Rafftrap, of whom I have heard so much and whose photo, taken with Mungo, occupies the top left-hand corner of Doris's dressing-table mirror; and a girl called Candy – very thin, freckled, and with the pin-prick pupils of someone on heroin. I am surprised to find Rafftrap so friendly. I suppose because I regarded Mungo as my enemy I expected anyone connected with him to be in some way hostile to me. I am also surprised at how intelligent he seems. He has curly hair and a round, rather flat face, and an engaging manner: he is telling me about a steam-bath he visited in a Tuscan hamlet and I am looking over his shoulder at Doris and noticing how dark her brown eyes are among all that fair hair and white skin, so that the image of her gets mixed in with Rafftrap's story and I see her eyes with the mist of the sulphur springs drifting across them.

'What news of Mungo then?' The words are spoken by Rod who has materialised at the end of the table.

'Oh, haven't you heard?' Rafftrap says brightly. 'He's meant to be getting in tomorrow night.'

'What, *here*?' I blurt the question out with all the force of my natural stupefaction. Doris looks away. Rafftrap is suddenly embarrassed: clearly he thought I must already know. Only Rod, oblivious or uncaring, blunders on with more questions about Mungo in New York.

I don't remember exactly what happened in the next hour or so. I remember being very angry and shouting at Doris and kicking a dustbin over in Greek Street. I remember sitting in a taxi saying over and over again, 'Why did I have to be the last person to know?' and Doris staring rather sulkily at the flap-seat in front of her, with the neon signs of Notting Hill flashing by behind her. But in my apartment I calmed down a little and Doris admitted she was tired of Mungo.

'I feel sort of responsible for him,' she said. 'It isn't really much of a sexual thing. In fact I think sometimes he even sleeps with other girls.'

'And do you like that?'

'I hate it.'

'Then why do you put up with it?'

'It's hard to explain. I think it's because I know that it's only his insecurity that makes him do it. I know that he loves me really and that he'd be lost without me; it's almost an agreement between us that I take care of him.'

'Take care of him?' I said, 'you sound more like a nurse than a lover.'

Doris shifted her position on the bed and her face took on a faint pout as she considered this. I always loved to watch Doris thinking. Her puzzlement inscribed itself in two delicate lines between her arched brows and the expression put me in mind of a traveller straining to understand a foreign language. I went and sat beside her on the bed; she didn't stir from her meditations and as I watched her I wondered how I should ever give up that delicate bowed neck and the overabundant gold tresses, and her perfectly smooth white skin.

'Don't touch me,' she said.

Overcome as I always was when I drew close to her, I had put out an absent-minded hand and touched a piece of her bare neck. I ran my fingers into her hair and kissed her behind the ear.

'Please don't, Herman,' she said, 'it makes me want you and I mustn't want you now. It must be over now.' She put her arms around me and held me tightly against her.

'Leave him,' I said, still kissing her neck. 'Leave him now while there's still time. You don't love him any more.'

'But I do love Mungo very much,' she said, breathlessly.

'You don't love him,' I said. 'You don't love him. You only love me.'

We were both so excited now that we could hardly speak.

'It's very difficult to break off something that's been going on for so long,' she said. I began to take off her clothes, talking all the time about anything that came into my head.

'Doris, it's the easiest thing in the world. You just have to be brave and act. You'll be surprised how quickly it happens. What's the point of drawing it out any longer? Once you know it's going to end sooner or later you might as well end it straight away. Putting it off any longer is just trying to run away from the truth.'

'Oh! Oh!' said Doris; and then, 'I don't understand. What's the truth?'

I went on pulling down her trousers from her tall hips, progressively laying bare to the orange light of the Baroda Palace the perfectly shaped legs which it had taken nature twenty-five years to make and would be another fifty in the unmaking. And just as I was sure Doris would never, at any time of her life, be more beautiful than now I was also certain I would never be more in love with anyone. I ran my hand along the smooth baby skin inside her thigh and her belly jumped twice; it was something which happened in seconds but which went into my memory like acid into a lithographic stone, so that years after all this whenever I speak or think about being in love, that moment begins to peel off in print after print of Doris's orange belly. And I hear my own voice, still constricted with emotion as it was then, saying, 'The truth is, Doris, that you don't love him any more. So it's much better to break it off straightaway.' And Doris making a little moan and whispering, 'Oh, yes Herman. Yes!'

I was woken up by the banging of dustbins in the street outside the window. Grey light seeped into the room, putting out like dirty water the fiery oriental glow of the Baroda night. Only in the ruddy gold mass of Doris's hair did a memory of those embers flicker. In sleep her face had a freshness and composure which suggested she had shut her eyes only a moment ago. I kissed her and said, 'Doris, wake up.' She rubbed her eyes, sat up and gave a little yawn.

'I'm hungry,' she said.

'You should be at home, Doris. What will your father say?'

She pulled the sheet up to her chest and yawned again like a little cat and said, 'Oh, it doesn't matter. I'll tell him I spent the night at Margot's.'

While the kettle was boiling she took a shower. I could see through the open door of the bathroom as I made the coffee the rough matter-of-fact-way she had of scrubbing herself, rubbing her breasts with no more respect than one would rub, say, the surface of a kitchen table. When her hair was wet it went a darker colour and lost some of its reddish hue. She got out of the shower and twisted it up into a rope and wrung it out like a dishcloth.

I said, 'The coffee's ready.'

She came into the kitchen and I gave her a bowl of coffee and poured some hot milk in it.

Doris lit a cigarette and sipped absent-mindedly. After a while she said, 'The Stuffed Shirts are playing tonight. At the Dance Dive.'

I put two slices of bread in the toaster and started looking for the marmalade. When the toast was ready I sat down at the table with her and said, 'Doris darling, I've got a present for you, which I want you to wear next to your heart.' I opened my hand, so that she could see in my palm the little silver chain and medallion which I had bought for her. Doris took the chain and held it up to inspect it.

'Herman, sweetie,' she said, 'thank you!'

'What do you think it is?'

Doris looked at me in a puzzled way. 'It's a necklace,' she said.

'And what's hanging on it?'

'A medallion.'

'Look at it carefully,' I said.

Her big hazel eyes fixed themselves blankly on the silver disc for a long time and then shifted inquiringly to me. I was reminded of one of those sad-eyed dogs waiting for a command.

'Here, on this disc,' I said, 'I have fixed my latest and best invention. You can only see it if you look at it this way.' I twisted the medallion and pointed to the faint trace which was the visible edge of the ear.

'You can hardly see it and that's its beauty. Nobody in this world has seen it except for me and you. Nobody even knows of its existence.'

Doris still looked mystified. 'Incredible,' she said.

'It's a listening device, like a sort of microphone only not attached to anything.'

'Yes, I've seen them before. Mark Rafftrap's group uses them. There are no wires. You can walk about the stage.'

'It's not quite like that,' I explained, 'because nobody can see this one. Even on the most sophisticated electronic tests, nobody can detect it. So you can hear what other people are saying, even when you're not with them. And they don't know anything about it.'

Doris held the medallion up to her ear.

'No, you don't listen to that. That's the bit you speak into. You listen somewhere else, to another machine.'

A shadow fell across Doris's face. 'Does that mean that if I wear it you can hear everything I say?'

'Normally it would, but in this case it doesn't because it's stuck on to silver and silver stops it working. I'm not trying to spy on you darling. I only want to make you a present of what's most precious to me in the world.'

She flushed with pleasure and kissed me.

'Thank you Herman darling. You're very sweet and I think it's very pretty.'

She put it round her neck and ran next door to look at herself in the mirror. When she came back she said, 'And are you really a spy then?'

'Yes, really.'

'And you do missions and all that?'

'That's right. It's quite simple when you know how.'

'And is it dangerous?'

'Very.'

'I think I'd like that,' she said. 'I like being really scared.'

Chapter 19

I knew Doris would be seeing Mungo that evening so I sat up very late trying to read Lipsky, but I was too excited and nervous to concentrate: excited because of the crucial decision Doris was taking – perhaps even at this minute – after which she would definitely be mine; and nervous because I couldn't help realising how much Dr Fitzer's drug had taken control of my life – while Doris had another boyfriend our liaison was only half serious; now it was becoming very serious indeed.

The next day, unable to wait till I got home for her to ring me, I decided to call her at work. When the switchboard put me through I heard her voice say, "Hellooooo! How nice to hear you. I didn't think that you'd call.'

'Of course I had to call.'

'How wonderful. I miss you.'

'So do I.'

A pause. Then I said, 'Doris darling, how did it go?'

For a moment the line went silent, and then she said in a very small voice, 'All right.'

'He wasn't too upset?'

'Sweetie, I can't talk now.'

'Can we meet this evening?'

'Yes! I'd love to see you.'

'Good. Come round after work.'

She came in a little late and breathless. When I asked her about Mungo I could sense that she didn't want to talk about him so I didn't press her. We sat on the sofa and watched TV. Later we made love and then it was time for dinner.

'Shall we get a takeaway or do you want to go out?'

'I can't have dinner. Mungo is expecting me.'

'I see. You're seeing him again tonight?'

'Till he goes back to America on Tuesday.'

Four days. I already knew that Dr Fitzer's drug made you

139

fall madly in love with the first person you met after you had taken it, but now I discovered that it redoubled its effect if subsequently you were separated from them. I started to become sentimental to a point which surprised me. I bought some of the records we had heard together on the jukebox in the café at Caldeya and played them at night when I couldn't sleep. In the daytime I found it almost impossible to concentrate on working. I was so obsessed with Doris that I even talked to Codrington about her – Codrington being the only person at the lab who'd met her. As I should have known, this was a bad idea. In his rugby-song soul, utterly devoid of proper feelings, he could find nothing more comforting to say than, 'That little thing? Well, I suppose I'd find her beautiful if I was in love with her.'

Of course it was a great relief to hear her voice when I rang her at work; but whereas usually Doris had plenty of time to chat, it seemed that just at that moment they were particularly busy in the office and she had to ring off almost immediately, saying she'd call back; and because they were so busy she never got time to.

The week-end dragged by. On Saturday I went into the lab and tried to work. On Sunday I had lunch with Pilar and Arachne. I was astonished to find that Arachne was much improved recently in many ways. She had given up her silly jibes about my throwing a basin of water at her and trying to run her over. Not only was she quite frank and polite towards me, but she seemed to have become much more intelligent and even quite witty.

Pilar was interested to hear that I had fallen in love. 'Exciting,' she said, 'and what's the lady called?'

'She's called Doris, Doris Shark.'

Pilar threw back her head and laughed; and in the flash of her teeth and her gold earrings, was it overweening of me to have detected a note of jealousy, of malice?'

'Shark! That's an evil-sounding name. In Venezuela, it would be an ill omen. No one would take her out. *Maldición*.'

'They would if they saw her.'

'And what does she do, this *maldición*?'

'She works in a typing pool.'

'The shark in her pool – beware.'

'I promise I'll be careful.'

'Liar. Lovers are never careful.'

I suppose Pilar was as beautiful as she'd been when we lived together – that brown face with the dark eyes set far apart didn't appear to have aged in any way; but now I was in love with Doris, the old thrill had gone away.

Monday was the last day of Mungo's visit and Doris came to see me after work. When she arrived, I was immediately aware that she was a hundred times more beautiful than I had ever realised and a hundred times more sensitive and intelligent. Almost as soon as she arrived she began kissing me in an abandoned way. This time I stopped her. Something inside me was angry with her for loving me and going on seeing him.

'It's been awful with Mungo,' she said. 'I can't make love to him.'

I don't know if she thought this would make me feel good; to hear her even speak of making love to Mungo – even of failing to – gave me a pain in my bones.

'It will be like a dream to see you freely all the time, every day,' I said.

She looked at me solemnly, with those big hazel eyes and said, 'Sweet thing,' and kissed me.

There was nothing particularly significant in the way she said this but to me it was significant. Somewhere inside me I felt it was wrong, but it was a feeling I couldn't put into words.

We went for a walk by the river and ate popcorn from a stall. Although it was dark already, the night was surprisingly mild and as we stood at the counter, a soft rain began to fall outside and to rattle on the iron roof of the stall.

'When does he go?' I asked.

She looked away and said nothing. I repeated the question.

'He's staying a few more days.'

'What!'

'What can I do?' she said, shrugging her shoulders. 'I can't refuse to see him, he just wouldn't be able to take it. It turns out he doesn't have to go back to America as soon as he thought.'

'How long is he going to stay?'

'I don't know. Maybe a few weeks.'

'A few weeks! Are you serious?'

'What can I do? It's not easy for me either.'

Suddenly I understood what was happening. Her gaze was fixed on the pavement at her feet where a few soggy hot-dog wrappings lay. She pulled one towards her with her toe and then pushed it away again. Behind her, outside the curtain of raindrops falling from the roof, one could dimly make out the big office blocks on the other side of the river, each one a monument to seediness and mediocrity.

'Are you in love with him?'

'I'm very fond of him. That makes it harder still.' She went on looking at the ground as she said this and then she raised her eyes to me and added, 'He knows something is wrong.'

I grabbed her arm in astonishment.

'Haven't you told him about us?'

'Not exactly.'

'You mean you're just leaving him guessing?'

'Sweetie, it isn't easy to say!'

'Good God!'

I took her by the arm and began to walk away from the stall. Ahead of us on the railway bridge a string of lights rumbled across the river into Charing Cross station. I began to explain to Doris that she must be brave enough either to leave Mungo or not leave him, that there was a point at which weakness became simply callousness. I think for the first time I began to dislike my passion for this girl.

'Where are we going?' she asked. 'It's still raining.'

To tell the truth I had forgotten about the drizzle entirely. We got into a cab.

There is something about the Baroda Palace restaurant which sets it apart from all the other Indian restaurants in London. Others may be more expensive or more chic, with cocktails and good-taste interiors and stars in the food guides, but for me the Baroda Palace with its 'velvet' covered walls, its tinsel-draped reproduction of Constable's 'Hay Wain', its coloured glass lantern and toothpick-holder on each table, in some way defines what an Indian restaurant should be. With reverence I accept that slightly stained cardboard menu, my eyes rest once more on its never-varying misspelt text as on an often-repeated prayer, and a feeling of completeness takes me over. Tonight the auspiciousness of the place did not fail me. Doris confided that she loved me and not Mungo at all, but that she wasn't brave enough to tell him. Very gently I pointed out that she hadn't any alternative; that it wasn't her fault if her affections had changed, and that all she need do was tell Mungo the truth. 'After all,' I finished up, 'he's not your enemy.' Doris brightened up quite a lot after this and we began to talk about a group called the Three Bears who were playing in a pub in Chalk Farm on Friday nights. She had seen them last week and said they were 'the best'. We agreed to go and see them again on Friday. I wanted to lean across the table and kiss her, but I knew she hated that sort of thing so I just sat and observed her: when she leaned forward to eat, a faintly greenish stripe cast by the glass lantern lay across her left cheekbone; and when she sat back it shifted down on to her neck, above the chain I had given her with the little silver medallion bearing my ear. Soon, perhaps even tomorrow, I would be able to kiss her as often as I wanted.

She promised to call me the next day but though I sat in all evening the phone only rang once: it was Pilar asking me and Doris to the first night of Arachne's latest play. I told her we'd come.

I tried to ring Doris at the office the next day but they said she hadn't gone in. In desperation I decided to call her at home, but there was no answer there either. When she didn't ring that evening, I decided Mungo must be preventing her from seeing me. Perhaps he was even keeping her away from work to keep an eye on her better. At last, after days of trying, I got through to her at home.

'Why are you phoning me here?' she asked. 'You know you shouldn't because of Daddy.'

'But you haven't rung me. And you're never at work. Doris, what's happening?'

'Nothing much.'

'When can I see you?'

'I don't know ... It's difficult.'

'I see.'

This confirmed my suspicion that Mungo was holding her a virtual prisoner.

I said, 'I have to see you. When's a good time?'

'It's very hard.'

'I understand darling. But when does he go out? There must

143

be a moment when you could get away. What about this evening?'

'I don't know. Mungo gives me cookery lessons in the evening.'

'Cookery? What cookery?'

'Mungo's into cookery since he's been in New York. We do it every night. Tonight's *bœuf en route*.'

'Don't you mean *bœuf en croûte*?'

'Well, bœuf something or other.'

'I thought you were a vegetarian.'

'You know I eat fish and white meat.'

'But Doris, *bœuf en croûte* isn't fish!'

'Well, maybe I won't eat it.'

The conversation wasn't going at all as I had planned.

'Listen Doris, couldn't I see you at lunch tomorrow?'

'Yes, maybe. Is it all right if I check though? I'm not sure right now.'

'O.K., fine. Shall I call you in the morning?'

'I'll call you. Leave your machine on.'

Normally Doris hated answering machines and never left a message on mine. So when she said this I knew the situation was quite serious. And when more days went by and no message came, I decided I had to come to her rescue. Unpleasant though it was, I would have to confront Mungo myself and force him to allow Doris to decide her own future.

I took this decision sitting at the bar of the Rangoon early one evening after work. Probably if I had been completely sober I would have planned what I did next a little more carefully; but fired by the spirit of dry Martinis I ventured out straightaway, telling myself it was the mark of a good spy to be able to act decisively at a moment's notice. Surprise is the essence.

Mungo's flat was on the top floor of a house in Ladbroke Grove. Just round the corner from All Saints Road, it was conveniently close to where he and Doris bought their grass: Doris used to point it out to me excitedly whenever we went past, something I'd always thought unnecessary at the time, but which was handy for me now.

Scrambling over a couple of low garages I dropped down into the garden behind the house. From here a drainpipe ran up a part of the building where kitchens had been added to the first three floors. It was not the sort of obstacle I should normally have chosen to tackle in the darkness but tonight I shinned up it as easily as a monkey up a palm tree. The roof here was on a level with Mungo's flat. There was a window through which I could make out the faint outline of what looked like a bathroom mirror. I opened it and let myself in, feet first. In the darkness I couldn't see what lay beneath me — a bath full of water into which I dropped, soaking myself up to the knee. This little surprise was followed by one far worse; something which felt like a pair of shears cutting through my lower calf and the side of my foot.

I let out a howl of pain, took a step backwards and fell out of the bath. My head went down on the tiles with a sickening crack. For a minute I lay there stunned, but the extreme pain in my foot prevented me from losing consciousness. Something hard was cutting into me there, something which wouldn't let go; and every attempt I made to pull it off only tore the wound further. Suddenly a blinding light went on. Doris was standing in the doorway. I looked down and saw I had a lobster attached to my foot. Doris screamed.

'Help me! For God's sake get this thing off me! Quick!'

I grabbed a plastic back-brush and dealt an almighty blow at the lobster, but hit the floor instead and the brush snapped in two.

'For God's sake, Doris, don't just stand there!'

'I'm scared of it!'

'Get me a knife from the kitchen! Or a hammer, a stick, anything!'

I began to limp across the room with the lobster still clinging to my foot. Through the door I found myself in the bedroom.

'Where's the kitchen?'

Doris pointed and gave a little whimper. Gasping with pain I limped and hopped my way to the kitchen where I found a big meat axe and cut off both the lobster's claws. But even now the damn thing wouldn't let go and I had to prise the disembodied claws off with my hands. My foot was a terrible mess of blood. One of the claws had gone through the bottom of my trousers and the other had pierced the leather of my shoes. I washed my foot in the sink and Doris brought me a bandage to bind it.

When we had dressed the wound, I asked, 'Why the hell is there a lobster in the bath?'

'We were keeping it alive for tomorrow's dinner. There are some shrimps and crayfish in there as well.'

'You might have warned me that you'd started a zoo in the bathroom.'

'How should I know that you would come in that way? I didn't ask you to come at all.'

'Well, I'm here now, and I'm not going until I get a few good answers. Good God! What the hell's all this?'

All round the room there were clothes-horses and chairs with white string draped over them.

'Spaghetti,' said Doris. 'We make it ourselves and hang it up to dry.'

My pain and exasperation were such that I was temporarily at a loss for words.

'I wish you would go away,' she went on, 'Mungo's coming back any minute. He just went out to get some algae.'

'Algae?'

'For the shellfish to feed on. Afterwards you cook them in it. It's all *nouvelle cousine* you see. Steam goes through it and it gets a taste of the sea.'

'Listen,' I said, 'I didn't come here for a cooking lesson. I came to take you away from that idiot Mungo.'

'He's not an idiot. Now do please go away. He'll be back any minute.'

'Has he been locking you up? Has he disconnected the phone? Oh my darling Doris I've missed you!'

I took her in my arms and she kissed me and I felt again the blissful melting feeling of being loved by Doris.

'Sweetie,' she said, and looked up into my eyes. I stroked her thick hair away from her face and tasted once more the softness of that wide mouth. Doris!

At that minute we were interrupted by the sound of the front door opening and there appeared before us that good looking face I hated so much in the photo, that lovely blond hair, that well-formed mouth with its evenly-matched teeth: Mungo. A second later I flew at him and we rolled on the floor, locked in violent combat. I think we would have battered each other's brains out had not the clothes rack, with all the spaghetti drying on it, fallen on top of us and tangled us up in so much wet pasta that for a moment we broke our hold on one another. At the first cessation of hostilities Doris ran blubbing between us.

'Stop!' she said between sobs. 'If you don't stop fighting I'll go away and never speak to either of you again.'

The appalling nature of the threat brought us to our senses. We both hung back, subdued by the lovely creature who was still sobbing between us. Now was the moment for me to be decisive.

I stepped forward and said to Mungo, 'Let's make a deal. It's disgusting to fight over Doris as though she was a piece of property. I suggest we let her decide which of us she wants to go with and both agree to abide by her decision.'

I was fairly confident that now Doris had me beside her all she had to do was say my name and then we could both leave. But to my surprise it was otherwise. No sooner were the words out of my mouth than she went and laid her head on Mungo's shoulder. There was nothing to do but leave with as good a grace as possible.

Chapter 20

When I told Pilar that Doris had left me she said, 'I thought so. I saw her having dinner with a young man the other night.'

'Where was that?'

'In a restaurant. I think it was in the Fulham Road. Goodness, Herman. Are you feeling all right? You look terribly pale.'

Suddenly I felt so sick that I had to go to the bathroom. I stood over the white bowl and looked at the word 'Twyfords' written on the side until the nausea subsided.

When I came back I said, 'I don't know why it's so awful to hear that. After all, they must have dinner every night but somehow it just makes one feel like death to be told so.'

'Have a drink, darling,' said Pilar. 'I think you need one.'

She was wonderful to me that night. She took me to see a film about beautiful teenagers robbing banks. The girl looked rather like Doris and there were many shots of her firing pistols. Although all of her friends were killed, she never got hit and walked away at the end, into the working-class district, wearing tennis shoes and carrying a plastic bag with all the money. The film was set in Spain and there was lots of stirring flamenco music. If only Doris had been Spanish instead of English, she would have had the wholehearted passions of that music, and she would certainly have loved me ... But then I remembered Doris *was* half-Spanish.

Later, over a Sichuan meal I couldn't eat I said to Pilar, 'Did the girl in that film remind you of anyone?'

'Not really. Why?'

'I thought she looked a bit like Doris.'

Pilar laughed. 'I suppose she had about the same amount of hair. Hardly the same colour though.'

'And the eyes. Didn't you think there was something in her eyes that was very like Doris?'

Pilar thought for a moment and then said, 'You're really miserable about her, aren't you?'

'It's my own fault, I know. I must have been mad to break in unexpectedly like that. No wonder she was frightened. And yet, you know, she did kiss me, right there in his flat. It must mean something mustn't it?'

Pilar took a prawn between her chopsticks and dabbled it pensively in the sauce.

'D'you know what I really think, Herman? I think you're wasting your time with that girl. Even if she loved you. Tell me truthfully, what is it about her that's so special?'

There was no way I could explain this properly without bringing in the drug I had taken and hence my activities as a secret agent. This would have been dangerous and even treasonable, so I said nothing except that Doris had many good qualities.

'I think you're being very immature,' Pilar said. 'There's nothing easier than to love someone you can't have, because it doesn't engage you to anything. But there's nothing so futile and unsatisfying. Forget about Doris, Herman, and think yourself well out of it.'

But I couldn't forget Doris. Ten times at least I dialled her number at work, sometimes getting as far as the switchboard operator and once even to Doris herself, before I put down the receiver. Then at last I did speak to her. She sounded surprised to hear my voice and appallingly matter of fact, as though it were years rather than weeks since we had been lovers. When I asked if I could see her she became even more cool and I felt as though I was being refused an appointment by somebody's secretary.

Opposite the offices of *Fashion* magazine there was a pub called the Fat Duck, and here I went one morning at opening time to watch out for Doris. When she eventually came out she didn't seem at all angry to find me waiting; in fact I think maybe she was rather flattered. I apologised for breaking into Mungo's flat and said that I'd missed her, and she just said, 'Oh yes,' in a non-committal sort of way. We went for a coffee at Maison Jackson in Soho: wooden tables and hard chairs which force you to sit bolt upright; weak coffee and heavy *pâtisserie*; on the walls, paintings of much nicer-looking cafés in Paris, as though to remind you that Maison Jackson falls a long way short of what it's trying to be. This is the place where Mark Rafftrap met the Hopi Indian who gave him the scarf which Doris now uses to keep her tarot cards in . . .

Coffee in front of her, éclair in hand, Doris wasn't nearly as distant as she had been on the phone. She told me that *Fashion* had bought the articles I had précis-ed for her, that Rafftrap and Mungo might quite probably be doing a film in London instead of New York and that she and Margot would have parts in it.

'Rod's really jealous,' she said, 'because Margot's playing opposite a dishy guy.'

'I didn't know Margot and Rod were having an affair.'

'Well they used to, and they still sometimes do, but not very often.'

She finished the éclair and wiped her lips, leaving a little fleck of cream at the corner of her mouth. Then she put on a new pair of sunglasses which were featured in that week's edition of the magazine. They looked awful.

'You're not wearing the necklace I gave you,' I said.

'The necklace? Oh, yes. That. I gave it to Daddy.'

'You did what?'

'I gave it to Daddy. When I told him about it he was very interested. Asked if I would lend it to him, so I said yes. Then I forgot to get it back. Don't worry. It's not lost. Anyway it wouldn't have gone with this shirt.'

'Doris!'

'What's wrong? I can get it back any time. Surely you don't expect me to wear it every day?'

'But Doris, you promised not to tell anyone! It's my secret, my most valuable possession in the world! Don't you remember? I told you if anyone knew it would be dangerous for me, maybe fatal.'

She put her hand to her mouth in a gesture which suggested she had forgotten about this. How odd she looked, with that studded leather bracelet round her wrist and the heavy black sunglasses!

'You promised to wear it under your clothes and never take it off. You promised.'

'Well that's all over now anyway. Listen, I'm sorry if I did the wrong thing. I'll get it back off Daddy and you can have it back again.'

'But it's yours. It was a present for you.'

'So what's the fuss sweetie? I don't mind not having it for a few days.'

That evening I was driving back from Arachne's first night in Camden when by an absent-minded detour, I found myself in Chalk Farm, in the very street where the Three Bears were playing. It was quite late and people were coming out of the pub when, just as I passed it, I caught sight of Doris and Mungo in the doorway. When I think about it now I am unable to explain my behaviour. I drove on to the traffic lights and then swung the car round and headed back in the direction I'd come from. As I reached the pub, Mungo and Doris were crossing the road. My foot, still swollen and sore from the lobster wound, suddenly seemed to be glued to the accelerator; there was a thump. I heard Doris scream. For a second Mungo's face flew towards me, his expression calm and mildly surprised, his hair weightlessly on end. Then his arm hit the windscreen which shattered, turning suddenly white and blocking my view.

Next thing I knew I was in the street and Doris was beating me on the chest and Mungo was lying on the bonnet of the car looking slightly bemused and miraculously uncut.

Two policemen ran up and Doris shouted, 'Arrest him! He tried to run us down. I hate him! He's mad! Put him in prison.'

The policemen looked at each other.

I heard myself say, 'Yes. Why not arrest me? Is it a crime to be in love with her? Put me in prison because I love her.'

One of the policemen said, 'Looks like a personal thing to me. Come along lady. We'll take you home.'

They opened the door of the police car for her and very firmly put her inside. When Mungo saw this he jumped off the bonnet of the car and got in too.

'You can't take that hooligan with her,' I said. 'He smashed up my windscreen.'

'If you don't want to spend the night in the police station,' said the policeman, 'you'll shut your mouth. Get in that car and drive it back home.' He gave the windscreen a whack with his truncheon. 'There you are. Look through the hole and drive carefully.'

When I got home there was a message on my answering machine from the Major, asking me to lunch at his club.

Of all the people I should have been on the right side of, Major Shark was the most vital to me. For although I had told Doris I was a spy, strictly speaking this wasn't quite true. Really I was an ex-spy and if I was ever to regain my former rank I needed the goodwill of her father. But this wasn't all. As the main arbiter of Doris's affections he was probably the only person in the world who could do anything at all to help me in her eyes. The trouble was that now Doris had given him my ear he must know I'd been lying to him all along, trying to keep it a secret from the Intelligence Service. This was hardly likely to recommend me as a spy. And now I'd gone and tried to run his daughter over in my car ...

It was with some trepidation, therefore, that I entered the gloomy hall of the Major's club. Although I'd never actually been inside one of these men's clubs before, I had an idea it would be immensely grandiose. Instead, I was surprised at how banal it was – one had the impression of being in a sort of private station hotel. I suppose I looked lost, because a man in uniform (again that feeling of stations) came up and asked if he could help me. I told him I was here to meet the Major and he showed me where to leave my coat. Somehow an atmosphere of old-world philistinism pervaded the very lavatories. Returning through the hall, I bumped into the Major who had just arrived.

'Newton!' he exclaimed, taking me by the arm. 'Go in, dear fellow, and order yourself a drink. I'll be with you in a minute.'

He seemed particularly bright and friendly for someone who had a double score to settle. Was this some obscure tradition of sportsmanship associated with the club?

I sat down and ordered a dry Martini to soothe my nerves. My foot had swollen up too much for me to get a shoe on it, so I'd wrapped a bandage round it and put a plastic bag over to protect it. I got an aspirin out of my pocket and swallowed it with the drink. The Major joined me, and began to talk about a race meeting that was taking place that afternoon. He was in a very good mood: last week he had bet heavily on an outsider – one of his personal favourites – and won. Normally speaking, I would have looked on this man as someone with whom I had nothing in common; but now he fascinated me because of his close connection with Doris. Armed with a toothpick he was engaged in spearing little cocktail onions from a dish beside him. Despite the fact that with his fat hairy hands, his sallow, grey skin and his darting eyes he bore little physical resemblance to his daughter, there was something in the way that he ate the onions, something in the compulsiveness of the action, which reminded me of the way Doris ate chocolates.

We rose to go into the dining-room. The Major, noticing my bandaged foot said, 'What's this? Stubbed your toe again?' and burst out laughing. His own jokes always pleased him the most.

To my astonishment he made no allusion either to my ear or to my unfortunate accident with Doris and Mungo. I suppose it was possible that Doris hadn't told him about the Chalk Farm incident – conceivably she didn't want the Major to know Mungo was back in London – but his silence on the subject of the ear was more than I could account for. I kept expecting him to bring it up at any minute, but the meal went on and he still talked about nothing but racing and himself.

It was only when our treacle tart came (the menu had a curious nursery tendency – one felt that the members might almost be in rompers under their pinstripes) that the Major said, 'The real reason I wanted to see you today is about your membership of the Knights ...'

I agreed with alacrity to become a member. Was it possible that I should get off so lightly? Apparently so, for the subject of the Knights led naturally to talk of my uncle, and this in turn to stories about General de Witt. The Major rubbed his plump hands together as the memory of a past era returned to him; he seemed to sit straighter, to become almost visibly younger under its influence.

By the time we drank coffee upstairs in the big panelled sitting-room, he appeared to be in such a good mood, and so obviously not about to attack me on any score, that it seemed the right moment to try and press my claims to be reinstated.

At first he was quite good-humoured about the idea: he smiled wryly to himself and said that he and his colleagues had decided the aphrodisiac had been a false trail and that Dr Fitzer hadn't in fact developed it after all. And when I pointed out that I'd seen it – or at least the remains of it – with my own eyes he just said, 'What on earth makes you think that was the aphrodisiac? As far as I can see all you found was some bits of broken bottle. Could have been anything at all, it seems to me.'

How could I, who had just committed myself to the Knights, tell him I had inhaled it myself and fallen straight in love with his daughter?

'In any case,' I said, 'aphrodisiac or no aphrodisiac, there are other loose ends I could tie up for you. That business of the weapons which Kolowski was involved in; it needs sorting out by someone, and seeing that I started on this case, why don't I finish it?'

Perhaps I had insisted too far. Perhaps I should just have counted myself lucky not to be his enemy. At any rate, when I made this last remark about the weapons, all the joviality went out of him and he said, 'I put you back in the laboratories, Newton, so kindly stay there. You've stubbed your toe on enough clauses in your contract already. Just try to keep your nose clean from now on, OK?'

I knew what this referred to and didn't pursue the matter any further. But another consideration prevented me from following his advice: Doris. The unfortunate accident outside the Chalk Farm pub seemed to have abolished whatever little chance I had of gaining her confidence. There was only one conceivable weapon left to me: Dr Fitzer's drug. Clearly, since it had made me fall in love with Doris it could equally well make Doris fall in love with me. My only hope was to recover it and then find a way of giving it to her. I decided to go to Barcelona in secret this time: the Major mustn't ever suspect I was there. If I was successful, it would be a coup which would be the envy of the whole Intelligence Service; and then even the unimaginative Major would see how right I'd been all along. But more important than that, I would have Doris.

A false beard and moustache were the principal elements of my disguise. When I bought them in a theatrical shop in Covent Garden I felt terribly conspicuous because I didn't know how to put them on like an actor would have, and I kept looking over my shoulder expecting to see the Major or one of his henchmen standing in the street outside. I bought sunglasses as well, which I thought were appropriate, and changed my hair by having it cut with a parting on the other side. In addition, I bought two dark suits made out of a rather cheap nylon with creases as sharp as a knife. I felt that this vulgar, slightly spivvy look went well with the dark glasses.

As soon as my foot was back to its normal size I began to wear the shoes and suits at work so as to get the feel of my new identity. And in the evenings I would put on the beard and moustache and walk about the streets and go to pubs. One evening I was strolling along Baker Street when I saw a tarot card stuck up in the window of a shop.

It was the one I had cut when Doris had predicted inheritance or marriage for my future. At the time she had said it might represent an older relative from whom I would inherit but now, as I looked at the picture of the old queen with her crown and her sword and her cup, I remembered something else that Doris had said about her: that this was the person who modified their character according to whom they were with at the time. I realised now that this was Doris. Underneath the card was a handwritten sign that read: TAROT CLASSES. INQUIRE INSIDE. I went into the shop and paid five pounds to enrol.

The occult in general had begun to interest me in a way that it never had before. In fact so did a lot of things which Doris did which I had thought boring or laughable before I met her. Even Space Invaders seemed quite fun in its way. There was a machine in the pub where I sometimes went for lunch.

Eventually everything was ready. I made up some excuses for Codrington about why I was going away, though of course I didn't tell him where. He listened to me and nodded and said,

'Is it a romantic journey?'

'Not at all. Why do you ask?'

'I just thought it might be because you've got yourself a decent suit at last.'

Codrington's sartorial taste was a mirror of his soul.

Chapter 21

My passport posed a big problem. It seemed likely that since my burglary of the Institute Myrna and Dr Fitzer would have told the police about me, and the police in turn would have warned the passport people. I therefore had to get hold of a new passport somehow.

Well, I knew, as everyone knows, that there's nothing simpler than getting false documents. I remembered reading about a runaway M.P. who had got the trick out of a description in *The Day of the Jackal*. But when you are suddenly faced with having to do it yourself, and quickly, all kinds of complications arise. For a start, what if you get caught? I had no idea what the punishment was for this sort of thing but I imagined it was taken pretty seriously in official circles; and I couldn't imagine the Major would be very delighted either. In training we had never dealt with this question – I suppose because if you are on a mission the service naturally takes care of all that sort of thing. Had the rules been tightened up since *The Day of the Jackal* was written? It seemed unlikely that somebody from the Passport Office hadn't read it. And if the loophole had been closed, they were probably on the look-out for people who were still trying to use it.

Another option was to buy a passport. I remembered the case of an artist I had known vaguely who one day tried to hold up a bank. The robbery was bungled, but he still managed to buy a passport to escape to Holland afterwards. 'It's easy to do,' my informant had told me, 'if you hang out in those pubs around Cambridge Circus.' Accordingly it was to one of these pubs that I went next, dressed in my spivvy suit and my new shoes and my sunglasses. As it happens I've never been much good at going up and chatting to strangers in public places. Though I've seen other people doing it with the greatest ease, I've always felt terribly intrusive when I've tried to do it myself.

But in this instance it was even more difficult because before plucking up courage I had to spot someone who looked as though he might be a member of the *malavita*. Actually the only person in there who looked at all shady was myself. Everyone else seemed perfectly ordinary and law-abiding. How could I go up to one of them out of the blue and ask where I could buy a false passport?

I had also read about a man who forged a passport with a children's printing set for a country he'd invented, and successfully travelled around the world on it. This seemed to have the virtue of showing a sense of humour, as well as being simple and practical to carry out, until I remembered a girl I knew who held an Andorran passport who told me that when she came to Britain the immigration people had never heard of Andorra and had to look it up. What if they queried my republic?

In the end I decided to alter my own passport. To the initial 'N' of my surname I added an oblique stroke so as to make it an 'M'. I also added a horizontal stroke to the last digit of the number, transforming it to a seven. There remained only the photograph: as it happened I had wanted to change the photo for a long time. I had had it taken at Waterloo station and the result was not flattering: the blue curtain in the booth gave me an unhealthy colour and one of my eyes was obliterated by the flash in the lens of my spectacles. In addition I had been caught with my mouth open in a way that accentuated my teeth. The photo was sealed in with a plastic strip which went the whole height of the page and around the other side as well. It would be impossible to remove this. Instead, I took a razor and very carefully cut round the edges of the photo, which left exactly the amount of space needed to insert the new spivvy picture with beard and wrong parting. On to this I drew freehand a continuation of the pattern in pink lines which ran down the right hand side of the page. The most difficult bit was making up the missing left halves of the crowns, and then covering this in another layer of plastic. It didn't look quite right but I hoped they wouldn't be looking too closely.

When I was a boy in Mexico my parents forced me, in spite of my natural aversion to domestic animals, to go for riding lessons every day. I believe they thought good horsemanship was an intrinsic part of the Latin American way of life and, not riding themselves, felt that at least their son should be able to. Every week-end, and every day in the holidays, I was taken with some other children for rides on a hacienda nearby. And every time at some inevitable stage of the dreaded lesson, the horrid little pony would bolt with me.

I was reminded of this feeling when I arrived at the airport, my heart drumming like four hooves, my whole body shaking and jumping about as though I was sitting on the pony's back hanging on to its mane with both fists. In addition I was yawning incessantly in a way which must have looked odd: I couldn't make out if the man at the check-in looked at me suspiciously or if I was only imagining it.

I was very early but I decided to get the passport business over straight away. I went into the toilets to have a last pee and check my disguise: the beard and moustache were fine, but you could see a join between them when I yawned. Then I went to the bar and drank off a large vodka before heading for the departure lounge. To my relief and surprise everything went as planned. When I gave my passport to the officer, he flicked a couple of pages over in a bored sort of way and handed it back to me without a word. I put my bag through the X-ray machine, walked under the metal detector, picked the bag up on the other side, checked in at the gate and boarded the aircraft. It all happened with an almost unreal orderliness – the sort of orderliness you get in Hollywood serials where the girl who tears off the end of the boarding passes has the manners of an aspirant beauty queen. It was only after we took off that the trouble began. The minute the cabin pressure changed, a baby in front of me began to bawl and kept it up mercilessly through the rest of the trip. I couldn't read very well because of my dark glasses so I had nothing with which to distract myself. What was even worse than the baby was the almost obscene fuss everyone made of it, including the airline staff who really ought to have discouraged such behaviour. By the time the plane landed I was so angry I didn't even feel nervous about the passport.

In spite of the complete success of my disguise, I thought it wise not to stay at the same hotel as last time. Also, now I was paying my way, it would have been rather expensive. Instead I chose a humbler establishment near the French Station. Here I shared rather primitive sanitary arrangements with my other guests, a tedious business, but one which I accepted resignedly, thinking of Sir Richard Burton in the caravanserai. My landlord was a surly fellow, suspicious, and with a slavish devotion to the rules of the house. When you took a shower (which cost extra) he appeared wheezing at the door before you were even dressed, demanding in an accusing manner if it was you who had used the *baño*, as he rather grandly called it. He smelt as though he slept on a bed of garlic and his veins, like his eyes, bulged grossly in a way that was reminiscent of certain amphibians.

My room was long and narrow with a tall window at the end. It had a single light in the middle of the ceiling, a bed which sagged uncomfortably when you lay down and a wardrobe with undetachable coat hangers. Here I unpacked my other razor-edged suit and my four new shirts. It was relaxing to be able to take off my dark glasses for a while.

I had a new, photographer's metal case with my receiver and tapes in it. Closing the shutters, I opened it up and tuned in to the bug I had left on Kolowski. It was still working: I could hear the sound of banging and some tinny music in the background and people talking a little way off. Was one of the voices Kolowski's? Yes surely that was Kolowski I could hear, and immediately my mind conjured up the scene: a tall loft, a photographer's studio with vast windows and at one end some studio lights and a backcloth. A radio is playing. By the door Kolowski's jacket is hanging from a peg, my ear nestling dangerously under its collar. Completely unaware of this the photographer and some friends are sitting round drinking beer; and in front of them Kolowski is on his feet giving voice with relish to some piece of intellectual tomfoolery in the way which is so typical of him.

'The test of time as measure of great art,' I can hear him saying, 'is a rank tautology. What interests me is that in our age art has simply degenerated into fashion ... The only real art of our time is the art of weaponry – our warplanes and missiles are the high point of contemporary culture, the bronze axe-heads and ceremonial daggers by which future generations will know us ...'

It is curious to think that under the mop hair and greasepaint of this tousled clown lies a KGB agent, methodical, crewcut and with a fanatical devotion to Marxism-Leninism.

His talk bubbles on, shallow and meretricious, and I sit on the bed watching the wheels of brown magnetic tape go slowly round and think of Doris. That she'd given my invention to the Major had hurt me not only because I had lost my secret but even more because Doris hadn't understood it and therefore had never really appreciated how original I had been. And the scene of my fight with Mungo among the drying spaghetti came back to me and once again I saw Doris go over and lay her head on his shoulder. As if to efface the memory I stopped the tape, leaving Kolowski like a waxwork conductor in mid-gesticulation. Now was not the time to dwell on past failures: if my mission was successful ... Whenever I thought about that, a vision of Doris by my side, walking through Hyde Park, arose in my mind. Her head is inclined towards my shoulder as we walk slowly along under the red and white flowering chestnut trees. The swallows are dashing about over the lake, and in the sky a few long, thin feathers of cloud have gone a pinky-beige colour in the last rays of sun. The air smells sweetly of cut grass and the heavy perfume of lilac. Every now and then Doris looks up with her enormous chestnut eyes; in the lapel of her jacket she is wearing a rose which I have given her. The stalls which sell soft drinks and lollipops are closing down now and the little boys who fly kites are going home. Doris and I walk on across the huge park until at a deserted bench under a tall and beautiful elm tree we sit down together. Doris twists the handle of her parasol as we talk. She is saying, 'I understand now that we were meant for each other all along ...'

In the vision she has a maturity, a womanly confidence, which is lacking in the real Doris but which I can imagine so easily that I feel it must, like an immigrant's mother-tongue, exist on a level outside our present discourse.

I knew my disguise was going to be at least half the battle. As long as nobody at the Fitzer Institute recognised me I would be able to inspect the new alarm systems and locks in the way that I had been trained to. But if anyone realised who I was I would probably be handed over to the police; or perhaps (I confess that my imagination fed on my nervousness) the Institute would take my punishment into its own hands: Dr Fitzer himself might administer some dreadful potion that would unleash, by means of his terrible metamorphic chemistry, a hideous sexual torture. And would he not be justified? I had betrayed his personal friendship, abused his trust, and attempted to appropriate for military purposes what he had developed to benefit mankind. And now I was trying to do it again, only this time for purely selfish motives.

I decided to make the initial test of my disguise at the Bar Boadas where I had put the bug on Kolowski and where I'd been often enough for them to know me by sight. To my great satisfaction, neither of the barmen showed the least glimmer of recognition during the half hour I sat there; and this despite the fact that I made a point of conversing with both of them.

Encouraged by this success the next day I went to the Institute itself. I chose four o'clock as a time when it was likely to be almost deserted because people would be having their after-lunch siesta.

In the hallway my disguise passed its first test. The lissom young man who normally sat at the reception desk passed me without a glance on his way out. Nothing had changed much in the Institute. Despite the double gloom thrown on everything by my dark glasses, I could still make out a number of familiar figures. As I made my way round the long stairs and corridors, none of them seemed to notice me and I began to breathe more easily. I made a quick survey of the doors and windows but I couldn't find any new security devices at all. Then I remembered I hadn't looked at the lift in the hall.

I went back downstairs. Here there had certainly been a new lock put on, but as I looked my heart began to beat faster – the door of the lift was not actually quite shut, so that the lock wasn't engaged. Here was a golden opportunity either to take an impression of the new lock or to put it out of action. But infuriatingly I had forgotten to bring with me the equipment which was necessary. On the spur of the moment, against all the precepts of my training I decided to take a big risk. I opened the door and went inside, staking everything on the chance that Dr Fitzer and Myrna had gone home for a siesta.

The laboratory seemed much smaller in daylight and of course it was far tidier than on the occasion of my last visit. The idea that I was literally within arms' length of Doris's falling in love with me made me quite light-headed. Perhaps there was also something in the appalling danger of my situation which contributed to this. I was chuckling aloud to myself as I recalled that hectic night when I first came under the influence of the potion. Here on this very spot the pyramid had broken and I had inhaled its fumes. And that was the shelf where it had stood before I picked it up. And there above it was the wrought-iron bracket on which I had banged my head. There was no bottle on the shelf now, none at any rate that I could see through the gloom of my dark glasses. I walked over to the shelf to take a closer look. One little pyramid, however small, would be enough for my happiness. I saw myself bending Puck-like over the sleeping form of Doris: a pile of golden hair on the pillow, a perfect complexion, an arm thrown out across the sheets. Silently I break the phial and pour the liquid on to the pillow by her face, and as it rapidly vaporises she opens her eyes with a little yawn and says, 'Hello darling ...' Then we are walking in Hyde Park again and sitting down under the elm tree and Doris is wearing a rose in her lapel.

'Hello.'

The voice, which carried a note of surprise, came from behind me. I spun round and saw, sitting at a desk in a tenebrous alcove, the shadowy figure of Dr Fitzer.

I suppose that ideally a spy should always have some emergency plan in the back of his mind to put into effect at moments like this. The truth was, I was so dumbfounded that I merely stood where I was and gulped back, 'Oh ... Hello.'

I must have walked straight past him when I came in: the disadvantage of my sunglasses was that they made it hard to distinguish any kind of detail in the shadows. Now that I took them off I could see him quite clearly. He had his shirt open at the collar and a silver charm round his neck and he was clearly in the process of writing something. His dyed brown hair was ruffled; he held a pencil and had another tucked behind his ear. On the desk before him were a mass of papers and several coffee cups piled one on the other with their saucers between them. When he stared at me with those hypnotic olive-green eyes I felt as completely in his power as I had been as a boy.

'We haven't seen you for a long time,' he said. 'They told me you were in London.' He paused. 'Please tell me what you think about this.' And he began to read from the paper in front of him an account of homosexual practices among some country's ruling class. When he had finished he said, 'What country do you think it refers to?'

I suggested the United States.

'Wrong,' he said with satisfaction. 'Imperial Rome.' He peered at me for a minute, then said, 'I say. Have you grown a beard or something?'

As I made no reply to this he went on, 'Well, it's very good of you to come and see us now you're back.'

By this time I had recovered my senses sufficiently to realise that by some miracle of misunderstanding Dr Fitzer seemed to have forgotten about my burglary – either that or he had mistaken me for someone else because of my disguise. Taking advantage of my good luck, I made no apologies or explanations for my sudden intrusion but simply went on chatting to him. All the time I was looking around frantically for signs of a pyramid-shaped bottle. It became evident after a while that despite his apparent pleasure at my reappearance, Dr Fitzer wanted to be left alone to pursue his researches; and it took all my skill to draw the conversation out further. If only I could see the bottle, I was sure I could divert Fitzer while I slipped it into my pocket. Such sleights of hand are the stock in trade of the professional spy.

At last my conversational skills could do no more.

'Well, well,' said Dr Fitzer. 'I must be getting back to work now. I'll ring for my assistant to show you down.'

At the mention of his assistant, a kind of strangled croak emerged from my throat like a record playing at too low a speed: a vision of Myrna came before me, stripped naked and chained to my hotel bed, not stirring lasciviously this time as I approached to pick up Burton's *Pilgrimage* but bursting her chains, sweat-covered, and falling on my neck with those strong hands of hers which had formerly practised gentler arts upon more delicate parts of my body.

'Myrna!' I said in horror.

163

'Myrna?' said the Doctor. 'No, no, not her. I have a new assistant now. I'm afraid Myrna didn't quite live up to my expectations. Do you know, about the time she left us, there was a burglary here and do you know – she accused *you* of doing it?' He shook his head sadly. 'I think she was involved with some bad people: apparently she took some madman to a hotel and he tied her up and left her there. I felt quite sorry for her really.'

Chapter 22

The Institute was shut on Sunday so I rented a car and drove up to Caldeya. Spring had definitely arrived now; one or two more cafés had opened and set up tables outside with big parasols saying 'Martini' and 'Cinzano'. However, I found that I resented these newcomers almost like an older-established member of the Caldeya foreign colony, and I stuck faithfully to the Galeón. It was noticeably fuller than when Doris and I had played with the flipper machine here. I wondered if any of the people Doris described had arrived yet, but I couldn't see anyone who looked at all out of the ordinary. Probably it was still too early in the year.

When I finished my drink I walked up the hill to the Mas dels Cavallers. The shutters were all closed up and the mimosa was over. In the garden the geraniums were in flower.

The house itself was deserted. Not even the yap of Screwscrew greeted me as I tried the door and walked round to the garden at the front. I could see the shutters of Doris's bedroom, their grey paint flaking a little in the sun, and I pictured to myself the darkened room inside where we had exchanged our first sweet embraces. Walking back down to the village I was filled with a strange conviction that Doris would come back to me and we would open those shutters together and go dancing again in the Fonda; and I felt an optimism I hadn't felt since she left me.

On an impulse I went into a telephone box and dialled the number of *Fashion* magazine. The girl on the switchboard recognised my voice and put me straight through to Doris.

'Hello,' I said. 'This is Herman here.'

Doris didn't seem to find this very interesting. My next step was meant to surprise her.

'Guess where I am?'

'Where?'

'In a phone box at Caldeya.'

'Oh, really.'

I could tell she was interested although she was trying not to seem so.

'Yes,' I went on, 'I'm down here on some important business, but it's absolutely top secret. In fact I can't say what it is and please don't tell anyone that I'm here. Do you promise?'

'Why not?' said Doris, in a way that suggested that she was intrigued.

'I can't tell you that on the phone. I just rang because I wanted to speak to you, because being here brought back memories.'

'Memories of what?'

'Memories of you ... and me ... down here.'

'Oh I see.'

'I miss you,' I said. 'Do you ever miss me?'

'Oh don't be a bore,' said Doris.

From where I stood I could see fishermen cleaning their nets on the quay, and I realised all this must seem a very long way away to her so I said, 'Listen, I'll call you when I get back to London. Is there anything I can bring you from Caldeya?'

'Well,' said Doris, 'you could bring me some of those almond chocolates from the shop on the corner.'

I went to the shop on the corner and bought three large boxes of the chocolates Doris liked. Even without my dark glasses, the man behind the counter didn't recognise me.

That evening in my hotel room back in Barcelona I became aware of an important new development on the Kolowski front. For lack of anything better to do, I played back his week-end on my tape machine and discovered a revealing conversation in Spanish. Kolowski and his interlocutor (whom I couldn't identify) must have been walking in the street because the noise of traffic was so bad I almost skipped over the whole thing at first; it was only when I happened to catch the phrase, *putas ametralladoras en Panamá* (whores of machine-guns in Panama) that I wound back to the beginning and made some adjustments on the built-in synthesiser which cut down on the booming and banging. Then cross-legged on the bed with the metal case in front of me I played over the whole conversation.

The meeting began with a few vaguely personal remarks of

the how-was-your-flight variety, but this lasted only until the other man whose manner was brisk and nervous was satisfied that no one was following them. Then the discussion took on a more serious complexion. Of course the nature of the business was not clear to me at first. Only gradually as I pieced together the information that they let slip did I understand that I had stumbled on a major drugs-for-arms deal: Kolowski's interlocutor was getting cocaine into Barcelona in exchange for arms provided by the Dove in Panama. Kolowski opened the meeting by announcing that the pay-off for the customs in Barcelona had to be raised. In addition he said that two 'Christmas cards' would be necessary, one in his own favour and the other in the favour of the Dove, both in numbered accounts at the Union des Banques Suisses in Geneva. In his case the sum was to be 25,000 Swiss francs and in the case of the Dove 50,000. Together with an extra 25,000 for the customs this would mean 100,000 altogether. The other man refused immediately. He said if it was like that then they had better forget the whole deal. Kolowski was asking for a huge extra sum, mainly to pay personal backhanders, and in any case over and above what had been agreed in London. Where did he think he was going to get all that cash? He only handled the 'snow'. Kolowski countered this by saying that the customs money was really the other man's expense: he, Kolowski, was only handling the Barcelona customs out of goodwill. As for his own payment, he was merely asking that some recognition of this goodwill be made: if cash was hard to find the extra money might be acceptable in 'snow'. A haggle over the amount involved ensued: Kolowski was demanding wholesale prices, the other man talked of street value. In the end they came to a tentative agreement that an extra kilo of cocaine might be made available. Kolowski was to confirm this with the Dove and the other man with the Hawk. It was at this stage that the other man asked when they were going to see the whores of machine-guns in Panama. Kolowski told him there was no need to worry; that he knew the barrels had already arrived and the gas plugs had left South Africa as automobile parts; and that the Dove was always as good as his word: when Christmas came all the weapons would be there. The other man grumbled and insisted nothing had arrived at all, not even the barrels, according to the Hawk.

'Well,' said Kolowski, 'there's no use complaining to me. I only handle the snow.' And then he said something momentous.

'I'll speak to the Dove about it when I see him on Monday week. We're having dinner at the Bengal Brasserie.'

If the Bengal Brasserie was the London restaurant I thought it was, this greedy little detail was going to be worth a lot to me – it might even be worth a reinstitution in the Intelligence Service. Come Monday I would have the identity of the Dove.

It was clear the '15kg.' I had seen in Kolowski's spiral-bound notebook referred to 15kg. of cocaine, and not to Fitzer's drug as I had imagined at first. The 'UB Suisses' must be Kolowski's backhander. 'Christmas' was the date the guns had to be in Panama. And so I was left wondering: did the 'Venus' of Kolowski's earlier conversation really refer to Aphrodite's Girdle, or was that also part of the drugs-arms deal? In other words had Kolowski been looking for Dr Fitzer's drug at all, or had I put this interpretation on an entirely different set of events? When I remembered Kolowski citing the passage about love-in-idleness from *Midsummer Night's Dream* I saw he had his fingers in both pies.

It seemed too early to sleep. I went outside into the night and struck out across the city on foot, brooding to myself about Kolowski's deal with the Dove, and about Doris. I wasn't really paying attention to where I was going, and after a while I found myself on the edge of the Barrio Gótico and I went into a bar to drink some brandy. One brandy led to another and I began to drift from bar to bar along those narrow medieval streets. Eventually I came to a place called El Tiburón. The windows were all steamed up but I could see the dim light of candles inside and hear muffled sounds of voices and guitars. I tried the door and found it locked, but since the place actually bore Doris's name (*tiburón* is Spanish for shark), and because I had probably drunk too many brandies already, I began to hammer angrily on the door with my fists in the hope of making myself heard to those inside. It wasn't long before the door flew open and two immense toughs were looking me up and down in a surly sort of way. Between them I passed into the club.

It was so dark in there I didn't take in much at first. Above the bar there was a string of blue bulbs which threw a cold and dim light on the rows of bottles behind it, and on the line of none too beautiful profiles which stood in front, and on the fat woman with thin straggly hair who dispensed the one to the other. The other part of the room where the tables were was even darker, with candles stuck into bottles which the years of dripping had transmogrified into amorphous mounds of wax. As in all such places the fug of tobacco smoke was unbelievable.

I found a table against a wall and sat down on a wooden bench. Peering at the woman who came to take my order, I realised that 'she' was a swarthy gypsy-looking man *en travesti*. She was a trifle unsteady, not only on account of her high heels but also, I thought, because she looked as though she'd had one too many drinks. Her wig was awry and her face was heavily farded.

Once she had served me she didn't go away but stood by the corner of my table and said, 'Buy me a drink, *guapo*.'

I bought her one mainly to get rid of her but the ploy backfired, because as soon as she had her hand round a glass of gin, the castanet player came over and I had to buy him a drink too. Next the guitarist arrived and with him, one of the toughs I had met at the door on the way in. They got a drink too, presumably on me. By now I had the feeling that the attention of a great part of the room was on me, or at any rate on my wallet. People seemed to appear from nowhere in a way that reminded me of the way beggars materialise in the East: and the transvestite waitress served them all.

But now an even worse apparition took place: from beside me a figure I hadn't noticed spoke up in a voice whose gravelly timbre and foreign pronunciation of Spanish was unmistakable.

'Well, pretty boy,' it said, 'it's been a long time since we met.'

For a moment I simply looked at her in blank astonishment. I didn't know what to say, the coincidence seemed so unfortunate.

'Myrna ...' I began; but my voice simply petered out.

'Yes,' Myrna went on. 'I haven't forgotten all the favours

you did me. I'm only too happy to have an opportunity to repay you.'

She made a move as though to hit me, and instinctively I put up an arm to protect myself. This evoked a bark of scornful laughter from Myrna, which was taken up by the onlookers like a chorus of yapping hounds. Myrna sat down opposite me with her arms crossed, and leered. To everyone watching, doubtless this looked very cool, but I could see the rage boiling in her black, squinting eyes and I was worried by the way the tough from the door went and stood behind me. Somehow I had to brazen it out.

'I came here to find you,' I said. 'Dr Fitzer didn't know where you were, but somebody at the Institute told me I might find you here.'

Myrna just went on sitting with the leering expression. I wished this interview could have taken place a little less in the public eye. I went on, 'I wanted to apologise about what happened last time. It was unfortunate. Very unfortunate. It was wrong of me but it was something I couldn't avoid. I know I have no right to ask you to forgive me, but please, if you'll only listen to my explanation I promise I'll satisfy you that I wasn't all to blame.'

'Oh really?' said Myrna, scornfully.

'I can understand why you're angry,' I said. 'Believe me, I would feel exactly the same in your place. Listen, all I ask is that we have a drink and talk it over. Then if you still don't want to forgive me, you can punish me in any way you like. Honest to God, I'll accept anything, if you'll first hear my side of the business.'

All this was a desperate bid to buy time. I called the waitress back and asked for another brandy for myself and one for Myrna.

This gave rise spontaneously to another general round of drinks on me; seeing my wallet as my only bargaining counter I gave the guitarist 50 pesetas to play. This was a good idea. The general attention shifted to the music, people began to clap in time, and the transvestite waitress started to dance, shaking and rapping on a tambourine. The flesh on her arms sagged and wobbled as she moved, and discs of sweat appeared at her armpits. Long strands of her wig kept getting caught in her paste jewellery and stuck to the heavy make-up. The song was about a woman who had been left far away in Seville: I wished the woman had been Myrna.

I hoped that by mobilising this musical *divertissement* I had created enough of a distraction to prevent Myrna from launching any very vicious assault, either verbal or physical. But I was wrong. The minute she saw my attention was on the dancer, she kicked me under the table and said she wished it had been in my teeth because at least if she kicked my teeth in I wouldn't be so ugly. Rage clouded my judgment. My foot lashed out, her brandy went in my face, I gave the table a shove which sent her reeling backwards into the guitarist. Suddenly everyone was shouting and pushing each other around. A bottle was broken, another table went over. Myrna picked up a stool and tried to hit me over the head with it.

I don't like to think how it all would have ended if Kolowski hadn't arrived just then. In the confusion nobody noticed him come in; he was suddenly there in the middle of us, shouting for quiet.

For a second everyone hung back and the pause was enough for Kolowski. He took me by the arm, told Myrna to shut up and sit down, said a few words to appease the waiter and gave some money to the guitarist. Now the two transvestites began to kiss and make up. A round of drinks was bought.

Myrna was not so easily appeased. She turned to Kolowski and said, 'This bastard wants teaching a lesson. There's no point in kicking him in the balls because he's virtually a eunuch anyway, so I thought I'd better use my fists to straighten his teeth.'

She was obviously quite ready to start all over again but Kolowski had other ideas.

'Listen, Myrna, Herman and I have business to discuss. Do me a favour just this once and leave us both alone.'

He called for my bill which when it came was enormous. I began to protest but Kolowski said, 'You've been causing trouble. Pay it.' So I paid.

Kolowski took Myrna aside for a word, then he came back to me and said, 'Let's go.'

He led me down a narrow street to one of the main boulevards and bought me a double black coffee in a bar.

Later in the street he said, 'Now, are you sober enough to walk, or do I have to put your head under that fountain?'

'I'm sober enough to walk.'

We walked back across the Barrio Gótico to his car.

'Lucky for you, Herman, I showed up.'

Until now I had been too preoccupied with the fight to wonder why Kolowski had rescued me. After all, he didn't owe me any favours and as far as I knew his loyalties were rather on Myrna's side.

'Thanks Kolowski.'

'Don't mention it. Any friend of the Major's is a friend of mine.'

Even in my befuddled and shocked condition this was a startling reply. It meant that Kolowski not only knew of my association with the Major but also that he wanted me to think he was one of us. Did he hope by this rather devious method to extract information from me? Was that why he had pulled me out of the bar fight?

I realised that I had better play my cards pretty close to my chest: this spying business is complicated enough when you're sober.

We arrived at Kolowski's car and got in.

'Instead of taking you back to the hotel how about if you came back to my place and we had a nightcap?' he suggested.

Clearly Kolowski was still keeping up the pretence of our being very friendly. But when a man has just saved you from the wrath of an angry woman, how can you refuse? We set off towards Montjuich to his flat.

Kolowski's place was very much in keeping with his assumed persona, so much so that I couldn't help admiring his professionalism. Everything about his flat suggested that he was exactly what he claimed to be: the walls were covered in cuttings from dissident newspapers and disfigured posters of Soviet leaders, as well as of people at the Fitzer Institute in various stages of undress. He had no curtains on the windows but he closed the shutters as soon as we arrived. In the corner I saw the orgone box which he had told me about.

'Have a go in it,' Kolowski said, 'it can't do you any harm.'

Gingerly I stepped into the contraption and sat on the little seat provided. It was surprisingly comfortable in there.

'Do you use this often?'

'Every day,' Kolowski said cheerfully. 'It's good for my liver. Apparently it cures cancer as well.'

He went into the kitchen next door and came back with two bottles of cold beer which he opened with his penknife. Then he swung his feet up on to the sofa and took a pull at his bottle.

'You've smartened up quite a bit since I last saw you,' he said, 'the beard improves your face no end. Tell me, why did the Major send you down here? I've wondered about it ever since you arrived but I just can't seem to work it out.'

'You tell me,' I said. 'What makes you think he did.'

It was only when the words were out of my mouth that it occurred to me it might be a mistake to admit even knowing who the Major was.

'How did I know he sent you?' Kolowski said in an amused way. 'Because he told me so himself. What he didn't tell me was why. He just said, "Listen Konstantin, I'm sending you down a chap who'll probably trip over his own toes and get himself into a mess. So keep an eye on him will you?" But that was the last time you came, and he never told me he was sending you back. So just out of interest, what exactly are you here for?'

I could see what the game was. The game was to insinuate that he was on our side as well, and his relaxed amused manner was somehow so natural and convincing that in normal circumstances I might have believed him. But only this evening I had heard good evidence to the contrary on my machines. I knew about the drugs-for-arms deal he was doing for the Russians and it was this evidence that I now set about using against him.

Of course there were a few embarrassing hurdles to get over first. I'm not used to talking to other men about going to bed with their girlfriends, and Kolowski – I suppose to prove some point about his bohemianism – made constant references to my evening with Myrna which for some reason he found terribly funny. In addition he made constant references to the débâcle in the Tiburón which was meant, I suppose, to make me feel I owed him something.

What I said next was wrong. But I had to do it for Doris and for the bench under the elm tree.

'Kolowski, I don't know how much you know about me. But I know a great deal about your Dove and your Hawk and your cocaine-and-weapons business with South America. Don't interrupt. I want you to hear me out to the end.

'Of course you know perfectly well why the Major sent me down here: it was to get the very formula for Dr Fitzer's aphrodisiac that you were after yourself. I spotted you from the start. Like me, you saw Myrna as the key to Doctor Fitzer's secrets and, like me, you cultivated her. On the night I burgled the Institute somebody else went in there first. The whole place had been searched and I have very good reasons for believing you did it. Now – don't say anything yet – I want to do a deal with you Kolowski. I want that aphrodisiac of Dr Fitzer's. If you give it to me I'll say nothing about the "Christmas" operation. It'll be a deal. But if you can't come up with the goods I want between now and "Christmas" you're going to find yourself in trouble. And don't think you'll achieve anything by having me killed. Everything I know is in letters which will be delivered to appropriate people if anything happens to me.'

'What on earth are you talking about?' Kolowski said, 'What aphrodisiac? What secret of Dr Fitzer's?'

'You know very well what I mean,' I said. 'The liquid in a pyramid-shaped bottle.'

'But,' said Kolowski, his silly smile returning, 'Myrna led me to understand that you'd tried it already and it didn't have the desired effect.'

'Don't be cute, Kolowski. I mean the one that makes you fall in love, and you know it. Like Puck gave to Titania, remember? You gave yourself away when you quoted all that Shakespeare to me. Hardly likely a Russian would know all that stuff off the cuff if he hadn't done his homework.'

'In Russia,' said Kolowski indignantly, 'we take poetry very seriously. We love poetry. We cherish it. Not like the West.' And he took a swig from his bottle of beer. 'Anyway,' he went on, 'if you want this stuff so badly why don't you ask Dr Fitzer? I'm sure he'd know what it was.'

'As a matter of fact I have asked him. But of course he denies its existence altogether.'

'Well then, what makes you think it does exist?'

This was actually very much to the point. Originally it had been the Major who had told me, but it seemed he had changed his mind on that point for reasons which were still obscure; so I could hardly call him as a witness.

'I know because I've tried it,' I told him.

'You have?'

'I took it by mistake one evening and it made me fall in love. Very unfortunate. Luckily the woman is someone very special, a real queen. But I need more of it.'

'Are you falling out of love already?'

'I need to give it to her.'

Kolowski began to laugh. He laughed to himself at first, so quietly I hardly saw it, and then with increasing vigour until it turned into his habitual guffaw. I got up out of the orgone box and walked over to the fireplace at the other end of the room and lit a cigarette. As I did so I knocked over the bottle of beer on the floor but neither I nor Kolowski bothered to pick it up, and it lay on its side exgurgitating its frothy contents on to the carpet in quiet pulsations. And I just thought, let him laugh, because he's going to have to work hard for me now. I felt proud of the great power my ear had conferred on me, perhaps for the last time; and suddenly Kolowski seemed rather ridiculous lying there with his dishevelled wig and bohemian disguise.

When his laughter died down he sat up and said,

'Eh well, Herman old thing, if there is some sort of drug like you suggest I'll keep an eye open for you at the Institute. But personally I doubt it.'

'You'd better get it Kolowski, or it'll be the worse for you.'

He gave me an odd look, rather as if he was humouring me in some way, and pulled out a packet of cigarette papers.

'A last joint?' he said, as he began to stick three of them together, two side by side and one along the top.

'I don't think ...' I began, and then broke off in mid-sentence because I had just noticed something that astonished me. In the way people do, Kolowski rested a flat surface on his knee to put the cigarette papers on while he covered them with tobacco and then sprinkled in the hash. He was in the process of performing this last operation when I realised that instead of the record or book that people usually use, Kolowski had on his knee no less an object than his briefcase! The briefcase with the faint KK embossed on the front which I had last seen in Caldeya when I delivered it into the hands of the Major.

Chapter 23

The following morning I was in the shower when I heard the hotel keeper banging at the door. At first I thought he was making his usual fuss about payment, and went on soaping myself down, but then I caught the word 'telegrama'. I washed off the soap and put a towel round me, and drawing back the bolt, took the blue envelope from his hand. He gave me an exophthalmic scowl. The telegram read:

WHAT DEVIL PLAYING AT QUERY RETUN
IMMEDIATELY = SHARK

I couldn't believe my eyes. How had the Major been able to track me down to this seedy little hotel when he didn't even know what country I was in? I read it again. The way it was written 'retun' instead of 'return' reminded me of the 'Barod. P.lace' sign under my window and I thought of Doris dressing in the orange dark. Now I would have to go back to London without the drug.

Landing at Heathrow was like going back from spring into winter. A pall of cloud hung over London, so low that the city was obscured completely, and the ground appeared as if from nowhere just under the wheels of the plane. The road into town was fouled up by an accident so it was dark by the time I got home. On my answering machine there was a message from my cleaning woman to say she had bronchitis and wouldn't be coming in. There was a message from the Major saying he wanted to meet me. Codrington had phoned. Pilar. My mother. But not a thing from Doris. I played the messages through again and surveyed my flat. To a successful man it may be comforting to return home and find everything exactly as one has left it: a feeling of having moved on is doubtless evoked, by the contrasting unchanged disposition of cushions on the floor, book open by the bedside, cup and cigarette end on the mantelpiece. But knowing as I did that I was no further forward with my plans, all this seemed infinitely depressing. Wearily, I lifted the receiver and dialled the Major.

I had expected him to be angry or at least impatient with me but to my surprise he spoke quite calmly, 'I can't afford to have you on holiday in Barcelona,' he said. 'Your work here in the laboratories is too valuable to us all.'

I couldn't help asking him how he had traced me, at which he laughed, 'Well, once Doris told me you were in Caldeya it didn't take me long to track you down. But Newton, there's another reason I had to get you back here: I'm afraid your uncle's not been at all well. Some sort of stroke, I believe. He's in the St Expeth's nursing home. I went to see him today and I must say he didn't look too good. I suppose you'll be looking in yourself tomorrow.'

'I suppose so.'

'Good. Take some time off work if you want. The old boy would certainly be delighted to see you. And Newton . . . '

'Yes?'

'I want to have a chat with you. Soon.'

'Whenever you want.'

'Hmm. Tomorrow evening then. At my house. Six o'clock.'

As a result of this conversation I did visit the hospital the next day. I was slightly surprised to find that my 'uncle' was in a ward rather than a private room and when I got there I had no idea which of the ailing old men he was. Beds lined the gloss-painted walls, and in each one an old gentleman was propped up on a mound of pillows. Any one of them might have been my uncle. With their piercing eyes and bristling moustaches now gone grey they retained an impressive vigour even in their decline – a robustness born of long campaigns fought across foreign deserts. I felt I was in the presence of that world which still had such a grip on the Major's imagination, a world where generals wrote and read in Greek pentameters and put down uprisings mercilessly, and which, like most epochs, had not been without its grander moments. I found a nurse to show me to my 'uncle'. He was wizened, with a long face and very pale blue eyes. His mouth went in where his teeth were missing; a false set stood beside him in a glass of water. A few white whiskers sprouted on his cheeks, and at the sides of his head he had some snowy tufts of hair. Otherwise he was as bald as an egg and the skin on his cranium was tight and blotchy.

It was clear at once that he was very muddled. At first he seemed to think I was a doctor; and when I explained in the clearest possible terms who I was, he put his teeth in and said,

'Ah, yes. Shark told me about you. A kind man Shark. A good man. Is she very beautiful?'

'Who?'

'Why,' he said with some surprise, 'Aren't you the one his daughter is in love with? You know the one I mean. Daphne. They say she's a pretty little thing.'

'You mean Doris?' I said. 'As far as I know she's in love with somebody called Mungo.'

I was trembling violently as I spoke and I must have turned as white as the hospital sheets but the old man was too far gone to notice. In fact he seemed to have forgotten who I was. He began talking about Hawtree, his house in the country. I suppose he must have thought I was his accountant or something because he said, 'Is it tax-deductible, d'you suppose? I don't understand these things any more.'

I explained once again who I was and he said,

'Yes, yes, I know. Shark told me. D'you suppose one could write the whole thing off as a loss? Yes, but against what, I suppose that's the question.'

I decided there was really no point in visiting him again. Possibly he had never had a very clear notion who I was; certainly if he had, it was now lost in the fog of anaesthetic and old age. I rather wished the Major hadn't insisted on bringing us together like this. What had he been telling him about Doris? Whatever it was, the old fellow had got hold of completely the wrong end of the stick.

The Major looked harassed when I arrived the next evening. Today the sun had been warm for the first time this year and because the trees were already half out the whole season seemed to have changed, not just the weather. But nothing about the Major responded to these beginnings of spring. His skin was the same paper grey, and the bags under his eyes were if anything darker than usual, as though he hadn't been sleeping. Responsibility sits heavily on old men, and he looked as though he had been shouldering more than his fair share recently.

He poured us whisky from a decanter and squirted in some soda. The windows were all closed as though it was still winter. There was the end of a smokeless fuel fire in the grate and a dismal sort of fug in the air. Around the room I could see traces of Doris: a copy of *New Musical Express* open on the sofa, with an ashtray on the floor beside it, containing a heap of lipstick-stained cigarette butts and chocolate wrappings. Some other chocolate wrappings had missed the fire and now lay beneath the grate among the ashes.

'Well, Herman, now that you're back at work, would you care to explain what persuaded you to take a holiday in Barcelona?'

The Major had only recently begun to call me by my Christian name and still reverted to 'Newton' when he wasn't thinking. Therefore the 'Herman' augured well for me.

I began without any apologies in the most businesslike way, to give an account of my doings. I didn't want to tell him that I had gone to find Dr Fitzer's drug: that part of the expedition was too immediately tied up with matters inimical to the Knights; also it had not been a great success. Instead I dwelt on the Kolowski episode, explaining that I'd managed to over-hear some new conversations of great importance.

As if by tacit agreement neither the Major nor I mentioned the ear I had kept a secret for so long and which Doris had given him. I suppose the old boy felt a bit sheepish about having wheedled it out of her and I certainly wasn't going to start making explanations unless they were demanded. So when I said I'd overheard Kolowski's meeting, the Major just nodded silently. I told him the details of the drugs-arms deal as far as I knew them: how the barrels were supposed to be in Panama and the gas plugs were due to arrive soon, and how Kolowski had cajoled another kilo of cocaine out of the Hawk and his team. There was something about the calm manner in which the Major received my revelations which led me to suspect that he already knew quite a lot about this drugs-arms gang – perhaps through British Intelligence's own sources.

When I told him about Kolowski's extra kilo he said, 'A kilo was it?' and nodded sagely.

I didn't mention the meeting in the Bengal Brasserie the following Monday because I wanted to take the credit for finding out who the Dove was myself.

When I had finished the Major said, 'You still haven't told me why you went back to Barcelona.'

'Because I was convinced that Kolowski was up to some monkey business and with respect, sir, I seem to remember you weren't entirely convinced. About his being a Russian spy and so on ...'

'I see.' The Major leaned forward with his elbows on his knees. 'Now look here Herman, I want you to get it into your head once and for all that this isn't a John Le Carré novel. If there were enemies of our country scheming against us in Barcelona, you can be sure I'd be the first to know about it. You have an unfortunate tendency to see a geostrategic offensive in the most trivial daily occurrence. These recordings of Russian conversations, for example, the ones you gave me in Caldeya. D'you know what they were?'

'No, sir.'

'Some Russian amateur dramatic group rehearsing *Midsummer Night's Dream*. Kolowski directing. So much for Russian spies. Now listen to me Herman. Spying is for professionals. I'm a professional: you're not. I put you on a job because you knew about aphrodisiacs. It was a false trail. I took you off that job. Now will you please get down to some work in the laboratory? I want inventions from you, not detective fiction. Is that absolutely one hundred per cent clear?'

'Yes, sir.'

'You're a bit harebrained in practical matters, but you're a brilliant inventor. I don't actually understand everything that you do but Codrington says it's first rate. Your work is valuable to the Intelligence Service. However, your spying excursions are not. Do I have your solemn agreement to cease henceforth from all such expeditions to Barcelona or anywhere else?'

It was galling to learn that Codrington was considered an authority by which to judge me; and equally galling to be dismissed as 'harebrained' in anything practical.

I said, 'There's more in this business than meets the eye, you know. Kolowski's briefcase for example. Do you know that he has got it back?'

'Newton! Did you understand what I just said? No more detective fiction!'

Wearily he got up and limped across the room to the drinks tray. Outside the window the sky was a deep, deep winter blue and the new leaves on the trees a vivid, very light green, and on the other side of the square the white houses had gone slightly yellow in the evening light. There was something strained in the air, some unresolved tension and I couldn't decide if it emanated from the Major or if it was just something uneasy about this moment in general, a kind of grinding of gears between afternoon and night, between winter and spring. The soda siphon spluttered. The Major came back to his ivy-chintzed armchair by the chimney and re-lit the cigar pensively. His sad gaze seemed to be directed at a photograph which stood beside his drink on the mahogany side-table: a black and white picture of him in his younger days, dressed in a beret and uniform and saluting a young woman (was it the Queen Mother?) who stood opposite him clasping her handbag in front of her in a slightly uneasy manner. Or was it the betting slip, half-folded beside it, which had attracted his attention? Apparently neither. Without breaking his stare he said, 'I can't help worrying about Doris. I discovered that chap Mungo was pestering her.'

Not knowing quite what line to take in the circumstances, I sipped my whisky and said, 'Ah, ah.'

'It gave me quite a shock,' he went on. 'My own daughter. In my own house . . . ' his voice trailed off.

I sipped my whisky again. Just above his dark receding head hung a lithograph of the Mas dels Cavallers in which one could make out quite clearly the windows of the room where Doris and I used to make love.

'Of course,' said the Major, 'he's gone away now. But it worries me all the same.'

'Mungo's gone away!' In my excitement I couldn't help blurting it out.

'Yes. I gave him a one-way ticket. No one fools around with my daughter.'

His voice was constricted with anger and he let out a series of nervous snorts – there was certainly something a little unhinged about this Knights of St Expeth business. I wondered if it was really such a good idea for me to join after all.

'But surely you don't want her to remain a spinster all her life,' I said.

'Not a spinster. No. When the right man comes along, he'll marry her.'

'Perhaps Doris thought Mungo was the right man.'

'Certainly not. If anyone decides who's the right one it'll be me: the thing is – how long can it wait? Young blood is impatient ... I suppose it'll have to be sooner than one supposed.'

He broke off these weary reflections and offered me another drink. We began to talk about my 'uncle' and I explained that he'd mistaken me for his accountant. The idea that he hadn't recognised me, though a matter of indifference to me, seemed incredible to the Major. Perhaps it irked him to feel that my uncle, whom he'd always admired for his sharpness of wit, could be losing his faculties. I think he considered my uncle to be a part of his generation although in fact he was some twenty years older, and I suppose that with his friends going senile and his daughter of marriageable age he was beginning to feel his years. Was this what prompted him to talk about retirement? He mentioned it casually, but in a way which suggested it had been on his mind recently.

'The modern age has got it all wrong really,' he said. 'Marriage is about children and property and so on, of which young people haven't any experience. The trouble is that by the time you've got the experience you're more the age for retiring, like myself. So parents have to help their children.'

When it was time to leave he said,

'Look here, Herman. Doris is very upset about all this business. Why don't you go up and have a few words with her? It'll be good for her to talk to someone her own age.'

To be told by the Major to go up and see her in her bedroom: the triumph over Mungo was sweet.

The bedroom being higher up was lighter than the sitting-room, with more sky outside. Through the windows the evening sun shone horizontally on to the walls of the room, bringing out in the pattern of brownish dots on the wallpaper some of their former redness. Doris's collection of cloth animals was scattered all over the bed and the floor and among them, in front of the dressing-table, Doris herself knelt, playing with the gerbil.

'Shut the door,' she said. 'And don't move or you'll frighten him.'

I shut the door as quietly as I could and stood absolutely still. Doris was leaning forward, as motionless as a waxwork with one hand stretched out in front of her, the palm towards the floor. Her jersey was pulled up to the elbow and on her slender forearm the gerbil sat looking about it and twitching its nose. From time to time it stared up at her and, as if it derived some sort of encouragement from her big brown eyes, took a few steps up her arm towards her elbow. As soon as it stopped again Doris's free hand moved very slowly up behind it, so as to block off its retreat. Soon the gerbil left the wax-smooth territory of her arm and began the ascent of the pink jersey; and behind it the barrier crept up, when it wasn't looking, like in the children's game of Grandmother's Footsteps. When it reached her shoulder it nibbled absent-mindedly at her hair and then passed underneath it and disappeared behind her neck. In the meantime, with almost equal caution I had been extracting my spectacles from my jacket pocket, and I was just putting them on in order to be able to observe better when the spectacle case fell on the floor. The gerbil scuttled down her back and across the room where it tried to hide behind the crystal ball.

'Cretin!' said Doris.

'Hello Doris.'

'What are you doing here?'

I explained how I had just happened to be dropping by and wondered how she was.

'I see. When did you get back?'

'Yesterday.'

She got up and went to sit on the bed. I thought she looked rather subdued but she might have been angry because I'd scared the gerbil. You couldn't tell with her because she kept her anger to herself.

I said, 'I wanted to ask you to dinner tomorrow.'

'I see. Where?'

'I don't know really. Maybe the Baroda Palace. Wherever you want.'

'Daddy told you to didn't he?'

'What?'

'Daddy told you to ask me out.'

'No, Doris, it was my idea.'

'He told you to come and see me because I'm depressed about Mungo.'

She glanced involuntarily at the photo of Mungo grinning his even-toothed grin out of a car window.

I said, 'He's gone away, hasn't he?'

'Yes. When he went we decided to be completely faithful. I promised that I wouldn't see you any more. So you see it would be sort of cheating to go out with you even if we aren't really going out together properly.'

I had to consider this last statement for a minute before I grasped what she meant.

'Doris, how long is Mungo going to be away?'

'Probably for ever. For a long time anyway.'

Behind the crystal ball the gerbil was shifting nervously, causing now its nose, now a shoulder or a section of its tail to appear vastly distorted in the glass. Doris seemed to be oblivious, her gaze fixed on the photo of Mungo.

At last she sighed and said, 'Did you see Screw-screw?'

'What's that?'

'Screw-screw. In Caldeya.'

'No I didn't. I went up to the house but he wasn't there.'

'He lives with Gemma in the village when we're not there.'

'I didn't know.'

'She's the cleaning woman. She lives in the house behind the garage. If she's not there you can get in over the garden wall. She leaves him in the yard.'

'Leaves who in the yard?'

'Screw-screw.'

'I see.'

'And did you get the sweets?'

'Yes. I've got them at home. Listen. Why don't you come over now?'

'I can't. I'm making dinner for Daddy.'

'Well tomorrow then.'

She shook her head.

'I made an agreement with Mungo,' she said. 'Anyway, how do I know I can trust you? You might try and run me over again in your car.'

'I don't know what came over me that night,' I said. 'I'm really sorry about what happened. But don't think I'm entirely to blame. After all, it's partly your fault for being so beautiful. I'm sure lots of men have gone a bit crazy over you.'

Doris gave her modest assent and a little flush of pleasure became visible about her face.

'So let's forget about the whole affair. Are you prepared to forgive me?'

'Oh, all right,' said Doris. 'I suppose so. But I'm not allowed to see you. I promised Mungo I wouldn't see you.'

'But Doris, darling,' I said, 'merely seeing someone isn't being unfaithful.'

She wriggled about a bit as though the idea made her uncomfortable and pouted in a sexy sort of way.

'All right then. But I don't want to go to your flat.'

'We'll meet somewhere else.'

'All right then,' said Doris. 'In the Rangoon, tomorrow.'

Chapter 24

'I hear your little barracuda lost her lover,' said Pilar.

'So I gather.'

It was difficult to sound nonchalant about it even over the phone. I clamped the receiver between my ear and my shoulder and reached for a packet of cigarettes on the table. Beside it were the boxes of almond chocolates I was going to give to Doris that evening.

'I heard it from her friend Margot,' Pilar said.

'I didn't know you knew her.'

'She's got a job at my hairdresser's. Apparently she'd heard you talking about Pilar's play and so we got talking. Pretty rough of her father, wasn't it? I didn't think that sort of thing happened anymore.'

'What sort of thing?'

'Didn't she tell you about it?'

'Not really. The Major mentioned something about a one-way ticket to the States.'

'Is that what he called it? Well, all I can say is you'd better watch out he doesn't give you one too. Apparently when he discovered they were lovers he went after the young man with a gun. As it turned out he didn't shoot him but the poor boy went off to America with a plaster on his nose and his arm in a sling.'

I said, 'Are you sure about that?'

'Well anyway that's what Margot told me. Apparently he's a member of some lunatic rightist group which goes in for chastity in a big way.'

'The Knights,' I said. 'I think I'm about to become a member.'

'You are? Well, you've certainly changed your ways then. Is it part of this new fashion for celibacy in America? Arachne says it's to do with AIDS. Apparently Puritanism in Europe only began when syphilis was introduced from the Spanish Empire.'

'That sounds highly improbable to me.'

'Oh, well. You're the expert on these sexual problems. All I can say is be careful with the Sharks. Father and daughter.'

'Don't worry,' I said, 'I can handle it.'

In fact this was easier said than done. To be quite exact I had no idea at all how to handle the Major. I could only hope that as a candidate for the Knights I was above suspicion; but the disadvantage of this was to make it even more of a treachery if I was found out.

Knights or no Knights, danger could not dissuade me from my rendezvous at the Rangoon that evening. I arrived in good time and drank a Mandalay – the cocktail of the house – while I was waiting. I had been here so often with Doris in the past that everything about this place and its false orientalism brought back memories of nights we'd spent together. Therefore it seemed fitting that our reunion should be among these stucco Buddhas and lamé-turbaned waitresses, beside the curling brass-railed bar with its Warholesque silkscreens of the Shwe Dagon-pagoda. In the smoked-glass mirror in front of me I could see the Space Invaders machine at the end of the bar just near the little cubicle where a girl sat taking the coats and making sure you signed the membership book. The door opened towards me, letting in new arrivals and then swinging shut again. At last it opened just a fraction and Doris slipped in. She paused for a moment on the threshold and said a few words to the coat-check girl, then without taking off her leather jacket, walked down the bar towards me, her abundant hair bouncing a little on her shoulders as she came. She had a new black and white check mini skirt, fishnet stockings and short boots with a leopardskin pattern.

She sat down and said, 'How lovely! You've brought the sweets!'

She wasn't at all sulky like she'd been the last time I saw her. In fact I've seldom seen her in such a good mood. We opened a packet of chocolate almonds immediately and I ordered her a drink. She didn't make any more remarks about the car accident, though she did refer once to my skirmish with the lobster.

A young man came up and asked her to come to a Chinese dinner he was giving on Friday. When she told him she was busy that evening he said he'd give the party on Saturday instead, and Doris said, yes, she thought she could go on Saturday. When he was gone we began to talk about Caldeya.

'Doris, I wish you hadn't told your father I was down there.'

She was quite surprised at this, and so I reminded her that she'd promised not to say a word about it to anyone. Her hand went to her mouth.

'Oh dear!' she said. 'I must have forgotten. Was it important?'

I explained that I had been on a mission and that in such cases secrecy is vital. If anyone got to know about these things you often had to abandon the whole operation.

'I warned you about that before,' I said, 'when I gave you the medallion.'

'Oh dear!' said Doris. 'I'm sorry about that. But I don't think Daddy believes you're a spy anyway. When I told him he laughed and said it was rubbish and you were a hopeless intellectual. But don't be hurt. I think it's very clever of you. Anyway, I got the medallion back: look!' And she pulled it out from inside her shirt.

The sight of this did a lot to restore my spirits. We began to talk about other things: a friend of Margot's had opened a clothes shop in her house which was open every day in the afternoon and till four in the morning on Thursdays. Could we go there? The jackets were incredible. Then there was a new club opening, done by Mark Rafftrap and some other friends. It was going to be all Salsa with Caribbean décor; they were doing a trial night to start with and if it was a success they might quite likely do it every week. Had I heard that they'd got Frogger and Pac-Man now in the bar of the Circus? She even wanted to join my tarot classes, and so did Margot. The only time she needled me was about my sunglasses which I still had from Barcelona. She said that nowadays everybody and his brother had a pair, and then burst out laughing in a deliciously mischievous way. All in all I could see that she was quite pleased to have me around now that Mungo was gone.

At this juncture, a most unexpected development occurred in the mirror behind Doris's head. At first I was only aware of something vaguely familiar out of the corner of my eye which drew my attention momentarily away from Doris. The next minute I realised that someone had just come through the door who didn't belong here, and I looked again in disbelief: curly black hair glistening with raindrops, a black leather coat, a pink umbrella, the figure yawed unsteadily but determinedly in our direction, its inebriated gaze self-correcting as it swayed, rather in the manner of a ship's compass: Kolowski.

'Why Herman, fancy finding you here. Hello,' he said, turning to Doris. 'I don't believe we've met.'

'Doris, this is Kolowski,' I said. 'Kolowski, Doris Shark.'

'Not the Major's girl?' said Kolowski. 'Well what an agreeable surprise! I'm Konstantin,' he added, retaining her hand in his and leering into her eyes.

'Do you know my father?' asked Doris.

'Do I know your father! I should say I do.'

He pulled up a chair and sat down heavily, hooking the duck's head handle of his umbrella on to the arm of a neighbouring Bodhisattva.

'Well, well,' he went on, 'this is quite a reunion. Something to celebrate. What are you drinking?'

'Mandalays,' I said.

'Mandalays? What's that?'

'Incredible,' said Doris. 'Try one.'

'Thank you my dear. I think I'll stick to the vodka at this stage of the evening. A very large one, Russian and straight up – like me!' He brandished his forearm in an obscene gesture and roared with laughter. It astonished me how he could be so vulgar in front of a woman – let alone one who was as innocent and beautiful as Doris.

When his drink arrived he winked at Doris and said, 'Your Pa and I are old buddies from way back. Guess what? I had lunch with him today. Talked about both of you as a matter of fact.'

Like many men who enjoy expressing maverick opinions Kolowski also liked to make up extravagant stories.

I said, 'Oh yes? Tell us about it.'

'Shall I?' He picked up his glass of vodka which arrived just then and sipped pensively. 'All right then. It's a story about a man who liked to spy on people. I oughtn't really to be telling you about this.'

'Oh, please do,' said Doris, 'I love all that spying business.'

'Well you see, once upon a time there was a man called Herman who liked spying so much he developed a very brilliant listening device so that he could hear what people were saying without their knowing anything about it.'

He paused and took another sip of his vodka. Doris looked at me with admiration.

'Now Herman here worked for your father and he was meant to tell him about all the new things he had discovered. Only in this case he didn't tell him, because he wanted it all to himself. But your father, being a very clever man, realised he had developed this thing and that he was keeping it secret. Naughty, naughty.' He shook his finger. 'And being a very clever man your father decided he would have to trick Herman into revealing his secret.' He hiccoughed, and then went on, 'Now, it so happened that at about this time Herman was trying to develop a particular sort of aphrodisiac which he believed would be the greatest invention since flying: and knowing this, your father told him someone else had already discovered it and sent him down to Barcelona to do a bit of spying. You see, your father thought that Herman wouldn't be able to resist putting his new toy to the test. And that would give him – your father – an opportunity to discover this toy. As neat an idea as we've come to expect from your Pa.

'To begin with, all went well. Our new spy, convinced that his aphrodisiac has been discovered, rushes off to Barcelona to find it. But now a complication arises: Herman here, in a blundering amateurish way, decides not to use his listening devices as he's been told to and instead conceives a plan to burgle Dr Fitzer's Institute. His methods are not chivalrous. On learning that somebody else's girlfriend – mine in the event – possesses the keys of the building, he seduces her into a perverted form of intercourse which involves tying her down and then urinating on her . . .'

'Kolowski,' I said, 'that's a filthy lie and you know it.'

'That's what the young lady said at any rate,' Kolowski replied smugly, and gave another hiccough.

I said, 'If you've got anything else to say you'd better come and say it to me outside.'

He let out a peal of laughter.

'My dear fellow. You sound like an officer in the Tsar's army. Remember I'm a Soviet. We don't fight duels. However, we do drink so don't be stingy. Offer to buy me another.'

'Get lost Kolowski,' I said. 'No one asked you to join us.'

'I say, don't be prickly. I know I've had a bit too much to drink already, but so had you if I remember rightly, on the last occasion we met. So let's have no hard feelings either way. I'm sorry if I've spoken out of turn and I won't say another word. It's a pity really, because I was just coming to the very important part played in the story by this lovely lady.'

'Oh, do go on with your story,' Doris said.

'Well, if you insist, all right ...'

'Doris, I think we've heard enough of his rubbish already. I happen to know that this man's a criminal and I don't want to hear another word of his stupid piffle.'

'I do,' said Doris.

'Aha!' said Kolowski. 'The lady's word must be our command. Very well. What happens next is that Herman here, still in blissful ignorance of his true role, blunders into the Institute and fails to find the secret. Not surprising really, seeing it never existed in the first place. Meanwhile, back in London, the Major is greeted with a pleasant surprise – a present from his very beautiful daughter in the shape of a silver medallion: nothing less than the elusive invisible listening device. The beautiful daughter had succeeded where all his own efforts and ingenuity had failed. I don't mind telling you Doris, he's very proud of you.'

Doris flushed with pleasure.

'You're lying,' I said. 'You made the whole thing up. The Major would never tell you anything because you work for the Russians.'

Kolowski laughed good naturedly and said, 'Wouldn't he?'

'Never.'

'Well then perhaps you're right. Perhaps I did make the whole thing up. Perhaps I'm just trying to make you look silly because I bear you a grudge.'

He looked at his glass thoughtfully for a minute and then, as the waitress passed, performed that gesture of his little finger which indicated a refill.

There was an uncomfortable silence. Doris fiddled around with the chocolate almonds and tried to break one in half. The waitress came back with the bottle of Stolichnaya and filled Kolowski's glass.

'Get out of here, Kolowski,' I said, 'before I throw you out.'

He drained his glass and got to his feet. There was something very ambiguous about his manner. I couldn't make out if he was poking fun at me or genuinely resentful.

He bent down and kissed Doris with obvious relish and said, in a filthy manner,

'*Au revoir, chérie.*' Then he leaned forward till I could smell the vodka on his breath and see the red frost-like tracery in the whites of his eyeballs and said, '*En garde*, Mr Newton.'

'Go to hell, Kolowski.'

He gave a little hiccough, 'By the way. Do you know what the funny part was? After you'd tied Myrna up that night she never wanted it any other way. Became an absolute fanatic for bondage. Ah well, life's full of surprises. That's the only thing that makes it worth living. And this,' he added, and I couldn't tell if the sweep of his hand was meant to indicate Doris, or the empty glass of vodka.

When he had gone Doris said,

'Herman, who is that funny man?'

'A cheap little crook. And he's not funny.'

'I thought he was sweet. That curly hair. He looked like the drummer in Watchamagotcha.'

The rest of the evening was made particularly sour by her evident desire to talk about Kolowski; jealousy was added to the other ill-sentiment I bore him. I answered her questions about him with absent-minded irritation, because the implications of what he had said now held my attention like an insistent mosquito in the dark. It infuriated me that he should have spoken about Myrna in front of Doris, especially since he'd added the lie that I'd taught her to be perverted when in fact I hadn't slept with her at all. The worst of this was that Doris probably didn't realise all this had taken place before I met her, or at any rate before I'd fallen in love with her, before I'd taken Fitzer's drug.

That night Doris left me outside the bar and went home alone. It had stopped raining now so I walked back to the flat across the wet city, turning over in my mind Kolowski's story and wondering how he knew so much about the Major. Could it be true that he and the Major had known each other for years? Was the Major in league with Kolowski? And was that how Kolowski got his briefcase back? I had to admit the evidence was damning. Yet I still couldn't bring myself to believe it. The Major was too genuinely in love with that old world of my 'uncle' and Hawtree and Lord de Witt to be mixed up with the enemies of that world. And what about the Knights? Surely a Knight couldn't be a communist! I had to assume that whatever Kolowski knew about the Major was information he received through Soviet Intelligence: I had read in Lipsky that agents often knew who their opposite numbers were. Well, perhaps that was how Kolowski knew what he knew. But what did he know? What about this story about the Major trying to trick me out of my ear? Of course, Kolowski might simply have made it up because he was angry with me about Myrna; but somehow it had a dismal ring of truth about it. Things became clear to me now which had always been inexplicable: the Major's obsession with listening devices, for example, and the way that he'd lost interest in the mission after Doris gave him my ear. For the first time I felt myself coming to believe what so many people had told me: that Dr Fitzer's potion didn't exist. And I realised that if (as I had always held to be theoretically true) a drug could make you fall in love just like the real thing, conversely, the opposite was also true: the real thing could be just like a drug. So there was nothing to explain about my passion for Doris; the bottle on the floor of the laboratory had been just some other chemical.

That night in my lonely bed visions of Doris kept appearing and disappearing in the way a hologram does when you walk round it. And mingling with them her father loomed before me insubstantially, suspended at his desk in mid-air and, like a hypnotist, swinging in his hairy hand the silver medallion bearing my secret. In the dream he didn't even look triumphant, only modestly satisfied, like a golfer who puts in an easy putt. This reptile, this bureaucrat, this *rond-de-cuir* – could he really have made a fool of me?

Chapter 25

The next days were awful. Doris hardly wanted to see me and I was convinced she was meeting Kolowski. I had begun to detest the man, and I looked forward impatiently to the meeting at the Bengal Brasserie when I would find out who the Dove was. I had already made up my mind that even if the Dove and the Hawk got away, I would make sure I had enough hard evidence on Kolowski to put him behind bars.

The only time I saw Doris was to go for a walk in the park on Sunday afternoon. Unfortunately the weather was not as balmy as I had imagined when I had envisaged this scene, nor was Doris so pliant and loving. There were no roses out so I picked a daffodil for her buttonhole. The chestnut trees had already put out their leaves and the oaks were just beginning to be covered in those little yellow-green tufts, like bunches of crumpled crêpe, which are the beginning of their foliage. It was only then that I remembered about Dutch Elm disease; there wasn't an elm tree left standing in the whole of Southern England.

A few spots of rain began to fall. Doris opened her umbrella. I had thought this umbrella looked familiar when we set out; now I remembered where I'd seen the white duck's-head handle and pink canvas before.

'That's Kolowski's umbrella.'

'I know. He lent it to me yesterday.'

'You saw him yesterday?'

'Yes. Why are you looking so surprised?'

'You said you were going to the Chinese dinner-party.'

'That was in the evening, silly. I had lunch with Konstantin. I really like him. He's really a sweet person.'

'Doris, he's a cheap little crook.'

'Oh, come off it Herman. What have you got against him? I mean, get real.'

We walked along the edge of the park towards Kensington Palace Gardens where the Russian Embassy is. I wondered if Kolowski was in there now. On our right, along the Bayswater Road practically every house seemed to be under demolition. Some had whole wings knocked off them, with the remains of floors still jutting out into nothing; others were laid bare from the front, as though someone had lifted a panel off a doll's house, revealing fireplaces, wallpaper, fitted cupboards and mirrors; it was appalling how symbolic and conspiratorial all this demolition seemed.

The next evening being Monday, I drove to my tarot class in Baker Street. It was held above the shop where I'd seen the advertisement, in a white room which was absolutely bare except for some rush matting on the floor. You had to leave your shoes at the door so the smell inside was not pleasant; the students, who were a clean-looking lot at first sight, were to a man afflicted by some appalling pedal disability. Our teacher, a pallid librarian with mousy hair and watery, pale blue eyes behind his spectacles, sat cross-legged at one end of the room and held forth. He had a little gold stud in his left nostril and wore round his neck an amulet in the shape of the Egyptian ankh.

He shuffled a tarot pack as he spoke, and claimed he existed on the astral plane as well as the terrestrial, and that he knew Krishnamurti well and had played with him as a little boy in that exalted dimension, although here on earth he had only met him once. He had a way of looking at you that made you think he actually knew a great deal more about you than he was prepared to let on. Probably this was the reason I found it easy to believe he had clairvoyant powers – a gift which he told me had been in his family for more than five generations.

He insisted upon payment in cash and went round collecting the money before we began. Then he disappeared into another part of the apartment, presumably to lock it away in a safe. I reckoned he must have taken a cool eighty or ninety pounds at least. Accordingly, after the first lesson was over I waited for everyone else to go and then I put a wad of cash worth about fifty pounds or so in his hand and asked him if he would do me a small favour. Before he agreed he counted up the money that I'd given him to make sure he wasn't being short-changed.

'In a short while,' I said, 'I'm going to send you a girl called Doris. She's very beautiful and intelligent but just at the moment she is rather lost in life. Probably it's to do with the fact that her mother died when she was young. As a result she finds it impossible to break away from the influence of her father who's a major in the army and a very strong character. But that's neither here nor there. The point is that she's in love with a young man who's gone away for ever to America. Now I want you to read her tarot. You can say anything you like but I want you to add one thing. Tell her to forget the man she's been with and go off with the new one who loves her so much. That's all.'

I knew that the voice of the occult would weigh very heavily with Doris.

All this had made me late for the Bengal Brasserie. I took a taxi down there and arrived around nine o'clock. Because I had no idea what time the dinner was meant to be I didn't know if I was still in time to see them arrive. I concealed myself at the corner of an alley opposite and kept watch on the door.

A few minutes later Kolowski arrived. There was nobody with him, so I knew that if the Dove wasn't already in there he would be arriving shortly.

It began to drizzle. I went into a pizza house and sat down at the window. From here I could see the big doorman with a red turban and handle-bar moustache, escorting the new arrivals under his huge umbrella up the steps of the brasserie. I was looking out for an unaccompanied man, but none arrived. Outside the pizza house I could see droplets of rain pass through the reflection of my face as if through a phantom, and the car headlamps made streaky reflections on the wet surface of the street. The rain stopped; a sliver of moon appeared behind the Tube station; a blue neon shop sign cast its deep electric reflection in a puddle outside the brasserie steps. Forty minutes had passed since Kolowski's arrival. It was time to go in.

From the doorway of the dining-room I had a clear view to the fresco at the far end of the room of Calcutta in its days as a small trading-post at the beginning of the eighteenth century. It was a far cry from the Baroda Palace: the huge room seemed to dwarf everything in it. All was harmony and spaciousness and decorum. The cane dining chairs were a pale green colour with pale pink cushions which matched the mouldings on the ceiling. Mogul-style screens inlaid with nacreous patterns separated the diners into intimate circles. Palms in brass pots. Old photos of rajahs. To one side a series of alcoves, with tables overhung by a striped awning.

I advanced slowly beneath the colonial-style fans, looking left and right into the tented alcoves which revealed themselves as I progressed. Suddenly, half-hidden by a screen on my left, I caught sight of the tousled head of Kolowski.

He is sitting at a table set beneath a niche in the wall, and his interlocutor, who must be the Dove, is still hidden by the screen. For an instant I stand there, hesitating between seeing and being seen; then I advance a little further, and round the edge of the screen appears the rest of the table, an ice-bucket and finally, the Major. He pauses with his fork in the air as he catches sight of me, Kolowski turns to face me too, and for a fraction of a second they are both frozen in astonishment as if caught in a photograph, their two heads leaning slightly together at the foot of a big brass peacock in the niche behind them. Then the Major nods casually in my direction and turns back to Kolowski and they go on with their meal.

No wonder the Major hadn't wanted me to establish the connection between Kolowski and the Russians! No wonder he'd first discouraged, then forbidden my investigations into the drugs-arms deal! I began to remember a host of little details: the Major pricking up his ears when I told him about the extra kilo of cocaine, Kolowski's briefcase mysteriously re-appearing in his possession; incidents which made little sense at the time but which were all too clear now that I knew the Major was a double-agent.

I also knew I had become dangerous to him. As long as I thought Kolowski was the only Russian spy in the affair I posed little threat to the Major, but now I knew the identity of the Dove, I went in fear of my life. The world of arms dealers doesn't have a reputation for pulling punches: it seemed probable that he would try to have me murdered or even worse...

Chapter 26

That night my 'uncle' died. The hospital rang at four in the morning to tell me and asked when the body would be collected.

'I don't know,' I said. 'Who's organising the funeral?'

There was a short silence.

'Well,' said the voice at the other end, 'he put you as his next of kin.'

When I hung up I put out the light but I couldn't get back to sleep. The Major's insistence on our relationship over the past year or so, which had turned him from a distant cousin into an uncle, seemed suddenly to take on substance now that I learnt I was his next of kin. All at once I was struck by how little I knew about him. How had he lived during the twenty years which lay between my visit to Hawtree as a boy and my last visit to him in hospital a few days ago? A few details of that ill-fated outing from school when I had been sick in his lavatory suddenly came to my mind: I see myself dressed in a green school blazer and shorts, rooting around with my racket among the long grass and sour-smelling cow parsley and unearthing a green-stained tennis ball. And this in turn leads to another memory: I am lying on a wide green lawn between my father and mother. The scent of a nearby lilac mingles deliciously with the smell of the suncream which my mother always wears in hot weather. She is holding the cine-camera which my father had given her for her birthday. Why do I remember these inconsequential moments with such clarity, when I can recall nothing of my uncle? I longed to know something more about him; perhaps if he hadn't been so insistent that I was his accountant I would have questioned him a little more in the hospital. Try though I might to bring some inkling of him back out of the past, nothing would come. All I could pull before me out of the orange darkness of my bedroom was the whirring cine-camera which my mother had been holding. She shouts to my father and me to move around and my father begins to gesticulate wildly, telling me to run to the beech tree; and off I go across the lawn to the tree and back again while my father, in white flannels and a panama hat, shouts, 'Faster, faster,' and the camera follows me as I go like the eyes of my great-grandfather's portrait which always hung over the fireplace in all of our houses. I dozed off at dawn.

Another surprise came the next day when I discovered I was my uncle's heir. His solicitors told me so on the telephone and asked me to go round and see them, if possible that afternoon. There were many things to do that day. The funeral parlour claimed most of my attention; I telephoned my mother and she said she'd send a wreath; I arranged for an announcement in *The Times*. Then there was the service itself: my uncle wanted to be buried in the same grave as his mad young wife who lay for some reason to do with her family under a marble sphinx in a cemetery in Chiswick. That evening I saw the priest. It was late when I got home.

As I ate my tandoori chicken and dal I thought of what my uncle had said to me in the hospital about writing his home off as a tax loss. Perhaps he hadn't mistaken me for his accountant after all, and had merely been trying in his muddled way to discuss the financial burden he was leaving me; for burden it was, as far as I could make out from the lawyers. And before I went to bed I got out my tarot pack and found the five of cups which Doris had said meant inheritance, or unsatisfactory marriage.

The day of the funeral was close and muggy. The sun shone weakly down on Chiswick through a haze of sooty humidity. There were about twenty mourners though I knew none of them personally apart from the Major and Doris. Doris wore a veil. Because the fashion was very much for black that year it didn't seem odd at all to see her dressed like this; in fact she'd worn the same dress at the Blackout not long ago.

The Major himself was grave and tired-looking, his complexion an unhealthy grey against his starched white collar and black tie. He sang snatches of the hymns in a deep voice and kept his eyes glued on the priest as if he were giving him an audition. I spent most of the service wondering how he had taken to my appearance at the Bengal Brasserie. He only looked at me once, rather suggestively, just before throwing a handful of earth down on the coffin lid.

There was no funeral supper afterwards. As we left the churchyard the Major took me by the arm and said, 'Come back with me now.'

I knew that my moment had come.

We got into the plum-coloured Jaguar and set off along the series of anonymous red-brick high streets which meander their way back into central London. The Major was pensive, repeatedly relighting his cigar from the ebony-knobbed lighter on the dashboard, answering my nervous attempts at conversation with a blunt 'yes' or 'no'. When we got to Earl's Court he suddenly said, 'I gather Kolowski's been blabbing.'

'You mean to me?'

'That's right,' the Major said, 'I'm sorry you had to hear it from him. I suppose I should have explained it to you myself as soon as Doris gave it to me.'

I realised he was talking about my listening device rather than the drugs-arms deal.

'Is it true then, what Kolowski said?' I asked.

'Yes. You see Codrington told me you were developing a new listening device, but that it was all so disjointed he felt sure you were keeping the missing links of the chain elsewhere. And it was such a promising and novel approach that when you dropped the whole thing we suspected you had actually perfected it in private and decided not to tell us about it. Inventors often have a tendency to do that, God knows why. You're a pretty kooky bunch. Luckily Codrington's an unusually smart fellow, and he spotted it.'

'So the mission you gave me in Barcelona was a trick?'

'That's right.'

'And Dr Fitzer's secret?'

'Never existed. I made it up. You gave me the idea yourself one day when you were explaining to me what you were trying to discover in the way of a special aphrodisiac. It struck me that if I said somebody else had already discovered it, that couldn't fail to catch your imagination. And knowing as I knew from our records that you were rather keen on spying

'... well, it seemed like a good way to get you to reveal your secret.'

'I see.'

'I expect you think I've been underhand. But remember, it was you who were underhand in the first place. You rather forced me. Your contract states quite clearly that your work is our exclusive property. We pay you enough for it anyway.'

This was true. Still I didn't see quite where this apologetic was leading.

'I got the idea from Kolowski,' the Major went on. 'Knowing he worked at the Fitzer Institute, and knowing that the Institute had its own patent medicines section, I decided it was the ideal place to send you. In addition Kolowski was there to keep an eye on you: something which was fortunate for you on at least one occasion, I gather. Yes, all in all, we haven't treated you badly. In fact I think there are things you should be grateful to us for.'

After this piece of softening up I was expecting him to get down to some hard talking but instead he said, 'In the beginning I didn't actually envisage sending you down there. I thought the training course, with the idea of the mission behind it, would be enough to provoke you into revealing your secret. I tried the usual techniques: those endless elementary questions about your speciality, in the hope that out of sheer boredom you would give yourself away. Remember, all I needed was an admission of guilt to be able to force you to abide by the terms of your contract.

'Well, you proved to be a tougher nut to crack than I'd imagined. Unable to trick you into telling me it yourself I had to go through with the charade and send you down to Barcelona. Now I had to come to Barcelona myself to try and find where you'd planted the bugs in the Institute. First I had a look round in your hotel room, but I couldn't discover any. Unfortunately you came back while I was there and I had to distract your attention for a minute in order to get out without your seeing me. Sorry about that.'

I remembered that 'distraction' of the Major's: it had forced me to keep my head on one side and my mouth open for a week. He went on, 'Next I went to the Institute to search all the places where you told me you'd left the bugs: inside the cover of the computer-monitor, on the inside of the blue filing cabinet, and the burglar alarm cupboard. Only when I got to the laboratory I discovered you'd lied to me: there weren't any bugs there at all.

'Now I thought I'd reached the end of the road. It seemed to me that once you saw the laboratory you'd be bound to realise I'd been in there looking for them. But even though you spotted me in the Ramblas you didn't manage to put two and two together. Of course, if you'd been a professional you would have, but incredibly, you decided that Kolowski was a Russian spy and blamed it all on him.

'Despite this piece of good luck, I had to return to London empty-handed. Really I was at my wits end how to extract the secret from you. But then I had a lucky break: out of the blue one morning Doris handed it to me on a silver medallion. Kolowski's already told you that part of the story.'

We arrived in the square where he lived. The Major parked the car outside his house and limped up the steps in front of me. We went downstairs to his study and he poured out the usual whisky and sodas. It was pleasantly cool down here despite the mugginess of the day. On the ottoman by the wall a yellow silk dress belonging to Doris lay crumpled under a pile of back-numbers of *Fashion*.

The Major said, 'The unfortunate by-product of all this has been your stumbling across another little piece of business I've been arranging with Kolowski. This is really what I have to talk to you about. For some James Bond spy-novel reason best known to yourself, you started barking up the wrong tree right away and thinking he was a Russian agent or something.'

I said, 'What exactly is Kolowski's role?'

'A very limited one. As you know, I'm involved in a deal to get arms to some people in Central America. It's an operation which my superiors consider vital in the struggle against Communism, and for our national interest in the region. Of course, these guerrilla fighters have only one currency: drugs. That's how they pay for everything. I recruited Kolowski to sell these drugs for us in Barcelona. He was already dealing in the stuff on his own account so he was quite well-connected in the drug world down there. Of course he's far too unreliable to be trusted with any of the details of the rest of the operation. I make sure he's kept in the strictest ignorance about that.'

'You mean this deal is actually instigated by the British Intelligence Service?'

'That's right.'

'And they are pushing drugs?'

'We have to pay for the guns somehow. This sort of manoeuvre can't very well go down on the Ministry of Defence budget can it? Look here Newton, I know all this sounds a bit dirty, but in the real world you have to get things done as best you can. I just want to make it clear to you that this is all absolutely secret. You signed the Official Secrets Act: I want you to make sure you abide by its terms a lot more conscientiously than you did by the terms of your contract. In the interest of the country it's essential that you keep your mouth shut. I don't want to have to shut you up altogether.'

He spoke the last sentence in a low voice which made it quite clear what he meant.

'I understand. I promise you I won't say anything.'

'And what about the taped evidence?'

'I'll destroy that too.'

'I'd like you to give it to me.'

'I will.'

The more I found out about this man the more he terrified me. His suave way of using expressions like 'distract your attention' and 'shut you up altogether' was more frightening than any violent talk. Yet what he had done to Mungo, what he might do to me, was really nothing compared to what he spent his whole life doing for the Intelligence Service. Now that I knew the sort of thuggery he really went in for I was sickened by his fine manners and his admiration of old-world values. I had an overwhelming desire to get out of his house, with its stench of cigar smoke and its gloomy leather sofas.

I stood up to go but the Major gestured to me to wait, saying, 'Sit down for a minute dear boy. I didn't bring you here to tell you about my doings in Barcelona. I just want to make the position quite clear to you. Sometimes we have to do things which aren't very pleasant but we do them because of the real values we believe in, which are more important than details of day-to-day business. I am speaking of our God, our country and our family.'

He had been fiddling around with his cigar while he said this; now he lifted his fat-ringed eyes to me inquisitively. There were no values in those eyes at all as far as I could see: there wasn't even any hatred or cruelty.

'You have just lost a dear member of your family,' he continued, 'and I gather that as a result you are a man of some quite substantial property. I always had a great affection for your uncle and I feel the same for you. These links between families are strong, but I think the time has come to make our own even stronger. I know you're in love with Doris and I have always thought of you as an eminently suitable sort of person for her. Why don't you ask her to marry you?'

All I remember was suddenly not knowing where I was, like sometimes when you stand up and black out momentarily. Now, though I didn't lose sight of the Major, the padded leather sofas, Doris's silk dress on the ottoman, all these things seemed to lose hold of their context; for a moment it seemed that this was the first occasion I had met the Major, in this same room a year ago when Doris had sat on the floor at his feet in a pink polo-neck sweater; and as I looked at the spot the carpet's ogival pattern melted and a patch of wet on the Fitzer laboratory floor swam up before me, its fumes acrid and nauseous; and there followed the aching nights with Doris, and the aching nights without her.

'And the wedding could be at Hawtree in the chapel . . .' the Major was saying. But I was far too thrown upside down to remember the rest of what he said: a whole lot of stuff about my uncle's house and the grounds, and my membership of the Knights . . .

Chapter 27

We were sitting on the sofa in my flat the next evening when I said, 'Doris, will you marry me?'

Doris looked up from the joint she was rolling and said, 'What for?'

This was not quite the response I had been looking for: somehow yesterday's conversation with the Major had made it all seem so definite. I explained that I loved her and that I hoped she loved me too.

She looked at me with her big eyes and said, 'I'm very fond of you, Herman, but I don't want to get married. You see, really I'm still a bit in love with Mungo. In any case, Daddy would never put up with it.'

'You're wrong,' I said. 'I'm sure he'd be very pleased.'

'He wasn't very pleased about Mungo. He sent him away to the States; perhaps he'll send you away too,' she added dispassionately.

'Perhaps he likes me better than Mungo.'

'Why should he?' asked Doris, and then, as though answering her own question, 'Perhaps he feels you're grander. In any case, I oughtn't really to be seeing you at all. That tarot teacher said I was to forget you.'

'Doris, that's impossible!'

'He did, really. He said to forget the man I'm with and to go with the new one who loves me so much.'

'But Doris, I am the new one. He means to forget about Mungo.'

'I don't think so. You see Mungo's gone to America. So he means to forget about you. And go with Konstantin.'

'Kolowski!'

'He says he loves me.'

'But Doris, I love you.'

She gave a delightful little laugh.

'Sweetie, you mustn't blame me. It's very complicated when you have a lot of people in love with you. It's not my fault.'

'But Kolowski doesn't love you. He's just an awful old lecher. You're no more to him than any other pretty girl he meets.'

'Yes,' Doris said thoughtfully, 'I used to think that. But the tarot teacher said he really does love me and I should go with him.'

After this I was so discouraged I didn't feel like proposing any more that evening. The next day I phoned the Major and told him that she'd refused me.

'Dear boy,' he told me, 'don't be despondent. All girls of her age are shy. Have another word with her this evening. In the meantime I'll speak to her at luncheon.'

That evening Doris came wearing a bright green dress I hadn't seen before, with green lipstick and black nail varnish. Nervous as I was about proposing again, it was a relief to see that she was obviously in an excellent mood.

I said, 'That's a very pretty dress. Is it a new one?'

'Yes, Daddy bought it for me this afternoon – seeing as we're getting engaged.'

'Doris! Will you marry me then?'

'Oh, yes,' said Doris dreamily, 'that would be incredible.'

She was so happy you couldn't imagine she'd refused me only yesterday. She skipped about, blushed, kissed me, asked about the ring, and did a thousand little things she was usually too sulky to contemplate. We went down to the Baroda Palace for dinner, and after dinner we went upstairs and had a bath.

'Sweetie,' Doris said, as she lay back and swished the suds up to her neck, 'Is it true you've inherited a stately home?'

'Yes, it is.'

'Just like the tarot said you would.'

While we were talking she had been lying with her head propped on the rim of the bath tub, lethargically abandoned to the heat of the soapy water. Her hair was piled up on her head and held in place with a chopstick from the kitchen drawer; only one lock had escaped into the water and now lay darkly against her neck and shoulder. Little flecks of foam clung to her chin and throat, almost indistinguishable against the pallor of her skin. But now two furrows of thought troubled the serenity of the composition: I realised that stately homes were something she was bound to consider grand.

So I said, 'Of course I'll have to sell the house to cover the debts. Really my uncle didn't leave me anything except financial problems.'

I didn't see why Doris should worry about the grandness of something we weren't going to end up with anyway.

But later that evening another aspect of this matter occurred to me. 'Doris, you won't say anything about my debts to your father will you? I think if he knew how little money I have it might come between us.'

'Yes,' said Doris thoughtfully, 'I suppose it might.'

Chapter 28

For the next few week-ends Doris and I were detained in London, either by my work or by concerts at the Circus, so that when we finally set off to visit Hawtree for the first time it was May, and one of the most beautiful days I can remember. When the sun is hot in England it doesn't hammer down like it does in the Mediterranean; instead, a warm buttery light spreads itself over the fields of green corn and flowering chestnut trees, the watermeadows in the valleys and the discreetly painted farm buildings on the hillsides. Everything in this landscape has been tended to: the fields have been drained by generations of farmers, the woodlands laid out for pheasant shooting. This countryside is like a species that has been so bred from the wild animal that its innermost nature is domestic. Its charm lies not in its naturalness, but in its informality: the hedgerows with their banks of cow parsley and campion, the great ash and oak trees struggling across its ordered pastures. The only foreign element in all this was the occasional picture of a bright yellow giraffe, symbol of an approaching Safari Park.

Doris sat next to me reading *Wedding* magazine and rolling an incredible number of joints. She was wearing a leather skirt – one of the shortest I'd ever seen in my life – and kept burning her legs when pieces of hash fell out of the cigarette. She always seemed to be in a good mood these days; even Hawtree didn't worry her, in spite of its grandness.

'It's funny isn't it?' she said. 'If Daddy thought we were going to sell the house he'd do his nut.'

I agreed it was very funny.

'And shall we have Mungo to the wedding?'

'I don't think your father would like that.'

'No,' said Doris, 'I don't suppose he would.'

As we drew near to Hawtree, the yellow giraffe signs

became increasingly numerous until eventually we saw one which said, HAWTREE SAFARI PARK I MILE.

'Doris, I have a feeling that my uncle may have turned Hawtree into a zoo. Did your father ever say anything about it to you?'

'No, but I do remember him saying the house was an ideal place to live.'

'My uncle must have done it to try and meet his debts,' I said.

'Perhaps,' said Doris, as though it was neither here nor there.

I wondered if I'd be able to keep the animals out of sight during the wedding. It looked as though everything was going to depend on the layout of the Safari Park in relation to the chapel.

At the gate of Hawtree House was a barrier with a little cabin beside it, where a youth in a leather cap sat chewing a toothpick.

When he asked for my money I said, 'I think you can let us through free. I'm the new owner, Herman Newton, and this is my fiancée, Doris Shark.'

The youth pushed back his cap and scratched his head. He seemed unable to take his eyes off Doris's legs.

'Sir Albermarle Newton was my uncle,' I explained.

'Never heard of him,' said the youth, switching his tooth-pick with a swift movement of his tongue from one corner of his mouth to the other.

'Well who owns this place then?'

'Dunno really,' the youth said, in a way that suggested he didn't much care either, 'Probably the captain, I daresay.'

'What Captain?'

'Captain Tebbit, innit?'

'And where is he?'

'Dunno. In the office probably.'

'And where's the office?'

'Up at the house, innit?'

I paid for a ticket and we drove through the barrier down an avenue of lime trees and then on into the open parkland beyond. We could see the house now up ahead of us: a vast pile of red brick gone black, covered in gables and tall disused chimney stacks. Doris was thrilled at the zebras which walked sedately ahead of us along the tarmac and even more so by the sight of a fat old lion that watched us go by with half an eye open from where it lay under some yew bushes.

'It's like the video of *Africa Unite*,' she said.

Halfway along the road there was a large car park where you could sit in the car and watch the animals browsing hay from large mangers. We stopped here and smoked another joint before driving on to the house itself.

When we arrived we somehow got caught up in a guided tour and had to follow round a succession of dismal Victorian rooms filled with big game trophies. I couldn't help being amused that my childhood ambition was being fulfilled in this way, but it upset Doris terribly to see so many animals stuffed: she considered the practice cruel. I tried to explain that they were already dead when it happened and that anyway they'd be sold along with the house and everything else, but it didn't really help. Poor Doris was visibly shaken.

We ended up in the refreshments room and although the bar was closed because of licensing hours we had a cup of tea and a chocolate bar for Doris. Better than this though was the Frogger machine. Doris cheered up a lot and we decided that even when we sold the house we'd keep the Frogger.

The chapel was at the back of the house, built in the Victorian Gothic style. The doors were nailed up and a notice on the fence around it told us it was closed to visitors. On the south side one window was boarded up and ivy had grown up on to the roof. There were beds of nettles everywhere around it.

I said to Doris, 'It may be closed because it's unsafe. In that case we could be married in London.'

Behind the chapel I could see deer in pens, and wooden sheds and a small concrete house. If the need arose the deer might pass as natural ornaments of the park, but it would mean getting the guests to the chapel without using the front gate.

'Captain' Tebbit had no real connection with the armed forces. The only things military about him were his bluff, rather bullying manner reminiscent of the parade ground, and a uniform which was as fictitious as his rank. He had begun his career as compère in a holiday camp, and from there he had graduated to the post of entertainments officer in a small seaside town on the south coast. Here my uncle discovered him and took him on as director of the newly-established Safari Park; or at least that's what the Captain said. My lawyers said there was something fishy about the way the whole thing was set up from the start. At all events 'Captain' Tebbit, with his red jacket and golden brocade, had been the driving force of the enterprise from the start. Within a few years he had gained control of the company; the move into the house had come at a later date when he advanced my uncle some more money. I remember he looked at Doris's legs practically the whole time; also that he made himself out to be my uncle's great benefactor. He explained that next year they were installing a miniature railway and that he had plans for a pub in the East Wing. Less promisingly, it appeared that the company belonged almost exclusively to him. My uncle had surrendered everything except a few non-voting shares which the Captain sycophantically invited Doris and myself to take up. We wouldn't have a seat on the board he explained – my uncle had given that up years ago – but we could come to the Annual General Meeting and listen to his report. And he hoped we were going to like my uncle's cottage which was very comfortable, and gave us the keys.

The 'cottage' was a little grey concrete bungalow on the edge of the grounds. The surroundings had been unattractively landscaped with miniature trees, patches of heather and prickly, stunted shrubbery. A strong smell of manure pervaded it from a series of pens and sheds where the safari animals were wintered and the young cubs and foals were weaned. Inside the bungalow my uncle had placed the few remaining pieces of furniture which remained to him and which, though certainly the best of his collection, looked ill at ease with their surroundings: an empire sofa and side-table dwarfed the sitting-room; two ormolu candlesticks and a rococo side-table seemed pointless beside the nylon-covered armchairs and fluffy red carpet. Behind the house was a lawn bisected by a concrete path.

Walking along it Doris said to me, 'I suppose we'll have to sell this place instead of the big house now.'

'I only hope it fetches some money,' I said doubtfully.

'Rabbits!' said Doris.

In the corner of the garden at the far end was a hutch, painted green, with a wire-netting run in the front. Here a large white rabbit was nibbling the grass while a number of bunnies hopped around. Doris opened the lid of the hutch and with a sure gesture, grabbed one of the bunnies by the ears and lifted it out.

'Look!' she said. 'He can't be more than one or two weeks old.'

She held the trembling creature against her lovely breasts with its ears down on its back and its little nose quivering. Its fur was clean with brown and white patches, almost the same colour as the brown of Doris's eyes and the white of her skin.

She kissed its tiny back and said,

'Herman, let's keep it.'

'But Doris, we've got nowhere to put it.'

'We could come and live here.'

'But you know I have to sell this place to pay the debts. Look, I'll get you some rabbits when we've got a garden or somewhere to put them. But just at the moment it's impossible.'

'It's always been my dream to live in the country,' she said stubbornly.

This was a new one on me.

'Doris you'd be bored stiff here. There are no concerts, no fashion, nothing.'

'We would live very simply, like rabbits.'

'It's all very well for rabbits,' I said. 'Rabbits don't do anything in life. But I have to work.'

'Rabbits do,' said Doris, 'they breed.'

Doris didn't forget the rabbits in a hurry. Or the Frogger machine. Scarcely a day went by without her referring to them, and she was already talking about 'our home in the country'. The maddening thing was that the Major used to talk about it in the same way; but once he discovered I was penniless, what would there be to stop him treating me like Mungo? To make matters worse, he was very keen to go and see my 'inheritance' as he called it. During the weeks that followed I resorted to every device to prevent him; but in the end he had his way, as he always did.

That evening Doris came over and informed me he was staying down there another day.

'He told me things didn't seem quite right,' she said. 'I don't know what he meant.'

But I knew what he meant only too well.

The summons arrived the following day. I was to have dinner with him that evening. Doris was to be there too, so I assumed he wasn't going to beat me up: it seemed that a fiancé got a more amicable send-off than a boyfriend. I knew Doris would accept whatever he told her and that she didn't really love me, and my thoughts that day returned in last-minute desperation to the idea of inventing a love potion.

When I arrived at dinner I was surprised to find that the Captain was one of the party. He was wearing a dark military coat this time, more suitable for evening, and he had a nasty bruise on the cheek and a cut above his eye.

'The Captain had a little accident,' said the Major, with an expression of concern, and then, his face breaking into a beam once more, went on, 'but you're all right now, aren't you Captain?'

'Yes, Sir,' he said, 'absolutely fine.'

After dinner the Major said, 'The Captain's got something to say to you young people.'

The Captain laughed nervously.

He began 'I want to give you . . . '

'Exchange,' corrected the Major.

'Exchange, rather. I want to exchange my share of the business for yours. As a kind of wedding present.'

'We call it a roll-over,' said the Major. 'You see it wasn't suitable for your uncle to have all the bother of running the company, so the Captain here took care of that part of it and your uncle had a more, shall we say, honorary participation. But now the Captain feels, as I do, that it's time for the younger generation to take their turn, and that it's more suitable for you to have the house and run the business, and for the Captain, who like myself is getting on, to take over your uncle's honorary role.'

I was so taken aback by this new turn of events I couldn't say a word. Doris was much more composed, not having really understood the position in the first place, and thanked the

Captain on our behalf. The Major went on to explain the tax advantages to Doris and myself of the roll-over. Then he opened a bottle of champagne and we drank to the partnership.

During the weeks before the wedding the Major drew up plans for the Hawtree Company. He didn't seem the least put out by my huge debts and viewed the Safari Park as a valuable money-maker.

'It'll be a lot of work,' he said, 'but we'll enjoy it. The miniature railway is definitely a good idea but I think we should organise some sort of rally or tournament as well which will draw bigger crowds. Then, when the Company's built up its profitability we can think about a conference centre in the west wing. We can even keep a racehorse and write off most of the expenses against the safari park.'

'Once I've paid my debts off,' I said, 'wouldn't it be much simpler just to sell it?'

'My dear Herman! What are you saying? Sell Hawtree? The seat of your family and your birthright! You can't possibly be serious.'

And so Doris Shark became my wife. The chapel at Hawtree was cleaned up for the occasion and the nettles were mown. I can see from the picture in our wedding album, though I don't actually remember, that the boarded window has been reglazed and the wall of the chapel bears a spidery imprint where a growth of ivy has been removed. Here, on the opposite page is Dr Fitzer, chatting incongruously with Margot, his wide champagne glass looking as though it is about to spill down her front, and on succeeding pages come Doris, clutching a bouquet and flushed with champagne; my mother on the arm of Kolowski; Captain Tebbit in his red uniform chatting to hugely bereted Rod, their eyes red from the flash of the camera; the Major, with a piled forkful of cold salmon. Underneath all of these Doris has written their names in her looping hand.

It is only three years since then, and the party has already almost dissolved. My mother lies with Oscar Wilde in the Père Lachaise cemetery; Captain Tebbit faded out of our lives as quickly as he had come into them; Kolowski and Dr Fitzer returned to Barcelona; my portrait of Pilar has been consigned to the attic. Margot and Rod used to come and stay at the cottage during the first year of our marriage and keep Doris company when I was away in London, but for some reason Doris has fallen out with Margot and only Rod comes now. The Major has retired to the big house where we usually join him for meals. Perhaps next year, when our baby is born we shall make a flat for ourselves in the west wing.

And Doris? I don't believe that she loves me, but she certainly likes me better than she did before. And it seems that this affection is enough. Everything slowly becomes easier and more natural. She happily accepts a lot of things about me which she used to dislike, and she loves her country life, and her rabbits and the Safari Park; and I love her.

And that is the story of how I married one woman who left me, and then married another who didn't particularly love me, but stayed. And I suppose it's as happy an ending as you could wish for. Sometimes, when I look back over these events, I am still struck by the thought that a drug might have brought on my old passion for Doris; and at such times the inventor in me can't help toying again with the idea of a love potion. Only now I have to put the question to myself: even if I ever did discover such a thing, would it really be any kind of solution?

A NOTE ON THE AUTHOR

Constantine Phipps was born in Yorkshire and has lived
in France, Italy and the United States. His first novel, *Careful
with the Sharks*, was published in 1985. He has also edited (for
Penguin Classics) a collection of stories by Rudyard Kipling,
The Day's Work.